P9-CRL-222

CONCORD PUBLIC LIBRARY
45 GREEN STREET
CONCORD, NEW HAMPSHIRE 03301

DISCARDED

Hoare and the Headless Captains

Also by Wilder Perkins

Hoare and the Portsmouth Atrocities

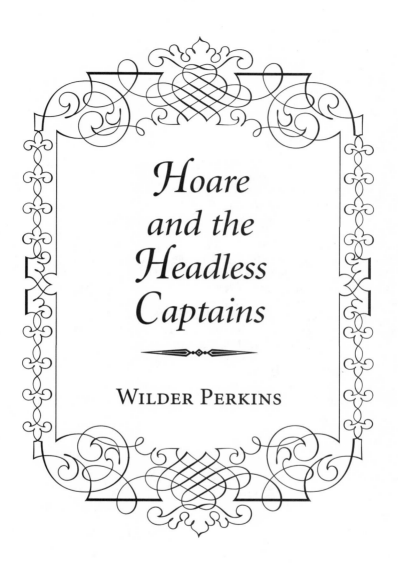

Hoare
and the
Headless
Captains

WILDER PERKINS

THOMAS DUNNE BOOKS
ST. MARTIN'S MINOTAUR
NEW YORK

FIC
PER

THOMAS DUNNE BOOKS.
An imprint of St. Martin's Press

HOARE AND THE HEADLESS CAPTAINS. Copyright
© 2000 by Robert Wilder Perkins. All rights reserved.
Printed in the United States of America. No part of this
book may be used or reproduced in any manner whatsoever without written permission except in the case of
brief quotations embodied in critical articles or reviews.
For information, address St. Martin's Press, 175 Fifth
Avenue, New York, N.Y. 10010.

ISBN: 0-312-25248-X

First Edition: January 2000

10 9 8 7 6 5 4 3 2 1

Hoare and the Headless Captains

Prologue

———✦———

COOM BACK 'ere, you Boye!"
On the moor just west of Dorchester, the shepherd watched his dog's behavior in astonishment. Never before had it quit work and run off like that. Even the bellwether looked up as if in surprise.

The shepherd reached out and cut a switch from a nearby pollarded willow as it blew in the heavy westerly.

"Coom oop then; coom!"

From within the Nine Stones Circle, Boye howled. The shepherd felt the hair rise on his nape. He dropped the switch, took a firm grip of his quarterstaff. The dog almost never howled, and the Circle was an uncanny place.

The shepherd stopped between two of the standing stones and gulped.

The dog Boye crouched in a great double pool of congealed blood between two bodies in naval uniform. One corpse lay at the foot of a huge ashlar at the center of the trodden circle. Its severed head lay beside it, gaping at the racing clouds. The other body sprawled on its back

1

across the rough, flat stone, its arms dangling on either side of the makeshift altar. Its head was nowhere in sight. Between the corpses, its own head thrown back, the dog howled again into the wind.

Chapter I

————◆————

TWENTY MILES to the south, Bartholomew Hoare, cruising in his pinnace in the Channel, knew he had bungled, and bungled badly. The sudden gust laid *Neglectful* nearly on her beam ends, to the ugly tune of crashing crockery in the cuddy below. There was no escaping it; he had misjudged the rate at which the weather to seaward would degenerate and the westerly storm strike the Channel. As a result, he and *Neglectful* were about to experience a very nasty October gale. He wasted no more time but brought her to the wind, reduced sail to a storm jib and a corner of mainsail, then hove her to and went below to lash down all the gear he could, wedge unlashable items securely, and pad everything breakable that had not already broken.

Remembering what had happened once last autumn, when he had neglected this precaution, he lidded tight the hod of cannel coal he kept for his galley stove. He lashed it to the side of *Neglectful*'s mast away from the stove itself. He would not have gritty black chunks and slurries fouling the cuddy again for months, not if he could help it. He put on his precious suit of Dutch foul weather gear, took two turns of line around ankles and wrists, pulled the suit's visored hood over his head, and fitted to his body a canvas harness well equipped with D rings from which depended short lengths of line ending in pelican hooks.

Just as he was about to double-secure the pinnace's cuddy hatch, he remembered something else. He reached back below, took up a towel, a jug, and a bag of biscuits. With one last look below to satisfy himself that *Neglectful's* innards were as snug as he could make them, he finished securing the hatch.

Neglectful was moving slowly but well. She rid herself easily of the seas from the west that were already sluicing across her deck and made a comfortable two knots nearly directly due south. Hoare could imagine she was looking forward to their mutual ordeal.

As it roared heavily across her larboard bow, the wind carried the spray down *Neglectful's* modest length. Hoare could swear that most of it was directed at his head and shoulders while he sat at her tiller, nursing her along. Wind and spray dropped for a moment whenever a rogue sea took her under its wing and put her under its lee before sweeping her skyward, leaving her exposed once more and rushing on toward its end. Hoare guessed the wave would crash ashore somewhere near Pevensey.

Whenever the seas passed beneath the yacht, lifting her into the wind, she felt the weight of the gale more deeply, and her moments of respite in the combers' lee began to become more welcome to Hoare. Depending on whether *Neglectful* was riding a crest or cowering in a trough, the gale either howled in her exiguous shrouds or moaned emptily above her reeling mast.

This blow was no squall. At this rate, it would build

for the next six hours or so, hold for another four, and then pass on to bludgeon Bonaparte's Frogs. Or so Hoare judged. But considering his failure to predict the strength of this blow, he had to doubt himself more than usual. It might be no more than four hours before he could safely fall off and run down, home to Portsmouth. It might be fourteen hours. Objectively, Hoare knew that this weather was nothing, but . . . in a twenty-six-foot boat, alone, at his age, surely he should be anxious—or, failing that, proud.

He wondered in passing if this blunder of his had not been intentional. Perhaps he had been trying to tell the world that he, Bartholomew Hoare, Lieutenant, RN, might be forty-three, mute, and beached forever by the Admiralty, but that, when face-to-face with Nature in the raw, he was any man's equal. Perhaps he was seeking an excuse to take shelter in Weymouth, where he could continue his suit for the hand of the widow Graves. In any case, he and *Neglectful* were in for a long watch together. He made his lanky, brown, silent self as snug in her cockpit as he could under the circumstances and hooked his harness into the eyebolts set into the coaming. The tiller under one arm and his bag of provisions at his feet, he let his memory take him four days back, to when Admiral Hardcastle broke the news.

"Now, as to *Royal Duke*." Rear Admiral Sir George Hardcastle, KB, paused to await Hoare's reaction.

That afternoon, Sir George wore his own hair, as he commonly did except on formal occasions. It was stone gray, cut short, and formed into a bang over his forehead in the fashionable Brutus cut. Brute he was often called, in fact, and he enjoyed the appellation, for he sought the reputation of being a grim and a merciless man.

To a large extent he had succeeded. Reputations too numerous to mention had been destroyed at his hand, leaving their owners—junior officers for the most part, but a sprinkling of Commanders and Post Captains as well—bereft, dangling more or less helpless on half-pay. Irrespective of whatever interest they might have, it collapsed when Sir George Hardcastle turned his adamantine will upon it.

"*Royal Duke,* sir?" Hoare remembered his Admiral's having once made passing mention of her and her late Commander—Ogilvy, if he remembered, or some such name. Oglethorpe, that was the name. What had *Royal Duke* to do with Hoare in any case, or he with her?

"Yes. Admiralty yacht, now lying in Greenwich. A hundred tons or so, brig-rigged. Eight brass four-pounders. Crew of thirty, more or less."

Hardly fit to stand in the line of battle, Hoare thought. And undermanned for even that trivial armament.

"She never takes the sea," Sir George had continued, "but rests in her home port, almost like a receiving ship.

"In fact, in some respects, she *is* a receiving ship, and in other respects a manufactory. For, you must know, *Royal Duke* serves the Navy as a mobile secret information bureau whose people maintain copies of all files relating to the efforts of foreign powers—Frenchmen for the most part, of course, but Swedens, Dutchmen, even Russians, Yankees, and Turks as well—to damage and defeat the Royal Navy by means of stealth.

"Pour me a glass, sir, and help yourself."

When he wished, as he did now, Sir George Hardcastle, Rear Admiral of the Blue, could address his listeners as if they were the House.

"She also includes a small corps," the Admiral continued, "who are charged with defeating, frustrating, and foil-ing the enemy's knavish tricks. This corps have not yet been put to the use for which they were intended, and Admiral Abercrombie has decided, among other things, that this must be remedied. Most of her crew are actually half clerk or assassin and half seaman, if that. All can read and write, though I am told 'tis hard to credit of some. Thus, she is manned in quite an unusual manner, as you are about to discover."

Here the Admiral had interrupted his discourse again, ostensibly to take refreshment but actually, Hoare suspected, to appraise his listener's reaction. He avoided making any but waited with suppressed amusement. Finally, Sir George grew tired of waiting.

"For you appear, sir," he went on, "to be well regarded in certain Whitehall corridors, as one of those experts in your own right. I imagine they believe you largely responsible for breaking up that gang that was blowing up so many of His Majesty's ships. Those affairs of *Severn*'s missing Master and that Bourbon Duke also stand to your credit. Accordingly, Their Lordships of the Admiralty have been pleased to put you into *Royal Duke*."

I am to go to sea again! Hoare cried to himself. To be sure, with a company of only thirty, *Royal Duke* could hardly support more than one Lieutenant, but even so, he would, under his commanding officer, of course, once again be an officer of a fighting ship. Or, more probably, he would be a mere supernumerary, one of those experts the Admiral had mentioned, though precisely where they thought his expertise might lie eluded him. Just the same . . . to be at sea again!

"Of course," the Admiral went on, "you could hardly expect to fill poor Oglethorpe's shoes in every respect. After all, he was a Post Captain, seventy-five years of age, and wise in the ways of the ungodly. No. The best rank

I—Their Lordships, I mean—have seen fit to bestow upon you is that of Master and Commander. You will read yourself in as soon as she makes Portsmouth from her present berth in Greenwich under the temporary command of her Lieutenant."

Hoare had simply sat there, bereft of words. Together, those three words *Master and Commander* put teeth into his new commission. His title was to be more than nominal: *Commander* was an appellation often used to recognize deserving Lieutenants who thereafter languished on half-pay for lack of an actual vessel to command. He was to be "Master and Commander," on active service, confirmed in command of his own vessel. He was only three-and-forty now; with luck, he would make post after all before he died, despite his disabilities of name and voice.

"While you will be Master and Commander in actuality," said Sir George, thereby figuratively nailing Hoare's rank to the mast of advancement, "you are not, yourself"— here he paused and read from a paper before him—" 'expected to issue spoken orders with respect to the working of the vessel under your command. Instead, you may give instructions to your Lieutenant, who in his turn will order the crew as conditions require.'

"In other words, in all circumstances where your lack of a voice would endanger *Royal Duke,* her mission, or her men, your Lieutenant will be—to coin a phrase—your executive officer. That will, of course, almost always be the case on deck and under way. You know that as well as I.

"However," Sir George added, "the case is hypothetical. *Royal Duke* can sail, but she must *not* sail. Lest she be taken by the French, secrets and all, she must never go to sea. 'This is the first and great commandment.' "

Hoare nodded. It was his crushed voice box that had cut short a promising career at sea and put him ashore—

forever, as he had believed for ten years and more. Well, half a loaf . . . To all intents and purposes, *Royal Duke* might as well be a mere idle hulk, but she would be his, his to command.

"The arrangement is unprecedented, sir," Sir George continued. "It demonstrates a highly unusual degree of trust on the part of Their Lordships in your ability to, er, navigate, so to speak, the uncharted waters on which you are about to embark. It will require an especially high level of mutual trust and accommodation between yourself and your Lieutenant. However, I reassure you that your command is not merely pro forma. It is de facto as well."

Sir George paused again, this time to admire his own mastery of Latin.

"And de jure, of course," he added triumphantly. Sir George was an accomplished and articulate flag officer as well as a grim and a merciless man, but, as Hoare knew, had gone to sea at nine and even as a midshipman had never sailed under the instruction of either a schoolmaster or a chaplain. An officer of the old school, he was more comfortable with action than discourse. Perversely, in Hoare's opinion, this inclined Sir George all the more to parade whatever classical crumbs he might have gathered up from under the tables of more learned men. It might also explain his excursions into periphrastic orotundity.

"In short, the duties of Master in *Royal Duke* will be assumed in practice, as a rule, by your First Lieutenant."

"May I ask, sir, who my Lieutenant is to be?" Hoare whispered.

"You may ask, sir, but you will receive no answer. I exercise my privilege of being irritating to my subordinates whenever I choose. Let you reveal yourself to the man, and he to you, when you read yourself in.

"I can state, however, that I briefly entertained the

9

name of Peter Gladden, who, as you will remember, was your colleague in defense of Mr. Arthur Gladden's recent court-martial. However, I chose to leave him in *Frolic*."

Hoare thought he could guess the reason. Peter Gladden was openly enamored of Sir George's daughter, and Felicia was known to reciprocate. Her papa the Admiral had given evidence that he did not oppose the connection; Mr. Gladden's parents were both wellborn and wealthy, and since Felicia, however good-hearted she was, was dumpy, spotty, and lacking in presence, he would be hard put to it to find a better match for the young woman. But, as prudent in his role of pater familias as in his position of Port Admiral at Portsmouth, Sir George had probably determined to separate the lovers for a spell before approving the union. Thus, any second thoughts on the part of either young person would have a chance to surface before it was too late altogether to cry off.

"Since your appointment will appear in the forthcoming *Chronicle*," the Admiral continued, "I give you leave to christen it as you please without necessarily waiting to read yourself in. You cannot draw your pay as Commander, of course, until *Royal Duke* has made port and that ceremony has come to pass."

That was true, Hoare knew. *Neglectful*'s former owner had fallen into that trap. When the brief Peace of Amiens had been signed with Napoléon, Their Lordships had refused to confirm him in rank and required him to restore every penny of his Commander's pay. Until the weary war had resumed, the poor man had had to scrape along on nothing except his winnings at whist and Hoare's payment for *Neglectful*.

"That will be all for today, then, Hoare," said Sir George with a wintry smile. "Go, make holiday; make merry. Put yourself in proper uniform, and wet your swab as you see fit."

Hoare was about to relive the christening of his swab, an occasion that, in keeping with the celebrant's advanced age, included Sir George himself and as many Post Captains and senior civilians as it did sprightly Lieutenants and therefore resembled a gathering of stately, convivial walruses. But a gust bore a sheet of cold October rain across *Neglectful,* and she heeled another strake. Hoare shook himself back to the present. He lifted himself stiffly, to scan the full horizon, first to windward and then, ducking under the boom and its straining trysail, to leeward.

Directly on *Neglectful'*s lee beam, tossing in the squall that had just passed overhead, a two-masted vessel emerged from the blowing rain. One mast was canted against the other; from both streamed the remnants of sails and rigging. As Hoare watched, the stranger was obscured by a fountain of spray, reappearing to show only a single mast remaining upright.

Timing his maneuver to coincide with the lee offered by an oncoming sea, Hoare eased both sheets and edged *Neglectful* eastward, off the wind. Trysail and storm jib, which had been straining before, were now pressed to their utmost, and her double backstays hummed in the following gale. *Neglectful* heaved, nearly pitchpoling, but gained her stride and rushed down the wind, the stranger growing in Hoare's vision as the two vessels neared. Another sea lifted between the two craft, reached the other, and hoisted her skyward as it passed under her, to reveal her condition more clearly.

It was perilous. Both masts—she had carried two lugsails, apparently—were over the side now, and she drifted, waterlogged and rolling heavily, bows-on to the seas, the wreckage of her top-hamper serving as sea anchor.

The floating wreck was less than a cable's length to leeward when she released a flock of birds. Hoare blinked in disbelief. Yes, they were birds, indeed, and no seabirds. They formed a confused cloud, seemed to veer upwind toward *Neglectful,* then gave over and let the gale carry them scudding off out of Hoare's sight.

Long since, Hoare had distinguished her people. There were two of them, clinging to the stumps of her masts so as to withstand the seas that were washing over their vessel. Both were waving frantically with their free hands, as though they must make absolutely, totally, utterly sure that Hoare saw them and knew their distress. He was close enough now to hear their faint cries, even against the gale.

This would call for his best seamanship. *Neglectful* closed the gap between herself and the wreck at a full ten knots, heaving and bucking in the scend of the following seas as if she were a wild mare. At top speed, Hoare lashed the helm lest she broach to while he occupied himself with the rescue. As they passed, *Neglectful* and the stranger would present their larboard sides.

Hoare snatched up a grapnel to which he had long ago spliced a light dock line and clambered forward into *Neglectful's* eyes. Shifting the clips of his harness onto her forestay, he stood erect, whirled the grapnel in a circle, and let it fly. Before the grapnel could even strike its target, he had dropped the line into a bronze chock, taken a turn, and braced himself.

The grapnel caught in the lugger's bulwarks. Hoare had a lightning memory of the last time that grapnel had been put to use; it had caught a Frenchman between neck and shoulder and pulled him off the schooner *Marie Claire.*

Now Hoare cleated the far end of the line to one of the sockets he had set to take *Neglectful*'s swivel gun at need. *Neglectful* lurched steeply to starboard, her timbers squealing in protest as the line drew taut and spun her full about, nearly in her own length, bringing her head to the gale, bucking in the seas aft of the stranger, her two scraps of sail a-thunder.

Between them, the three men heaved *Neglectful* and the dismasted lugger close enough to each other so that the castaways could scramble across their own swimming deck, take a purchase on *Neglectful*'s jib-stay, and drop onto her bowsprit. The first man made it without incident, but the second missed his timing and went over the side with a shriek of despair, carrying Hoare's grapnel with him, into the widening strip of Channel between the vessels. He had kept a tight grip on the grapnel, however, and the other two men readily dragged him aboard *Neglectful,* spluttering but no wetter than he had been before his bath.

Especially in foul weather, the Channel hereabouts was a no-man's-land, so until now Hoare could not be sure whether he had saved French lives or English ones.

"Jesus, Mary, and Joseph," the swimmer gasped, crawling after Hoare into the stern sheets, where Hoare could take the con once more. The sentiment might be Papist, Hoare thought, but the words were English. At least, then, he did not face the risk of being overpowered by ungrateful guests and carried off to some Breton port.

The first castaway looked back at the lugger, dwindling in the distance and wallowing visibly. "There goes me livelihood," he said bitterly through chattering teeth.

Hoare gestured to the two to go below and mimed eating, drinking, and dry clothing. They looked puzzled.

"Can't ye talk?" the first arrival shouted at him. Like so many people, he must assume that anyone who could not speak certainly could not hear. Hoare shook his head, smiled an apology, and repeated the motions. The swimmer went below, but the owner waited while his livelihood raised her weary bows into the air and disappeared behind a roller. She did not appear again. Thereupon, the owner joined his companion below.

Hoare kept his yacht's course easterly, scudding before the wind, even though wind and seas were far outpacing her. He knew *Neglectful*'s cleverly formed transom would prevent her from being pooped.

The choking reek of coal smoke, sweeping horizontally from the little yacht's Charley Noble, was followed quickly enough by the more welcome smell of soup a-heating. The gale had not let up, but it had not strengthened, either, and *Neglectful* rode smoothly enough that Hoare's guests— probably as good seamen as he, if not better—had judged it safe to light her galley stove. Hoare had no spare oilskins, but he had several loose heavy garments that would fit any wet visitor well enough. It was no more than half a glass before the bereaved owner, clad in Hoare's thick Shetland sweater, stuck his head out *Neglectful*'s cabin hatch and reached his host a cup of thick, hot soup, in one of his own thick, hot mugs. It was welcome; events had moved so fast that Hoare had not thought to breach his emergency cockpit supply.

In his other hand, the rescued owner held one of the Roman-style wax tablets that, together with numerous other devices, Hoare carried about for easy communication whenever his feeble whisper could not be understood.

"Name's Dunaway, your honor," he said, "Abel Dunaway. Owner of the *Fancy* lugger—though that means nowt this day."

Dunaway handed the tablets to his rescuer. His mournful, tanned face bore a week's growth of grizzled beard, and a shag of gray hair dropped into his eyes. He made himself comfortable in the cockpit, face-to-face with Hoare. In *Neglectful's* narrow cockpit, their knees all but touched.

"Just the same, sir, I owes you for me life, and Jamie below as well, though he must speak for himself. The boy Jethro Slee went overboard this morning, when a thicky murderous gale hit.

"I should never ha' sent him forward to reef the fore-sail; he went overboard. When I bore up to fish him out, we broached to, and her mainmast went by the board. 'Twere all my fault, my most grievous fault, and I don't know how I'm to break it to his da." Dunaway fell silent and studied his borrowed mug.

"May be lettin' up" he observed after a bit. "What d'ye think, sir?"

Hoare smiled into the growing darkness and shook his head. In point of fact, the moan of the wind in *Neglectful's* rigging had risen a half-tone. It was nigh time to heave to completely.

"Sorry, sir," Dunaway said. He handed Hoare the waxen tablets. "To whom do I owe my life, then?"

Hoare scribed his name in the wax, added "Lieutenant RN," then recollected himself, scratched the title out, and replaced it with "Commander, RN." He had been a Lieutenant for twenty-two years and still found it hard to remember that he now rated the courtesy address of "Captain."

"Captain," he said to himself. "*Captain.*"

Dunaway managed a grin. "A new creation, I'll warrant, *Captain,*" he said, as if he had been reading Hoare's mind. Hoare nodded again and returned the grin.

"*Fancy?*" he wrote. "Smuggler?" He knew very well she was no fisherman. There had been no sign of nets or trawls aboard the lugger, and her rig had been better suited to another calling.

"Fisherman," Dunaway said. Hoare shrugged.

A heavier sea came within a hair of breaking over *Neglectful*'s stern. Cleverly formed or not, her stern sheets risked being overburdened within minutes.

"Sea anchor," he wrote. He tapped Dunaway's hand and pointed to the tiller with raised eyebrows. The other nodded.

"Aye aye," he said.

Hoare crawled forward once again, securing the idle grapnel as he went. Timing his moves to coincide with one of the periodic lees afforded him by the sea, he cracked the forward hatch, reached down, and dragged out *Neglectful*'s seldom-used drogue. He hitched its pendant beside the useful grapnel, took in the scrap of storm jib, and signaled Dunaway to let the yacht work herself around into the wind. He gave the sea anchor ten fathoms or so of scope and cleated the line before crawling aft again.

Since she was no longer running with the wind, *Neglectful*'s rigging began to shriek instead of merely moaning, but she rose willingly to the seas, now breasting them instead of fleeing them. Her trysail held her in place, so that once he had lashed the tiller again, she would do her duty as long as Hoare called on her to do so. He motioned Dunaway below and followed him, catching up his bag of sustenance as he went and securing the cuddy hatch behind him.

Neglectful's builder had not designed her to accommodate more than two. With three sizable men below, she was cramped. A man-o'-warsman, as used as any sardine to living bump-bottom with his shipmates, would have hardly been troubled, but Hoare had never gone to sea as less than a very junior mid. He saw that the proximity of two companions would become irksome in no time and resolved to set them ashore as soon as the weather permitted. Meanwhile, he accepted the fresh mug of his own pea soup that Jamie, the swimmer, offered him. Strangely, the rich smell of the soup blended cozily with the smell of wet wool that both his guests gave off as they began to warm up and the pervasive reek of Stockholm tar.

"Thank you," Hoare whispered, as much as to see if he could make himself heard above the muffled cacophony here below as to give the man a polite response.

"No; thank *you,* sir," Jamie said. His voice was unexpectedly cultured, but with a slight accent. French perhaps? His unweathered face was open and innocent. "Bose Mr. Dunaway and me 'ood be feedin' the fishes long since if it were not for you."

"A grand piece of seamanship," interjected Dunaway. "Both Jamie and I owe you our lives."

"Permit me, sir, to drink your healf in this most uncommon good soup," Jamie added.

"Permission granted," Hoare whispered with a smile. "If you'll steer your mugs this way, I'll even bless 'em with this." He wedged his own mug securely in his corner of the padded starboard locker, withdrew a jug from its bag, and, having drawn the cork with his teeth, poured a noggin of black rum into the others' extended mugs, remembering to christen his own before restoppering the jug.

"What brings *you* to sea, sir, alone, in such weather, if I might be so bold?" Dunaway asked.

"Pure foolishness Mr. Dunaway. I am about to take command of one of His Majesty's ships"—here he must take a breath—"and I knew that from that moment my time will no longer be even as much my own as the Port Admiral's office has allowed me these past years.

"As . . . a man who makes his living from these waters,

17

you may find it hard to credit that there are some of us who fish almost as much pleasure out of them as you do cod."

More, almost certainly, Mr. Dunaway, Hoare thought, *considering your real calling.*

"And the name of your vessel, sir?" Dunaway inquired.

"*Neglectful,* Mr. Dunaway. Today, that is." With this, Hoare steered the conversation into very familiar waters.

"Today?"

"Today. Lift up one of the floorboards under your feet, if you will, and look at its underside. Any one of them will do."

Dunaway did as directed. He snorted with surprise.

" '*Inconceivable,*' " he read.

"Yes. I also call her *Insupportable,* or *Molly J,* or *Dryad,* or *Serene,* or *Unspeakable.* I change her name according to my mood of the moment—most often at the outset of a voyage, but sometimes, if the luck is bad, in midpassage as well. As you see, I keep several trail boards below, and face the spares into the bilges for a cabin sole. It makes no difference to *her;* she answers to none of them. She just answers her helm, and very well, too, at that."

He knew these lines by heart.

Dunaway gave a bark of laughter.

"I recognize you now, Mr. Hoare. I should ha' done so earlier. You're the sharp cove as caught that Frog Moreau and his gang."

Dunaway and the man Jamie exchanged a glance. The stuffy, warm air in *Neglectful*'s cuddy grew a trifle ominous.

"Do not be foolish, gentlemen," Hoare whispered. "I know who you are, and you know I know it. . . ."

He interrupted himself to take a breath, as he must from time to time whenever venturing more than a short sentence or two.

". . . Pray do not make war on me; it would not be worth your while."

He displayed a small pistol he had won from the mate of an American brig only a year ago.

"As long as your trade does not diminish His Majesty or his Navy, and as long . . . as long as I am not under orders to suppress smuggling, your trade is no concern of mine.

"I would like your word of honor, both of you, that you will permit me to land you both, unharmed and secure . . . at the first landfall we make where a landing can be made without risk to my little *Neglectful*.

"Failing that, I shall be forced to shoot one of you and require the other to leave this little patch of dryness in the middle of a very wet Channel."

With this, *Neglectful* gave a little extra lurch, as though she agreed with Hoare.

The two guests exchanged another look; Jamie shrugged.

"You have our word, sir," Dunaway said.

"Will this do, or shall I beat back up into Weymouth?" Hoare asked his passengers the next morning. The gale had gone its way, yielding to an easy westerly breeze. The tiny harbor of West Lulworth lay a mile on the larboard beam, next to its landmark, the Durdle Door.

"Don't trouble yourself for us, Captain Hoare, sir," Dunaway said. "What with this and that, we'd as lief not even pass through Weymouth. No, Lulworth will do just fine. Fact is, I've folk in Lulworth.

"Now, by your leave, Jamie here and I will shift out of the clothing you so kindly lent us and be on our way."

Without too much difficulty, Hoare persuaded the two

men to keep their borrowed gear for the time being, carry their own still–soggy garments, and send Hoare's clothing to him in Portsmouth.

"It will reach me at the Swallowed Anchor," he told them. To tell the truth, he wanted to see if they were as trustworthy as he hoped, for he could see the opportunity of putting their apparent skills to use in the future. But then he remembered.

"At *Royal Duke,* I mean after she enters port," he said. He was no longer to lodge ashore. He had a ship, or would have, soon.

Hoare dropped *Neglectful*'s useful grapnel again and let out its line while swinging her inshore, driven by the still-heavy breakers. He had Dunaway raise her sliding keel into the trunk that split her cuddy fore and aft, so she was able to grind none too gently onto the shingle. Her passengers could now step ashore all but dry-shod.

"Our thanks again, Captain," said the owner, gripping Hoare's hand with both his own before he disembarked. "Call on Abel Dunaway of Langton Herring, by Weymouth, whenever you have the need."

The man Jamie followed suit. "Thenkee, sir," he said now, in no unfriendly tone, knuckling his forehead awkwardly. He followed his skipper ashore, leaving Hoare to heave *Neglectful* up to her grapnel through the surf. He took reefs in mainsail and jib and fell off before the wind toward Portsmouth and home.

Chapter II

⟫◆⟪

FRANCIS DELANCEY, the Port Admiral's Flag Lieutenant, smirked at Hoare. Delancey wasted no time
but ushered him into his master's presence.

"You take your God-damned good time, sir, in obeying the orders of your superior officer," the Admiral declared. "I've cautioned you before: I will have no man
loiter about at his ease while I await his attending me at
whatever hour it pleases his slovenly self."

The heaps of paper on Sir George's desk did not appear
to have changed in the ten days since Hoare had last seen
it, nor did the Admiral look any less restless. Delancey gave
Hoare a sour look and departed.

"Man's in a temper," Sir George said of his aide, sailing
out of his own little squall as easily as he had sailed into it.
"Your friend Gladden took my Felicia aside the night before *Frolic* weighed anchor, having received my permission
to pay her his addresses. As if the slyboots hadn't been
'payin' his addresses' to the poor fat thing this year and
more! Puts Delancey quite in the shade, just when he

thought he was about to have a free run at my little girl. Ha!

"Anyhow, as I told you the other day, I'd thought to put young Gladden into *Royal Duke* as your Lieutenant, but the incumbent brought her in yesterday, as I suppose you noticed, and when he reported here, I had second thoughts. What would I do with *him,* after all?"

This was ominous. If Sir George felt he must ask the question, even if only rhetorically, what else he could do with *Royal Duke's* present Lieutenant if he were to put Gladden there in his stead; what sort of monster awaited him?

"Here are your orders. Now, take yourself off and read yourself in. I'm busy."

Back in the anteroom of the Port Admiral's office, Hoare must eat 'umble pie and ask Delancey where his command might lie. The Flag Lieutenant replaced his sour look with a sneer.

"Look yonder," he said, pointing.

Admiral Hardcastle had assigned *Royal Duke* to a mooring a mere cable's length offshore, a mooring that could have taken *Victory* through a hurricane with ease. The little brig dangled from it like a fierce mouse with its teeth clenched in a tomcat's tail. Hoare left Admiralty House, his precious orders in his hand, and once on the Hard hailed a wherry, with an ear-piercing whistle through his fingers, to take him out to his tiny command.

The wherry man first looked him askance, as if to ask, "Wouldn't it be quicker to swim out to her?" But, after all, every one of His Majesty's ships that was fit to sail had been shoveled out of Spithead to back up Nelson's fleet, and the roadstead was all but empty. Empty as the Admiralty's cupboard. These days, the pickings for watermen must be thin, indeed. An occasional light, spitting sprinkle, moistened them on the way.

"*Royal Duke!*" the wherry man cried at the end of the perilous voyage, in answer to the hail from the yacht's watch signifying that he had her Commander aboard. The man treated Hoare as if he carried two swabs instead of one—and that one on the inferior larboard shoulder—and offered him a hand to help him aboard. But to reach *Royal Duke*'s flush deck would involve no climb at all; the boarding port that was opened for him in her bulwark was below his chin. Hoare handed the man the customary shilling and reached his portmanteau up to a hand on deck.

After pausing for a heartbeat to savor what was to come, Hoare hoisted himself aboard his command—his command!—with a single heave of his arms. The thin skirl of a boatswain's call sounded, followed by a thunder of booted feet as all hands formed to receive him. He could easily have out-tweetled the piper with his own silver whistle, the one he used to signal those persons he had trained to its calls.

But where was his Lieutenant, that mysterious, unemployable monster whom Sir George must perforce leave in place for lack of anything else to do with him? The person facing him was a mere midshipman.

"Welcome aboard, sir," said the boy in a surprisingly big voice, raising his round hat in salute. Wishing he had only half as much voice, Hoare looked at the speaker more sharply. This was no mid, as he had first thought, but a Lieutenant. Moreover, he was no lad, either, but a man of at least thirty. He was less than five feet tall.

"Permit me to introduce myself, sir," said the minikin.

"Harvey Clay, at your service. I look forward to serving under you, sir."

"Thank you, Mr. Clay," Hoare whispered. He felt unutterably pompous as he continued, "It is, indeed, a pleasure to make your acquaintance, and I am happy to have you under my command.

"I shall inspect the ship's company."

In a double rank facing him, Hoare's second surprise now presented arms—no fewer than six strangely uniformed men.

"Who the hell are these? Or what?"

"Our Marines, sir."

Hoare had never seen a Marine in any uniform other than the regulation bright red coat and white breeches. These men's coats and overalls were a dull green. Instead of pipeclay and twinkling brass, their accouterments were finished in lusterless black. Their Sergeant presented his gleaming halberd as smartly, nevertheless, and the men presented arms as crisply, as any other contingent of Jollies he had encountered. Hoare passed on to the crew.

He had long since decided that eye-to-eye contact was his best way to make an instant appraisal of another's character. The first one or two seamen offered no surprises, being the kind of cheerful grinning horny-footed creatures Hoare had known since he was twelve. But here he left familiarity behind. He was stopped by the appearance of the third hand. Cheerful and grinning like the others he might be, but this man had the longest, hairiest arms Hoare had ever seen on a human being.

"Who are you, sir?" Hoare whispered. The man looked at him from under his beetling brows in a startled way; perhaps he had never been called sir before in all his days.

"Iggleden, sir. Foretopman." An appropriate rating; the

man might have been a gibbon. He bared enormous yellow teeth in a grin and brought his right hand to his low, hairy forehead in salute. The movement was an impressive one.

"Second-story man, sir, as well," said Mr. Clay. Iggleden must have overheard, for he grinned still more widely and bobbed his head.

What had this little Lieutenant said? Hoare withheld comment and continued his inspection.

The appearance of the remaining hands on *Royal Duke's* spotless deck was equally unexpected. Hoare found himself viewing a row of men who, while they looked fit enough in their varied jumpers and petticoat breeches, must hardly ever have faced wind and weather. Except for a blackamoor and one manifest Oriental, their intelligent faces were noticeably paler than that of the typical tar, and three of them actually wore spectacles. In the navy, this was unheard of. The Oriental might be a Japanese, or he might be a Chinese; Hoare had never been able to tell one nation from the other, let alone identifying individuals.

Hoare now found himself staring into the green eyes of a woman, an unmistakable, full-bosomed woman, and a fine-looking woman at that, as he could not help observing. Her eyes were level with his own, which made her nearly a six-foot woman. She wore a seaman's roundabout jacket and loose trousers, not as if she had dressed up in costume for a masquerade or a prank, but because they were simply what any seaman or seawoman would wear.

"And who have we here, may I ask?"

Like Iggleden before her, but more gracefully, she knuckled her forehead.

"Taylor, sir, Sarah Taylor. Master's Mate."

"And your duties?"

"Cryptographer, sir. And geometer, when needed."

25

What?

"A superb navigator, sir," Clay murmured. "Theoretically, that is."

Those cautionary words reminded Hoare of Sir George's admonition: Hoare must keep close to his desk and never go to sea.

A neat turn of phrase, Hoare thought. Perhaps he should keep a little commonplace book for clevernesses of the kind and pass it on to his biographer when he died famous.

In addition to Taylor, two other hands were female. The Royal Dukes were, as Sir George had told him, indeed, "*manned* in quite an unusual manner." So that was why the Admiral had all but bitten his tongue to keep from laughing out loud.

"You must explain all this to me later," Hoare told his Lieutenant, handing him the commission still clutched in his hand. "First, however, I must read myself in. At least, I shall begin to do so; you will be so kind as to read the balance on my behalf when my voice gives out."

"Aye aye, sir," Mr. Clay said in an undertone. Then, in his normal, enviable full-bodied voice: "Off hats. Fall in aft." The Royal Dukes broke ranks and gathered around their vessel's mainmast.

Hoare began. "By the Commissioners for executing the office of Lord High Admiral of Great Britain and Ireland, et cetera, and of all His Majesty's plantations, et cetera. To Bartholomew Hoare, Esquire, hereby appointed Master and Commander of His Majesty's ship *Royal Duke.* . . ."

Clay took the paper that Hoare handed him and continued.

" 'By virtue of the power and authority to us given, we do hereby constitute and appoint you Commander of

His Majesty's ship *Royal Duke,* willing and requiring you forthwith to go on board and take upon you the charge of Master and Commander in her accordingly, strictly charging and commanding all the officers and company of the said ship to behave themselves, jointly and severally, in their respective employments with all due respect and obedience unto you, their said Captain, and you likewise to observe and execute the General Printed Instructions and such orders and directions as you shall from time to time receive from us or any other of your superior officers, for His Majesty's service. Hereof nor you nor any of you fail as you will answer the contrary at your peril. And for so doing this shall be your warrant. . . .' "

After twenty-two endless years, Hoare thought as he listened to the dignified ritual, he was in formal command of one of His Majesty's ships, with a firm grip on another rung of the ladder, and within reach of his Post-Captaincy.

Mr. Clay concluded his reading of Hoare's commission, folded it, and returned it to his Commander. "And now, men, three hearty cheers for Captain Hoare! Hip-hip . . ."

"Huzzay!"

"Hip-hip . . ."

"*Huzzay!*"

"Hip-hip . . ."

"*Huzzaaaay!*"

At the last cheer, all hats flew into the air, one of them flung overboard by its exuberant owner.

"Thank you, men," Hoare whispered tritely, "and women." Then, with a glance at his Lieutenant, he gave the signal for him to relay his next words at an audible level. When Mr. Clay obliged, one or two hands looked mystified by the process. "As you can hear, I never speak above a whisper, so I shall usually relay my orders through

Mr. Clay. I do have certain signals, however. . . ."

He broke off, withdrew his boatswain's pipe, and blew "All Hands."

"You know that one, I see," Hoare whispered, Clay echoing his whisper out loud for the crew at large. Hoare pocketed the pipe. "But you do not know this one. . . ."

Putting two fingers of one hand to his mouth, he emitted a piercing, rising whistle. Clay jumped, and so did a good half the crew. There was also a fluttering noise dead aft, behind Hoare's back. He forbore to turn in search of the noise's origin.

"That," he continued, "was my summons to Mr. Clay. I have many more such signals, which I wish you to learn in time. You will find me firm but fair. Do your duty, and you will have nothing to fear.

"Dismiss the hands, Mr. Clay."

Hoare took the next few minutes to walk the flush deck of his new command, guided by his new Lieutenant. She was a conventional Navy brig in half-scale. If he remembered *Beetle* correctly, she was perhaps less cluttered than her sisters. *Beetle* had been Hoare's very first ship; she had made his fortune for him before he was nineteen. It was all very well that *Royal Duke's* eight brass four-pounders, bowsed tight against her low bulwarks, gleamed to perfection in the October sun. All the same, they looked like toys and would have little more striking power than so many firecrackers. Her broadside would be a fearsome sixteen pounds, equal to no more than the blow of a single one of a frigate's main guns. *Hardly fit to stand in the line of battle,* Hoare repeated to himself.

Two strange high wooden cases squatted in her stern sheets. They would surely carry away at the first sign of a breeze. Whatever they were, he must have them stowed elsewhere—if, that is, *Royal Duke* was going to sea, a supposition that was already beginning to stir in Hoare's mind. For now, though, he suppressed issuing an order to have the obtrusive cases pitched overboard, since upon closer inspection he saw that the cases were neatly divided into pigeonholes. That, he realized, was exactly what the boxes held—holes, pigeons, for the use of. In fact, a few were occupied by murmuring birds. One occupant and then another took wing, circled, and returned; the fluttering that had taken place at his whistle a few moments ago explained itself.

Belowdecks, Hoare found *Royal Duke*'s architecture bewildering. Forward of the guarded doorway to the cabin suite that was to be his own new home, a clean sweep reached into her forepeak. It was low but surprisingly spacious. Unlike every other vessel's he could remember, her 'tween-decks was well lit; thick glass prisms were let into the overhead at frequent intervals, and several skylights admitted the cool October sunshine. Its overhead itself was high enough to accommodate Hoare's height without his needing to stoop. Long hanging tables, interrupted only by the brig's masts and flanked by hanging chairs and benches, stretched along her center line.

But it was the arrangement of compartments stretching the full length of the space, on both sides, that was most unusual. Between their louvered doors—there were no fewer than eight to a side—the brig's builder had set ranks of cabinets and bookshelves.

Several of the crew had already reseated themselves at their tables and were at work over various papers, while others looked over their shipmates' shoulders and still others had congregated into groups. One of these had gathered round a messmate who seemed to be doing magic tricks for them. *Any ship's officer who was attentive to his duty would have sent these people about theirs,* Hoare thought, and was about to chide Clay but then realized that perhaps they *were* about their business.

The woman Taylor—"Master's Mate," as she had named herself—had donned spectacles to resume a task that apparently involved the use of mathematical tables and an abacus. Double the length of her neighbors' queues, her own thick sandy pigtail reached the bench on which she sat. *A Mate, indeed,* Hoare thought.

All in all, the 'tween-decks space of HMS *Royal Duke* reminded Hoare less of a man-o'-war than a counting-house or some other kind of lay monastery that, like those of the early Irish Christians, accommodated both sexes in mutual, uncomfortable celibacy. If his command was intended to be a countinghouse, what was he doing here, he who had never in his life more than walked through one? His heart sank.

"May I show you your quarters, sir?" came Clay's voice at his side.

"If you would be so kind, Mr. Clay."

The other went to the glossy teak door set high in the after bulkhead of *Royal Duke's* great main compartment and signaled the Marine sentry to open it for his commander. The man wore the same uniform as his mates. On this second sight, Hoare found it oddly familiar.

"What's your name?" he asked.

The marine looked about him to see whom his Captain might be addressing. "Me, zur?" he replied at last.

"Yes. You."

"Yeovil, if you please, zur. Gideon Yeovil, of Harrow-barrow. That's north of Plymouth. . . ."

"Very good, Yeovil. And . . . isn't that a rifle you're carrying?"

"Yes, zur. We Johnnies in *Royal Duke,* zur, we'm all Riflemen."

That explained the green uniform. It was the same as the one some unknown genius had designed during the late American war, for the first Riflemen in the Army. Hoare had seen it in Halifax then, but hardly ever since. As sharpshooters, Riflemen were better off unseen, and the lobster coat had drawn fire as a whore did sailors. Hoare wondered if the same principle might not save lives among the soldiery in general but set the idea aside as absurd. After all, he supposed, Lobsters were meant to stand there and be shot at. But not *his* lobsters, by God. Now that he had his very own live, unboiled green lobsters, he would guard their lives just as they guarded his.

Hoare stepped into a blaze of sunlight pouring through the cabin windows. Struck not only by the sun, he stood stupefied. Though he must still stoop, this was luxury.

The book-lined space might be lower than the Captain's quarters in a fifty-gun, two-decker fourth-rate ship of the line and half the breadth, but it was little shorter. It was laid out in a similar fashion. A wide, heavy table stood before a comfortable chair just forward of the glazed window opening onto *Royal Duke*'s gallery, *his* gallery. Other chairs stood about the black-and-white diaper-patterned canvas laid on the deck underfoot. Suspended from one overhead beam was an enormous construction whose purpose eluded him. It was evidently still another chair—but a chair for what? It could have held a young elephant.

"What on earth is *this?*" Hoare whispered.

"Sir Hugh's special chair, sir," Mr. Clay replied. "Admiral Abercrombie was wont to visit Captain Oglethorpe quite frequently when we lay in Greenwich."

"Sir Hugh Abercrombie must be a very big man."

"A very great man," Clay said in a neutral voice. Personal size, Hoare realized, might be as sensitive a topic for this wee man as commercial sex or whispering was for himself. He would have to be very mindful of this.

He was about to ask Mr. Clay to assemble the officers when he remembered that in addition to the two of them, if his memory was correct, *Royal Duke* counted only King's warrant officers in her complement, plus, of course, the seamen and a boy or two. He decided, instead, to query Clay about their mission.

"Take a seat, won't you, Mr. Clay?" Clay complied. Hoare noted in passing that the poor man's toes did not reach the deck when he sat.

"Did Captain Oglethorpe leave a servant when he died?"

"Oh, yes, sir. Whitelaw by name."

At the sound of his name, Whitelaw himself entered, bringing with him a tray of delicacies: a decanter of what looked like a tawny port, glasses, and a plate of biscuits. He was portly, but portly in the way of a wild boar: heavy, solid, and probably extremely strong. He placed the re-freshments on the table and withdrew without a word.

"Tell me about yourself, Mr. Clay," Hoare whispered when he had poured each of them a glass.

The little Lieutenant was quite willing to speak of himself. When he first went to sea, he told Hoare, he was no smaller than other midshipmen of the same age.

"I simply failed to grow," he explained, apparently feeling no more embarrassment about his stature than Hoare did about his silence.

Hoare needed little time to learn that his Lieutenant was mentally quick. Though small, he looked physically fit—nimble, in fact. He had, he said without affectation, been out twice and obtained satisfaction each time.

"I chose swords both times," he said. "My adversaries were so surprised at being up against such an unexpectedly long reach on the part of such a miniature opponent that, on each occasion, I drew first blood with no ado."

Since one of his maternal uncles was an Admiral and an Earl——. "My stature may be negligible, sir, but my standing is not." Mr. Clay's interest had sufficed to overcome any reservations the examining board might have had about his lack of stature, so he eventually found himself a Lieutenant. But since his commissioning, Mr. Clay had never seen action. Most of his service had been in auxiliary vessels or, naturally enough, in cutters, brigs, and others of the smallest men-o'-war.

He had been seconded to *Royal Duke* a year ago. He knew her crew and her mission from main truck to keelson, for the late Captain Oglethorpe, as he faded out of life, had lately relied more heavily upon him every day. In these last months, Mr. Clay said frankly, he had commanded the yacht in all but name.

"And to tell you the truth, sir," he said, "I am happy to be relieved of full responsibility for both the vessel and her business. A person with my limited experience in the world of statecraft has no business meddling in the sorts of affair that come aboard us here."

Of these affairs, there were four important ones at present, Clay explained. The first was the dissection and improvement, for similar use against the French, of the clockwork timers whose provenance Hoare himself had just run down in the course of a previous Herculean labor for Admiral Hardcastle. The second was the plugging of an information leak that had appeared among the clerical staff in Portsmouth. The third was an inquiry into a sharp reduction in morale and hence in productivity among certain mateys in the Navy Yard. The fourth involved breaking the cipher that Hoare had encountered during his inquiry last spring. Clay had sensibly delegated the day-to-day pursuit of each mission to a different individual.

"If I may, sir," he said, "I propose that we summon each in turn to tell us about his task. Or hers in one case, for Taylor is responsible for the cipher."

"Very good," Hoare said. "Let us begin with Taylor, then. Will you pass the word for her?"

Taylor still wore her spectacles but had pushed them to the top of her head. Hoare thought they made her look like a highly premature grandmother.

"Be seated, if you please, Taylor," Hoare whispered. Clay's face took on a surprised look, as if he was none too sure that *Royal Duke*'s Captain was wise to address a hand with "please," let alone inviting her to be seated in his presence.

"Tell me," Hoare asked, "what progress have you made in deciphering the set of messages . . . that originated with the affair of the infernal machines last spring?"

"Almost none, sir," she admitted. For her impressive size her voice was quiet, her accent ladylike. A gentlewoman in reduced circumstances, perhaps?

"I am convinced that the key to them is a passage in some text carried by both sender and recipient. The Bible is the most common key, as you must know, being the most widely distributed text. But I have tried both the King James and Douai versions without success."

Not only ladylike: prim. A bluestocking, then, disguised as a sailor.

"But why are you using English translations of the Bible when the messages are almost certainly in French?" Hoare asked.

"In *French,* sir?"

"Yes. You knew that, surely. In the covering letter I enclosed with the messages, I informed the Admiralty that at least two of the men using the cipher spoke French and that one left a French Bible next to his worksheets."

"That information never reached me, sir," came the quiet voice.

"I can corroborate that, sir," Clay said. "I received the material and inspected it before handing it on to Taylor. There was no covering letter, just the messages."

So, Hoare thought, *someone had slipped up, either at the Admiralty or in Portsmouth.* Was it by carelessness, he wondered, or intention? Could this have to do with the information leakage problem? Whichever and whoever it was, the omission had kept *Royal Duke*'s cryptographer from deciphering the messages. The delay might have serious consequences, for while the writer himself might have been put out of the way, his unknown master remained at liberty. Furthermore, the prospect of still more French agents lying doggo in his working network was disconcerting.

"Is there a French Bible aboard?" Hoare asked.

"I'm sure there is, sir," Taylor said. "If you'll give me leave, I'll ask McVitty to find it and begin forthwith."

"Do so, Taylor. But who is McVitty?"

"Our librarian, sir," Clay interjected. "The short, square woman with spectacles."

"Good heavens," Hoare said. "Thank you, Mr. Clay. Carry on, Taylor. And look first in Kings."

"Aye aye, sir. I remember—Jehu and Ahab. Second Kings, chapter nine, verse twenty. Thank you, sir.

"But, sir, I must point out that there are surely as many editions of the Bible in French as there are of our own King James version. Would it be possible to obtain the particular volume to which you just referred?"

"We shall try to get it for you."

Taylor's legs were not to be seen beneath her sailor's wide breeches, Hoare thought, *but yes, her stockings were surely blue.*

"Shall we go on to review the timers, sir?" Clay asked.

Before Hoare could assent, a knock came on the cabin door. Hoare gave Clay a meaningful look, intended as an instruction to call, "Come!," but it took the other a full second to realize what was being asked of him. When Clay finally spoke the magic word, the sentry Yeovil appeared.

"Mr. 'Ancock here says as how there's a signal from Admiralty House, sir," he said, looking squarely between his two officers.

"Very good," Hoare whispered. "And, Yeovil, if I whistle like this"—he uttered a gentle chirruping noise—"it means for you to come straight in."

While he had the man's attention, he went through several other signals and had him repeat them.

"I want you to teach those signals of mine to your messmates tonight," he said.

"Aye aye, sir," said Yeovil. "An' Mr. 'ancock? He was actin' like the message was urgent."

"My God. I was carried away. Have him bring it, please."

"Hancock's our pigeon fancier," Mr. Clay murmured. "And one of our signalmen, since we have no young gentlemen in our complement."

"Sir, Admiralty House signals for you to report to the Port Admiral forthwith," Hancock said. Hoare found him hard to understand, for he had few teeth remaining, and those rotten. His breath was horrible.

Hoare thanked Hancock but took up his hat and fled the confinement of his new cabin as swiftly as he could, Clay trotting behind him.

"Never let that man into my quarters again, Clay,"

Hoare said. "Have my gig manned, if you please." Clay thundered the order.

Hoare had saluted his command's nonexistent quarterdeck and was about to swing down into the gig when an exciting thought came to him.

"Tomorrow, Mr. Clay, be so kind as to send two men to the man Guilford at the small boat dock in the Inner Camber. Have them inform Mr. Hackins of the Swallowed Anchor . . . that I shall now be living aboard *Royal Duke* regularly. I shall settle my account with him on my return." (Breath.) "They are to pack up the gear in my rooms and bring around my pinnace—er—*Neglectful*. I shall attach her to *Royal Duke* as tender."

That had been a three-breath sentence for Hoare—too long for comfort.

"Aye aye, sir," Clay said, and doffed his hat in salute as Hoare dropped over the side into the gig.

That will be enough to make all stare, Hoare said to himself as the gig's crew rowed him awkwardly ashore. Surely *Royal Duke* would be the first Admiralty yacht to have her own tender. Yet he knew that, even with the continuity provided by *Neglectful,* he would miss the peaceful, monotonous life he had lived at the Swallowed Anchor. What, he asked himself, was he to do about his ward, the tubular little Jenny Jaggery? He had promised her father, Janus, that he would care for the creature, yet she would hardly belong in *Royal Duke.* He must take counsel with Eleanor Graves the next time he saw her. Perhaps she, like the dauntless partridge she was, would take the child under her wing into her personal pear tree.

• • •

"I didn't expect to see you again so soon, Hoare," the Admiral said. This was, Hoare thought, *the very first time Sir George had failed to chide him as a laggard.*

"We have another unexplained killing on our hands. Or two, rather. A message has just reached me to the effect that the bodies of Francis Getchell, Captain of *Agile,* twenty-eight, and his cousin Benjamin, Captain of *Argilla,* thirty-two, have been found in the Nine Stones Circle near Winterbourne Abbas."

"This is dire news, indeed, sir," Hoare said. He had known both officers, liked one, and admired the other.

"You know Winterbourne Abbas, of course."

"I fear I am not acquainted with the gentleman, sir," Hoare whispered.

"It's a place, Hoare, not a person. Nor, to be candid, did I know of it. Rabbett had to enlighten me; it appears that he used to nibble the farmers' cabbages thereabouts."

Rabbett, Hoare knew, was a minor clerk in the office of the Admiral's secretary, Patterson. Heracles, when Sir George was in a jovial mood, was Hoare himself.

"I'm little acquainted with the inland geography hereabouts," Sir George confessed. "I'm a Staffordshire man myself. It seems Winterbourne Abbas lies west of Dorchester. The Nine Stones Circle, Rabbett tells me, is one of those ancient British temples, a miniature Stonehenge, if you will. You *do* know of Stonehenge?"

"Yes, sir."

"Well, I am told the two Captains were en route from London to Plymouth by hired coach to rejoin their ships. A shepherd found their bodies in the Circle, beheaded and robbed. They were both under orders to join Nelson. Since Nelson is already desperate for frigates, this strikes him a hard blow at a bad time. The two vessels will sail, of course, but neither First Lieutenant has enough experience to be put in permanent command. Their Lordships are taking two jobbing Captains off half-pay to replace the dead men. With frigate Captains in such short supply, you can imagine *those* fellows' caliber. Barrel scrapings, I'll warrant.

"Nobody saw fit to inform me about this until this morning, which is why I did not call it to your attention during your previous visit. However, that is beside the point. What *is* to the point, sir, is that I am requesting your new command to take it upon itself to investigate these killings, find the perpetrator or perpetrators, and bring him or them to justice. Sir Thomas Frobisher thinks himself King in the region. You know all too well what he thinks of the Navy, and of you in particular. I can hardly rely on *him* to pursue this outrage with the requisite energy."

Hoare heard Sir George's next words with only half an ear. The Nine Stones Circle was in Dorset. Weymouth was in Dorset. The recent plot to blow up His Majesty's ships had been spawned in Weymouth, by Edouard Moreau. Moreau had been all too hobnob with the frog-shaped Sir Thomas, who, as Sir George had said, considered himself the absolute ruler of southern Dorset. Ever since Sir Thomas had goaded Hoare into an ill-timed jape about bat fanciers in the Midlands who flew their treasures against flies and used the prey to nourish their pet frogs, the Baronet had loathed him.

Sir Thomas was a rare breed, both a Baronet, the title he had inherited from his forebears, and a made knight like Sir George himself. When they had last run athwart each other's hawse, the knight had elected to encroach upon Hoare's destruction of Edouard Moreau and insisted on riding victoriously all the way back to Portsmouth, ahead of the troop of horse marines bearing the renegade's body, leading his own mesne of retainers. In fact, the two knights,

Sir Thomas Frobisher and Sir George Hardcastle, had held an oral passage at arms thereafter, in this very office.

The thought had passed through Hoare's mind before that Sir Thomas might be "Himself," as he had heard agents call the mysterious personage believed to lurk behind Moreau and perhaps others. Could this be a new initiative on the part of Himself?

"You are not attending, Mr. Hoare!"

"Sorry, sir. What you were saying made me recollect Sir Thomas Frobisher to mind."

"Him? The man's mad, mad as King George. If he had his way, he'd be King Thomas the First, that's what. 'Crown of Ethelred,' indeed! But, *as I was saying,* I cannot *require* you to accept this request. After all, I do not command the movements of *Royal Duke.* She and now you come directly under Admiralty orders. In principle, I have only the same administrative responsibility for your ship as I assume as Port Admiral the moment the anchor of any of His Majesty's ships is dropped at Spithead.

"No, I can only *request* this service of you, Heracles. Of course, I am reasonably confident that, if pressed, Sir Hugh Abercrombie would accommodate me. If I took steps to do so, nothing would be lost but time, I assure you."

"Happy to be of service, sir, as always," Hoare whispered.

"Very good. Carry on, then, Heracles."

In another of his classical moods, Sir George had dubbed Hoare "Heracles" by reason of the endless series of tasks that he was required to perform. This meant, as the Admiral had happily added, that he himself must be the hero's eccentric master and monarch, while Patterson, flag secretary, was Talthybius, the herald who brought the missions to lay upon Heracles' back. Clumsy, in Hoare's opinion, but it made Sir George happy, and that was no small task itself.

"Aye aye, sir." Just as his hand was on the doorknob, a thought struck Hoare, and he turned.

"May I borrow Rabbett, sir, if need be?"

"*Rabbett?* What on earth . . . oh. Of course. Excellent notion. I'll have Patterson hold him in his hutch for you. Don't let the Whispering Ferret get him."

The Admiral chuckled. He knew, it seemed, that Whispering Ferret was one of the names used by people who bore an antipathy to Hoare. The Admiral, in fact, knew a great deal.

"Now *go.*"

"Here you are, sir." Outside the Admiral's door, Patterson held out a folder of papers. And, in response to Hoare's whispered request, "Yes, of course. I'll hold Rabbett for you, sir, by the ears if I must."

As the gig rowed him back to *Royal Duke,* Hoare found himself wondering, not for the first time, what it was that made people persist in jesting and japing over others' unusual names. Surely they must realize that the name's owner had long since heard every possible weary play upon it. Moreover, the jester often went in harm's way. Mr. Clay's understated story this noon had demonstrated that. For his own part, even before Captain Joel Hoare had arranged for his son to go into *Centurion,* 60, as midshipman, young Bartholomew had run a jeering schoolmate through the thigh with a carving knife.

Hoare shrugged. He was used to the weary custom by now and had learned ways of either diverting or damaging those who offended him. So far, he had avoided killing anyone in his affairs of honor.

The nights were drawing in, Hoare noticed as the gig shoved off. It was more than halfway to its destination when he saw that *Royal Duke* was now accompanied by another, still smaller, more familiar vessel. So Mr. Clay had already complied with Hoare's request and had *Neglectful* brought over from the little estuary where Hoare had kept her. Very brisk of Mr. Clay. Hoare made a mental note to have a spare rifle put aboard her; his own had been missing since he made that first momentous call in Weymouth. The rifle had, he supposed, been carried off to France in Moreau's schooner *Marie Claire* after her owner had died in the surf off Portland Bill. It had been a work of art, but since there would be no replacing it this side of the Atlantic, he would have to make do with one of the Marines' standard-issue Baker weapons.

Neglectful's larboard bow, Hoare saw, bore a fresh, raw, newly painted patch.

"I'm pleased to see our new tender, Mr. Clay," he said as he returned the Lieutenant's salute. "But somebody has been mishandling her."

Clay's face reddened in the dusk. "Yes, sir. Joy, sir; boatswain. Timothy Joy."

"*Boatswain,* is he? And he can't bring a boat alongside without tearing her sides out? He should be disrated."

"Aye, sir. But . . ."

"But what?" Hoare demanded.

"We haven't a better. He's our quarterstaff instructor. And he's excellent with the brightwork and a superb marlinspike seaman."

"Hmph."

"He's waiting to report to you, sir." Clay nodded toward a wrinkled man who stood beside *Royal Duke's* mainmast, twisting his hat anxiously in both hands. When Hoare beckoned to him, he came up and knuckled his forehead, looking at his enormous boots, shamefaced.

"Well, Joy, I see you've managed to practically wreck

our new tender. How long have you been rated boat-swain?"

"Gone these forty years, sir," the wrinkled man said.

"Forty years? And you still can't bring a boat alongside without staving her in?"

"No, sir. 'Twere me eye, sir. I can't judge distances no more, sir." Joy raised his head, and Hoare saw that where his right eye should have been was a red, oozing hollow.

"Very good, Joy. Carry on, now."

"Beggin' your pardon, sir, but I've a message from the shore."

"Well?" Hoare asked.

"From Miss Jenny, sir. She says like she's learned to write all her letters now, as far as K, and please will you remember about the kitting you promised her?"

At the mention of "Miss Jenny," Hoare's heart forgot his rage at the inept Joy. He had not forgotten the kitten. He thanked Joy and dismissed him once again.

He turned back to Clay.

"If you can find no more suitable man for this ship's boatswain than a one-eyed antique like Joy, Mr. Clay, we shall have to take a very hard look at our readiness for sea."

"Aye aye, sir," was all Clay could say.

"I bring us a new assignment, Mr. Clay," Hoare said. "Come below, if convenient, and I'll tell you about it."

Chapter III

—————

I N HOARE'S cabin, the silent Whitelaw already awaited them, once again bearing biscuits and port. Hoare did not believe he had yet heard the man speak. Was he, perhaps, even more totally mute than his master?

"Well, Mr. Clay, it is *my* turn to inform *you*." So saying, he conveyed to his Lieutenant all he had just learned about the affair in the Nine Stones Circle.

"All too little," he concluded. "I propose to make at least the first investigation myself. But I would like your recommendation of a man—not a woman at this time, if you please—to serve as my deputy or amanuensis. I have never worked with one, and it is clear that I must learn how. In your experience, which of our crew is best suited to handle this mission?"

Clay gave Hoare's question a full fifteen seconds' consideration before saying, "Thoday, sir."

"Of course, today," Hoare said in a displeased voice. "Tomorrow at the latest. There isn't a moment to be lost."

"Tho*day* is his name, sir. Accent on the ultimate. His father was one of Sir John Fielding's best men—the 'blind beak,' you know—and Titus Thoday takes after him. Experienced, cold, sharp. Rated Gunner's Mate, nominally."

"Very good. Let's have a look at him."

Hoare chirruped, and Whitelaw reappeared.

"Get me Titus Tho*day,* Whitelaw," Hoare said. But first . . ."

Hoare demonstrated to Whitelaw a few simple signals besides the chirrup that he had found useful in dealing with persons waiting on him—the trills on his boatswain's pipe he had developed with pink Susan Hackins at the Swallowed Anchor, for example. He was already confident that the silent man would need no rehearsal. In fact, the brief experience told him that Whitelaw might well foresee his master's requirements before he knew them himself.

"Now, get me Thoday," he concluded.

"Aye aye, sir." These were the first words the man had uttered. *That settled one question: Whitelaw was not mute, but merely taciturn—a rare but welcome characteristic for a Captain's servant,* Hoare thought.

Had Hoare been anyone but his Commander, the demeanor of the person who appeared within moments would have been quite intimidating. Thoday stooped to clear his head in what Hoare considered a condescending way, even though *Royal Duke's* low overhead made the stoop necessary. Thoday's nose was a beak, his eyes an icy pale gray, his thin lips habitually compressed. He accepted as merely his due Hoare's invitation to be seated and listened in silence until Hoare finished his story for the second time in half an hour.

"I shall accompany you ashore tomorrow morning, sir, when you depart," Thoday then said. Neither Hoare nor

Clay had said a word about Hoare's coming journey, nor did Thoday seem to doubt that his Commander would accommodate him without boggling.

"We shall require an assistant with local knowledge," he continued.

"Lemuel Rabbett is one of Admiral Hardcastle's clerks," Hoare said tersely. "He is a native of the area, and he has been told to make himself available. I hope you'll find that satisfactory," he added with mild sarcasm.

"I shall find out quickly enough." Thoday's voice was hard, but it bore a faint hint of approval. "We can pick him up in the morning, as we leave town."

Thoday rose to his feet.

"And now, gentlemen, I have my preparations to make—as, no doubt, have you."

"A bit above himself, isn't he?" Hoare asked as the cabin door closed behind the Gunner's Mate.

"You will find, sir, that most of my, *your* crew have little innate respect for rank," Clay said. "They are something like the Americans in that respect. But, fortunately, our people at least know what correct behavior is and generally choose to adopt it when strangers are present, so no self-esteem is lost on either side.

"I am given to understand that Thoday is an excellent gunner as well, although he has had no chance to demonstrate his prowess with our poor little popguns." *So Mr. Clay was a secret fire-eater*, thought Hoare.

Aloud, he whispered, "We shall have to correct that as soon as I return, shan't we?"

They had ordered an Admiralty chaise to be ready to leave at the turn of the watch, so Hoare would not even have time to shave. Whitelaw picked up the portmanteau he had yet to unpack for his Commander and, lugging it, led the way from *Royal Duke*'s cabin into the misty evening.

At the boarding port, Whitelaw handed the bag to Thoday, who accepted it without blinking an eye. Mr. Clay doffed his hat in salute.

"Since you have issued no orders to the contrary, sir, may I presume that I should continue with the projects assigned us before *Royal Duke* left London?"

"Exactly. But I would like you to add some drill with her—er—great guns."

"Even without her gunner, sir?"

"*Especially* without her gunner, Mr. Clay."

"Aye aye, sir." Hoare thought to see an ironic smile on Thoday's thin lips. Was there an undercurrent of something here? he wondered.

"Give way, all," said the coxswain.

Before the chaise departed Portsmouth in the chill of late evening, Lemuel Rabbett had to undergo Thoday's inquisition. The little clerk showed himself as full of local knowledge about the Nine Stones Circle, and the copses and heathy moors in which it was set, as any harbor pilot must necessarily be about his local waters. Not so long ago, he explained, the area had been largely enclosed and left fallow to support the growing flocks of several local landowners. As the party already knew, it was one of the shepherds whose dog had sniffed out the bodies of Captains Francis and Benjamin Getchell. In his boyhood, Rabbett had roamed the area, studying the birds and his namesake coneys, and he knew most of the lonely men, as well as their dogs.

The Nine Stones Circle, he told them as the chaise

trundled through the moonlit October countryside, was itself something of a magnet for the curious. He had even heard that strangers gathered in and around its nine stones at the equinoxes and solstices to conduct ungodly rites. After all, the Poor Lot Barrows lay only a few miles farther west, and everyone knew that there, on those same occasions, the wights came out to dance with the neighboring witches.

Of course, if one were to ask Rabbett his opinion, only the locals believed in that sort of thing. A native of Dorchester himself, four miles distant, Mr. Rabbett knew perfectly well there was nothing in it. Besides, since neither an equinox nor a solstice was at hand, as the Naval gentlemen surely need not be told, the Captains' deaths could have had nothing to do with any Satanistic celebrations in the Nine Stones Circle.

"Nonetheless," Rabbett said, "it's odd, is it not, gentlemen, that All Hallows' Eve is not so many days away?"

And so on and on, throughout the night. Rabbett must be habitually nocturnal. He left Hoare, at least, only a few minutes in which to nap. Whenever he woke, Thoday was sitting opposite him, awake, erect, and silent, and Rabbett was talking.

The bodies of the Captains Getchell, Hoare had been told, were reposing at the Church of All Angels. Here the chaise drew up before sunrise, just as a sleepy sexton trudged into sight.

The sexton made no trouble about letting them see the two corpses. The weather had been mercifully cool, so the odors of corruption were still faint. Nevertheless, Rabbett gagged and pressed a kerchief to his face.

"Have the relatives of the dead men been notified, do you know?" Hoare whispered to the sexton.

"Ye needn't whisper, sir. There's only one of 'em as 'as ears to 'ear with, and 'e ain't listenin'.'"

For, as Hoare had already been told, only a ragged stump remained on one of the bodies, windpipe and neckbones projecting obscenely with the shrinkage of the tissue from around them. The other head had been replaced on the neck, where it no longer seemed to fit. The owner had been struck fiercely from behind, his occiput being crushed and part of his brains splattered. The single pair of eyes that remained, now mercifully closed by those who had found the bodies, must have almost bulged from their sockets. Blood and brains stained both uniform coats, suggesting to Hoare that the missing head would display the same injuries. Their coats had been stripped of their gold braid and buttons, their shoes were missing, and their stockings— and their breeches, of course—stained and ruined. Coat and breeches pockets had been turned out.

"Oh, dear me," Rabbett said from behind Hoare and Thoday. The latter looked at each other and shrugged; there was little these sad, dead shapes could tell them. As they turned to leave, Hoare saw Thoday cross himself. This explained something about the gunner—but hardly everything.

"You did not answer my question . . . except with an untimely impertinence," Hoare whispered to the sexton. "Kindly restrain your misplaced humor and give me a civil answer. Have the relatives been notified?"

"I don't know, sir," the sexton said. "Ye'd be better talking with Vicar, or the Capting. He be crowner, he be."

"The Captain?"

"Aye. Capting Spurrier. Ye don't know the Capting? Well, 'e'll put you right, 'e will."

"His whereabouts?"

The sexton cackled. "Ye'll find him in town hall, if anywhere."

But Hoare's itch to view the scene of the crime was too strong to resist. Captain Spurrier must wait to "put him right," whatever that meant. Rabbett knew that Mr. Trowbridge was vicar at the Church of All Angels but could not enlighten Hoare about Captain Spurrier. Hoare directed the chaise's driver to take them west to Winterbourne Abbas.

The morning sun, still low, was casting shadows ahead of them when the chaise put the scattered cottages of Winterbourne Abbas behind it. The Circle, a broken ring of high gray fangs, appeared out of the ground fog, reminding Hoare of a giant's skeletal lower jaw buried to the teeth in sand, except that here the "sand" was cropped greensward. Once there, and a wandering shepherd found, the two seagoing men needed Rabbett to interpret the heavy local dialect. No, this man was Emmon Tredegar. It was his wife's cousin Dym they wanted, for it was Dym and his dog Boye who had found the horror in the ring. Dym and his flock were probably down over the coombe yonder. The man pointed vaguely northward.

There was no road that way, only a path that wound lazily off into the distance. The three left the chaise in its driver's charge and plodded on in single file, half-asleep, pausing every so often to negotiate a stile. At last, the barking of a dog brought them fully awake. Hoare caught sight of a man standing lofty among his surrounding sheep, their owner's reddle mark blood-red above their dirty tails. Between the strangers and the flock it owned, the dog stood its ground, calling, *War! Fear! Foes!* at the top of its lungs. Rabbett, who happened to be in the lead, uttered an odd whistle that appealed to Hoare's ear instantly. Apparently the dog was of the same mind, for it quieted, sniffed Rabbett's hand and then, in a more intimate manner, that of each of the two other intruders, and led the way through the flock of its bored-looking, bleating charges to its master, tail waving proudly in a victory signal.

Dym Tredegar, when they managed to communicate with him at last, squatted and offered around some of the hard, strong yellow cheese in his scrip. He must explain first that while he was, indeed, Emmon's wife's cousin, he was also Emmon's own cousin. That understood, he was happy to tell his tale once more to these strangers. He knew the story well, and he was a skilled raconteur, though sometimes unintelligible to foreigners like Hoare. At these points, Dym must turn to Rabbett for an interpretation.

" 'Twas was early mornin'," Dym said, "just about the same time of day as it is now. Boye here got up to some tricks, and I could hear he was in the Ring, so I went to see what 'twas so moithered him.

"Well now, ge'men, what did I see but two other ge'men, a-wearin' coats almost like yours, sir"—he pointed at Hoare with his chin—"a-layin' on their bellies, there . . . and there, dead as the stones around 'em, in front of that there stone in middle of Circle. I didn't need to touch 'em none to know that, for I could see, plain as plain, they didn' 'a' but one 'ead between 'em. And that 'un 'ad been a-chopped off. It was like two butchers come up behind 'em like they was oxen for the slaughterin' and dopped 'em in back of their 'eads. And so down they'd went, a-dumpin' their blood all over the green in Circle, and the flowers a-layin' scattered roundabout, all in their garlands."

"Where was the other head?" Hoare asked.

"Not to be seen, sir," the shepherd answered through Rabbett.

"Their hats?" Thoday asked.

"Not to be seen, sir."

"Their pockets?"

Dym glowered, stubborn as one of his sheep. Then, as if he realized that these men were not accusing him of looting the dead, he relaxed again.

"Their pockets was turned out, sir, if that's what you mean. And their shoes was gone, too. Wouldn't 'a' been first time that green's drunk 'uman blood, I'll warrant." He shook his head. "Nay. You ask Mye Dabbleworth about that; she be wise enough for all of us."

Mye Dabbleworth, Dym explained, was a wisewoman who collected greens by night—moonlit nights especially, like the nights this week—and preferably there in the Circle.

"She coom all the way up from her darter's house in Dorchester. She used to live in Winterbourne over hill, but when Squire enclosed commons the folk was all evicted. Not that dere was that many . . ."

Hoare let Dym maunder on. He had found that one could never tell when a compulsive talker would drop a gem instead of a turgidity. But Hoare got no more good from Dym, nor apparently did Thoday, so they retraced their steps along the path and over the stiles to the Nine Stones Circle.

Once there, Thoday began to range the heavily trodden enclosure at an awkward stooping canter, grumbling to himself every so often as he went, while Hoare and Rabbett watched. Hoare almost thought to hear him snuffle as if he were a true sleuth, a bloodhound. He picked up some of the wilted garlands, sniffed them, grunted in a puzzled way, dropped them. He examined several of the stones closely, paying particular attention to the flat-topped ashlar that stood waist-high in the center of the ring, left the Circle to trot as far as the lane where their chaise and its driver still stood, inspected the ruts around the chaise, and returned inside the ring of watching stones. There he walked more cautiously around the enormous double bloodstain before the ashlar.

"It's a disgrace," Thoday declared, "how the men who took the bodies to Dorchester trampled the ground hereabouts. The tracks of their great feet are all over the Circle. They might have been *trying* to destroy the evidence."

If they were Frobisher minions and Sir Thomas was what Hoare thought he might just be, they might well have been doing precisely that.

"But it's plain as the Great Charter," Thoday declared. "The carriage was held up somewhere east of here, possibly in Dorchester, and highjacked with its passengers. The man-thieves numbered at least a dozen; we can hardly call them kidnappers, can we, in light of their captives' mature years?"

No more than jesting Pilate did Thoday pause for answer, but went on, "The victims' arms were bound, and they were brought *here.* They were hauled out of the chaise *here;* their shoes were removed *here;* they were unbound and clubbed from behind like vermin in a drive as they attempted to escape—*that* way. Shots were fired. One ball struck someone sitting on the chaise—the criminals' driver, I should suppose.

"The killers then beheaded the bodies, robbed them, and clambered into the chaise with their dead companion. They drove off westward, having parted company with the lone horseman.

"That is all the scene of the crime can tell us. It is peculiar, by the by, that though the greensward is badly torn up by human footprints, only a few participants actually stepped in the blood. As you can see, the effusion was considerable."

"I certainly would want to avoid wading about in blood," Hoare murmured.

"Perhaps, sir. Perhaps not." Thoday's voice was mildly scornful. "But a party of some ten or fifteen persons would have had some difficulty in dodging pools of that size. Shall we go, sir?"

"I don't understand how you discovered so much so quickly, Mr. *Tho*day," Rabbett said timidly. He accented the first syllable of the gunner's name.

"Elementary," Thoday said. "And it is Tho*day,* if you please, as in *today*. Moreover, one does not pronounce the full diphthong. But to answer your implied question, I shall show you how I did it. You will then tell me how obvious it was. Come." Thoday led the way out of the Ring.

"As you can see, the tracks of our chaise overlie those of the Captains' vehicle, and the latter—which are deeper than ours, there having been more men in it than would have made for distant travel in any comfort—extend beyond it. Their chaise stood long enough in one place for its wheels to have sunk in slightly but then moved a short distance forward, perhaps when the horses were startled by the shooting of their driver. By then, however, all the passengers had disembarked."

"You deduced that because the ruts are shallower," Hoare said.

"How obvious!" Rabbett declared.

"Indeed," Thoday said. "Excellent, Captain Hoare. Very good, sir. But, actually, you can see the confused tracks of at least four men as they stepped out of the vehicle. Now the Captains walked, at pistol-point, I presume, into the center of the Circle. They were forced to their knees—you can see the marks here, if you look closely—and required to remove their shoes."

"Why?" asked Hoare.

"It is impossible to tell, sir, from the tracks alone." Thoday's raised eyebrows reproved Hoare for a childish question.

" 'How do you know?' is what I meant."

Thoday shrugged. "Very seldom can mere tracks reveal motives, sir," he said. "One can only speculate, which we shall do in due course. It may have been a matter of ritual, whereby to go unshod before divinity showed humility and respect. The presence of out-of-season flowers, some of which were plaited into garlands, demonstrates that a rite of some sort was celebrated. There is something that puzzles me about the flowers, however. I wonder . . .

"But, to continue: the criminals cut the lines binding the Captains' arms—'why' is again a matter for speculation—and urged the prisoners to flee.

"They gave the demoralized brother officers a lead of a second or two. They fired shots, perhaps to speed the victims on their way. One of the shots struck the driver of the death chaise, as the spray of dried blood beside the tracks shows. Then the killers leaped after their prey, competing, I suspect, for first blood, and struck them down. Like vermin, as I said, or, more likely, like sacrifices. Human sacrifices. The rest I have already told you." Thoday folded his arms and stood silent.

"Amazing," said Rabbett.

"Elementary," said Thoday.

"Where do you suppose their chaise is now? And the driver's body?" Hoare asked.

"*Bodies,* you mean, sir," Thoday said. "For there were two drivers: the original driver from London and the man who replaced him at the reins when the chaise was highjacked."

"Of course," Hoare said.

"Of course, as you say," Thoday echoed, his voice

heavy with sarcasm. "As to your question, nothing here can tell us. They could be anywhere between London and Penzance. Perhaps the heavy-handed men of the local law, who destroyed so much of the evidence here, will be able to redeem themselves in my—*our*—eyes by having found something relevant beyond our horizon here. So we must retrace our steps to Dorchester and confront them. Shall we go?"

The three men stood in the middle of the Circle for a moment while Hoare made up his mind what to do next. He made much of studying the sketch map of the district that Rabbett had made for him.

"Let me see. There is no place hereabouts for us to set up headquarters. Dorchester is about five miles away—"

"Four, sir," Rabbett said.

"But I know of nothing there that would help our hunt for the killers. On the other hand, Weymouth is only a little more distant, six miles or thereabouts, it would seem—"

"Ten miles, sir," said Rabbett.

Hoare turned on the clerk. "*Will* you hold your tongue, sir? Six, ten, whatever distance, Weymouth is a major station . . . for the excisemen, and it may have been smugglers that killed the Getchells. The Weymouth men are likely to be able to point out possible suspects."

Which was more than the civil authorities in these parts were likely to do when he, Bartholomew Hoare, was the suppliant, Hoare thought. He stood in bad odor in Dorset.

"Yes," he said. "We shall make our base in Weymouth."

Thoday looked at him aghast.

"I protest, sir. Have I not just told you—"

"You do not, by God, take that mutinous tone with *me,* my man." This was Hoare's best commanding voice,

56

a rasp that he found it excruciatingly painful to produce. He used it seldom, therefore, mostly when, as now, a subordinate provoked him when he had not been expecting it.

"You do not *tell* your superior officer anything whatsoever except when asked. . . . You shall remember to keep your place, or it shall be the worse for you."

As Thoday stood silent and dumfounded, Hoare whistled for the Admiralty chaise. Weymouth might be, as he had said, a center for useful intelligence, but he knew a rationalization when he heard it, even if it was his own. Weymouth was also the home of Mrs. Eleanor Graves.

"On our way to Weymouth, of course," he said, "we shall retrace our steps to Dorchester. While there, we will talk with this Spurrier, who is apparently the person charged with finding the Captains' killers. . . . Then, Thoday, we shall find out what he has discovered, with particular reference to the missing drivers, the missing chaise, and the missing head."

Hoare finally ran Captain Walter Spurrier to earth at the Mitre Inn, where he was taking an early nooning or a late breakfast. He was also jesting in an intimate way with an admiring young woman of parts. It was not clear to Hoare just what Spurrier was Captain of; the scarlet uniform coat, heavy with bullion, bore cherry-colored facings. Hoare did not recognize the regiment. Judging from the shape of the saber dropped carelessly on the inn table, Spurrier's high boots, and the scar that ran from a ravaged left ear through his reddish side-whiskers to the corner of his sensuous mouth, he was a cavalryman or an ex-cavalryman. If he had not been seated, Hoare could have sworn he was swaggering. *All in all*, Hoare thought, *if ever a man was cut out to play the villain in some fustian Gothick novel, Spurrier was he.*

Whatever his regiment, Spurrier was visibly unimpressed by Hoare's own uniform. Though Spurrier removed his spurred boots from the low table before him, he did not rise. He looked Hoare up and down with cold heavy-lidded eyes—Hanoverian eyes, they might have been.

"Navy chap, I see. What brings you this far inland? This might be countryside for the Treasury's men, but you haven't the look of a tide-runner. Impress Service, perhaps? If so, you're not welcome here. Be off."

"Two dead Captains bring me, Mr. Spurrier," Hoare said. "One of them with his head gone astray. A missing chaise, in the Admiralty's service. And two drivers, one of them an Admiralty servant."

"Navy doesn't keep very good track of its property, does it, Bella, me dear?"

The young woman of parts giggled and jiggled.

"Not surprising you feel you must reveal your mission only in a whisper." Captain Spurrier's tone was just short of insolent.

Giggle. Jiggle.

Hoare sighed. The man obviously saw himself as cock of the walk here in Dorchester, and perhaps he was. Hoare itched to put him in his place but needed information. As long as his insolence grew no greater, Hoare felt, he must needs abide it. So he limited his riposte to fixing the idle Captain with his faded gray eyes narrowed and level, his brown face frozen. The basilisk stare as much as said, far more directly and credibly than Hoare's shattered vocal cords could have managed: "I have been defending my good name on the field of honor since I was six and my lack of voice since the Glorious First of June. I am still alive, though my voice may not be, and my name is as good as it was when my father gave it me. Draw your own conclusions, sir. Get yourself killed if you must. It is of no consequence to me."

The silence, and Hoare's stare, stretched on, and on, and on. In due course, Captain Spurrier sobered and rose to his feet, his chair toppling behind him. The young woman of parts forgot to giggle and stooped to right the chair. She hastily brought another for the visitor.

"My muteness *is* an unfortunate matter, sir," Hoare said in a placatory whisper as he seated himself, "even more for me than it is for you, I assure you. . . . My whisper has less to do with secrecy, however, than it does with an injury. I am sure you understand . . .

"Now to return to the matter of the missing head and the chaise. . . . I refer, of course, to the deaths of Captains Francis and Benjamin Getchell. Naturally, the Admiralty is much concerned. What can you, as . . . ?"

"Deputy Sheriff of Dorset for the Dorchester region— under Sir Thomas Frobisher, of course. And you'd be . . ."

"Your servant, sir. The name's Hoare. Bartholomew Hoare, at your service. In *all* respects," he added warningly. "What, I ask you once again, can you tell me about the deaths of the two Captains Getchell?"

Captain Spurrier was not prepared to be stared out of countenance again.

"I must consult my journals, sir. Will you be pleased to step over to my quarters?"

He led his unwelcome guests across the High Street to what might have once been the house of a prosperous merchant, with a black front door. Grasping an oddly phallic handle, Captain Spurrier opened the door and gestured to the others to precede him.

Hoare nearly coughed as he stepped into the shadowy hallway; beside him he heard Thoday sniff. A few times, particularly in the parish church of Sainte-Foi in Quebec where he had wedded his dear dead Antoinette, Hoare had been present at High Mass. Now he smelled the same cloying, pungent odor of cold incense. Why, he wondered, would Walter Spurrier, bold Captain in the Something Horse, burn incense in his quarters?

If the room to which Spurrier led Hoare was his place of business, it was a peculiarly furnished one, dark-paneled and lit by stained-glass windows as if it were some sort of chapel. Next to a great Bible on a stand, a wide, cluttered desk stood in the stained-glass window. Moving quickly, Spurrier strode to the desk, displacing a chair as he passed it so that it hindered Hoare and Thoday's path. When Spurrier threw a large piece of embroidered fabric over the desk, the breeze of its falling blew several papers to the heavily carpeted floor.

Hoare bent to retrieve them, nearly bumping heads with Thoday and his host.

"Thankee, gentlemen," Spurrier said when they handed him the papers.

"Now, let me see," Spurrier said. He seated himself at the far side of the desk and lifted one corner of the cloth. It looked to Hoare like some kind of garment. "Yes. Yes. Here we are."

He drew out several rumpled sheets of paper and pretended to inspect them.

"Says nothing here about any Getchell," he said. "You've probably been led astray."

"They were brothers, Mr. Spurrier. Getchell was their name. And I have not been led astray."

Uninvited, Hoare took a seat at the desk opposite the Captain and gestured to Thoday to follow suit.

Spurrier cleared his throat. "Now then, sir. What, more precisely, would you wish to know?"

"Our intention is the same as yours, of course," Hoare

whispered, "to lay the culprits by the heels and see them hanged. But if you don't mind . . . I'll have my colleague, Mr. Thoday, tell you what we know so far and what we would like to know. The spirits are willing, but, alas, as you pointed out so wittily just now, my voice is weak."

Spurrier turned to Thoday with something of a patronizing air.

"Enlighten me, then, my good man."

Unruffled, Thoday summarized the events he had described to Hoare and Rabbett in the Nine Stones Circle, without disclosing his method. When he was finished, Spurrier looked visibly less patronizing.

"I suppose you have evidence for what you have just told me?"

"Indeed," Thoday said.

"For instance, you claim that there were three murders."

"Four, sir. The two Captains whose bodies now rest in the Church of All Angels and two drivers."

"Four, then." Spurrier's voice was impatient. "How do you know about the third death, or the fourth, for that matter?"

"The Navy driver remains unaccounted for. He has simply been either abducted—which would serve the criminals no purpose—or killed, which they would have found far more convenient. The driver who replaced him was struck by a bullet, either aimed or accidentally, and died on his seat."

"Why are you so sure he is dead and not just wounded?"

"The blood he shed, Captain, was under high pressure. It spurted from him like water from a fire hose or, to use an analogy that will surely be more familiar to you, like so much horse piss. It was his heart's blood. Even a skilled surgeon—had one been present, which I beg leave to doubt—would have been hard put to it to stanch the flood in daylight, let alone moonlight. No, the second driver has already gone to his reward, as an unwelcome witness of the other killings."

"Tell us, if you please, what has been found of the other bodies, the missing head, and the chaise," Hoare said.

Again Captain Spurrier made much of looking through his papers.

"Er, I can tell you very little. One of the villagers in Grimstone says he heard a carriage and pair going north through the hamlet during the night at a gallop, but he saw nothing. Probably because he didn't want to see anything. In these parts, seeing too much can be dangerous. However, let me see. This is Saturday. The inquest is to be held on Tuesday. By then, I am confident that my men will have gathered all the evidence there is to be found. Meanwhile, no stone will be left unturned, I assure you. Of course, you are welcome to attend the inquest.

"In fact," Spurrier added, seemingly as an afterthought, "as coroner I may find it necessary to ordain your attendance, in light of your man—er—Thoday's findings. I still have my men out scouring the countryside, of course."

Hoare doubted that. Out of either natural indolence or concern for the wishes of some hidden master, Captain Spurrier would most certainly spend less of his time turning up stones on the trail of the men who had killed two Captains in the Royal Navy than he would turning up the skirts of the young woman of parts.

"Of course, Captain. I am, indeed, assured. Until Tuesday, then."

Captain Spurrier bowed to them from his doorstep and watched his two guests climb into their chaise, where they joined Rabbett.

"Weymouth, driver," Hoare whispered as he boarded.

"Will you be needing my services for a bit, Captain Hoare?" Rabbett asked before the driver could begin to obey. "You see, my mother and father dwell here in Dorchester, and it is more than a year since I have paid them my respects. I would be happy to walk to Weymouth from here. It would take me little more than two hours."

"Very good, Rabbett," Hoare said, "but put yourself to use while you are here. Lurk about whatever lurking spots you believe will bring you the most information . . . and bring me anything you can learn about what people are saying about this affair."

"I can do better than that for you, sir," said Rabbett. "My mother is gossip with half the womenfolk of Dorchester. I could have her tune her ears to the matter."

"Very good, Rabbett," Hoare said. "Until later, then." With a rap on the roof of the chaise, he signaled the driver to shove off.

This would be excellent. If Rabbett's ears were long, surely his mother's would be longer. So Hoare mused, then chided himself for succumbing, even if only in thought, to the selfsame idiot wit with which others had plagued him all his life.

"The Captain's papers, sir," Thoday murmured as the chaise rolled down the highway to Weymouth. "The ones he let fall from his desk and we helped him recover. . . ."

"Yes?"

"Had I dared, I would have retained one of them, but Captain Spurrier's eyes were on them, and I have yet to pass muster with Blassingame."

"I do not understand you," Hoare said. "Who is Blassingame, and why should you pass muster with him?"

"Beg pardon, sir. Mark Blassingame is sailmaker and

prestidigitator—magician—in *Royal Duke*. Among other things, he teaches filching."

"Good heavens," Hoare whispered. He remembered the man now; he was the one who had been performing magic tricks before a group of shipmates in a corner of *Royal Duke*'s working space.

"But what about the paper you wanted to filch?"

"I have seen Taylor—you remember Taylor at least, our student of codes and ciphers?—studying papers with the same texture and bearing the same distinctive writing pattern as the one I saw here just now. I am quite sure that the text was laid out in five-letter groups. I am therefore of the opinion, sir, that Captain Spurrier failed to conceal a ciphered message from our eyes. Moreover, sir, what was Captain Spurrier doing with a cope in his office?"

"A cope, Thoday? A clergyman's robe? Isn't that what a cope is?"

"Yes, sir. It was a cope he used to cover the materials on his desk. And a peculiar-looking cope it was, too."

"In what way?" Hoare asked idly. He was half-asleep.

"The embroidered figures looked sacrilegious, sir, if I may sound so fanciful."

Chapter IV

━━◆━━

*T*HE CHAISE'S driver found the steep scarp leading down into Weymouth town a hard stretch to manage. At last, he had Hoare and Thoday disembark.

"I won't have you gentlemen's blood on *my* hands if she oversets," he said. At the foot of the scarp, however, he let them back aboard, so they were able to enter Weymouth in dignity instead of dust.

The depressing piles of neglected construction materials that Hoare had noted in the streets last summer had merely grown more grass. It was questionable if the King in Kew, sane again now but still bewildered, would soon return to his favorite watering place. But Hoare knew where he was now, so he could direct the driver to the Dish of Sprats. There Hoare dismissed him, telling him to return early Monday.

Joseph Parker, proprietor of the Dish, recognized Hoare and seemed pleased to see him again. Parker evidently viewed him and Titus Thoday as men of equal standing, for Thoday's appearance greatly belied his station.

Nonetheless, Hoare surprised his host by calling for two rooms instead of sharing one with his companion. Hoare was ready to travel with Thoday and dine at the same table with him but drew the line at sleeping with an enlisted man when he need not.

Before leaving the Dish of Sprats, Hoare suggested to Thoday that he see what the folk in the town hall might have to contribute about the Nine Stones Circle affair. Hoare himself planned to call on Mrs. Eleanor Graves, then board the cutter *Walpole* for a glass of Captain Israel Popham's burgundy and some information.

At his own assignment, Thoday demurred. "I think, sir, that we would be well advised to leave the world of clerks and countinghouses to Mr. Rabbett when he arrives. After all, that is the world of his calling, just as this district is more or less his geographic world. I have lines of my own that I might be better employed in following."

Thoday did not choose to be more specific, but Hoare must agree with his observation about Rabbett, so he changed his order to Thoday accordingly. Moreover, Hoare knew that word of his return to Weymouth would reach Sir Thomas Frobisher's ears within minutes, if it had not already done so. The Knight-Baronet would have instructed every one of the town's functionaries to cast every possible impediment in Hoare's way. So he withdrew to prepare himself, by sluicing his head and combing his coarse hair, for his next piece of business: paying a call upon the woman who held his heart.

Eleanor Graves still wore the dull black of mourning for her murdered husband, Simon. It did not suit her sallow complexion, but then, Hoare admitted to himself, he had yet to see her becomingly clad. She received him in the

66

drawing room of the house she had shared with her late husband, sitting on her customary round, resilient tuffet. As usual, she looked rather round and resilient herself. Once again, Hoare was amazed at how dearly he had come to love her.

She was accompanied by a family of three ill-assorted cats. A strange rumble filled the room, as if the tumbrels of the Terror were passing in the cobbled street outside. The kitten, a glossy, tidy little black beast, was attacking the tuft at the end of its mother's tail. It resembled its mother not at all; the latter was large, awkward, and flustered and bore random growths of whitish fluff on her body and limbs. An enormous gray animal crouched beside Mrs. Graves, watching his family and giving off a benign thunderous purr. This, then, was the source of the tumbrel sound.

Hoare reached down a hand as he passed the gray beast. It stretched up its head to meet the hand; the tumbrels seemed to draw nigh as they bore pinioned royalty to a ghostly guillotine.

Mrs. Graves pointed at the kitten after allowing her hand to be kissed. "Order," she said. "Out of Chaos." She pointed at the mother. "By Jove," she said, indicating the monster.

"Jupiter *tonans,* as I can hear," Hoare whispered.

"What happened to the rest of the litter?" he inquired.

"I cannot say," she said. "The dam, Chaos, would have no faintest idea. You might inquire of Order.

"But I must ask you how you do, Mr. Hoare, or, I should have said, *Captain* Hoare," she added. "And what brings you to Weymouth?"

"I do well enough, thank you," he said. "Once again, it is a crime that brings me."

"Leaving your little yacht behind?"

"I came by land this time and left *Alecto* behind."

"Now you have named the poor inoffensive thing after a Fury," she said. "Why, pray?"

"She has towed behind *Royal Duke* since I took command of the brig, dogging her trail as if she were one of the three dire sisters pursuing Orestes."

"An unkindness to both vessels, it would seem to me. My felicitations on your advancement, just the same. My friend Miss Austen apprised me of it, though *you* did not condescend to do so. But there. . . . How does little Jenny do?" she asked.

"The landlord's Susan is caring for her well enough, teaching her her manners and watching her diet," Hoare said, "but I am not in the child's good books just now . . . for I must now sleep aboard my command, as is required of all Masters and Commanders in the Service, and may no longer lodge at the Swallowed Anchor. So I am rarely there to see her to her bed and give her her nightly blessing. She is not amused.

"Also, I have placed her in a dame school, for it seems she has never been taught her letters. She objected very strongly, until I promised her a kitten if she learned to write . . . her alphabet. So just now, I imagine, she is sitting at the inn kitchen table, her little tongue stuck out, struggling bravely. I am told that she has now reached *K;* it may be so."

"K stands for 'kitten,' I suppose. Hmmm," Mrs. Graves said. "I have sealed Order's fate, then."

"Which one of the Fates deals with kittens?" Hoare asked.

Eleanor Graves put her head on one side thoughtfully. "All three of them, I should say. But surely not Atropos in *this* matter, Mr. Hoare—"

"Bartholomew, please . . . Eleanor."

"Very well. Bartholomew, then. For Atropos decides the time of one's death. And I cannot be Clotho, who spins the thread. Clotho must be Chaos, the creature's dam. I must then, must I not, be Lachesis, who measures the kitten's life? Well, I shall assume the role. Order is yours, then, to take to Miss Jenny when you believe your fosterling is ready."

"I hope Order and her new mistress will come back to you soon afterward," Hoare said.

"Not yet, Bartholomew, not yet," she murmured.

"Er, no. I agree. First, Jenny must earn her kitten," Hoare whispered.

"That is not precisely what I meant, Bartholomew."

Eleanor Graves offered Hoare tea, which was brought by an old acquaintance, Eleanor's abigail, Agnes. The widow seemed pleased rather than otherwise to know he would be remaining in the area for some days but did not probe into the nature of the crime he had mentioned. She did not invite him to dine.

Perhaps, Hoare thought, as he proceeded on his next errand, *he had made some progress in his campaign for Eleanor Graves's hand.* She had not objected to his using her Christian name and had willingly adopted the use of his own. She had quietly accepted his offer to accompany her to church tomorrow, it being a Sunday. She could hardly know he was no churchgoer.

Captain Israel Popham of the revenue cutter *Walpole,* a lieutenant in the Customs Service—his "Captaincy," like Hoare's own, being the mere courtesy due his command—received him like the old friend he was. After toasting Hoare's new swab in his own fine contraband Bordeaux, he sat back to hear what his guest might have to say. At

Hoare's mention of the Nine Stones Circle, he whistled softly and thoughtfully.

"That's a very interesting spot, sir, on several counts. You've been there, I take it?"

Hoare nodded.

"Then you know it has an unearthly air about it, as though the spirits of the old . . . but I wax poetic. It's an odd place, to be sure, and the folk thereabouts steer clear of it, especially of nights. Especially of a moonlight night. Ghosts walk there, they believe.

"Now, I know for certain that there are those of the Upright Men who make use of that superstition as a cover for their work. My predecessor in *Walpole* told me of catching a gang of 'em sorting out a cargo in the Circle itself.

"I'll tell you who would have more to tell you about the place. He's an acquaintance of yours, in fact."

Popham paused for a sip and watched his guest, evidently waiting for his curiosity to get the better of him.

"Very well, Mr. Popham, who?" Hoare whispered at last.

"Dunaway, that's who. Abel Dunaway," Popham said. "You may remember fishing him and a friend out of the Channels t'other day."

"I'll be damned," Hoare whispered.

"Yes. The old rascal and I are ancient adversaries. He wins some, I win some, and nobody's hurt—so far, at least. He's probably won more than I know of. As long as Sir Thomas Fat-Arse is the law hereabouts, Dunaway's safe enough in the courts. Just the same, a bad little bird chirped in my ear not so long ago, and my men took up a nice parcel of his brandy. Have a drop?"

Hoare demurred.

"Speaking of birds," he said, "one of them told me that Dunaway's passenger—Jamie, he called himself—had an odd accent. . . . As though he were French, perhaps, trying to talk cant. And the lugger bore a cargo of pigeons. I saw them escape."

"Oho!" Popham said. "Was Dunaway outward bound, d'you think, or homeward?"

"Homeward would be my guess, though I cannot be sure. I never thought to ask. He and his man, or his passenger, would still have been clean-shaven, wouldn't they, if they were fresh from home?"

"I'd imagine so. In that case, old Dunaway is getting into deeper waters than he should, wouldn't you say? Perhaps your waters rather than mine?"

"It might be," Hoare said.

"I wouldn't take it amiss if someone were to pass him a friendly warning, if so," Popham observed.

"I'll do so gladly, since I want to chat with him in this other matter. If you'll give me his whereabouts," Hoare said.

"Well, I hear he's been flitting up and down the coast between Plymouth and Dymchurch, looking for a vessel to replace his lost *Fancy*. When he settles, it's usually within hail of the White Hart along the shore there, under the castle. Weaver's woman there brews the finest ale in Dorset. It would be a kindness, Captain, for you to speak with him. After all, his regular trade is all in the day's work, so to speak. So long as he don't overreach himself, there's no one the loser. Except King George, of course."

"I said as much to the man's face," Hoare said.

The two King's officers laughed, touched glasses and tossed them off, and bade each other farewell. Hoare went ashore to find Dunaway's lair.

• • •

Weaver at the White Hart denied all knowledge of anyone named Dunaway until he learned that Hoare had been the man responsible for saving the latter's life and that of his passenger. He then revealed that while Jamie had long since gone, Dunaway might be only down the road a piece, over to Easton, where he had heard a suitable vessel might be found. He should return any moment now. Meanwhile, would the officer care for a spot of the needful?

Hoare's stomach rumbled, reminding him that he had had nothing to eat since breakfast in Dorchester.

"You brew your own ale, Mr. Weaver, I think."

"Indeed. My old woman's ale is what brings Mr. Dunaway to our doorstep, and many another besides, if I do say so."

"A mug of her ale, then, and a platter of eggs, if you please."

The proprietor and his potboy were a bit greasy for Hoare's taste, but the White Hart's ale was as rich as had been promised and vanished quickly. Just as the last scrap of Hoare's egg followed it, Dunaway appeared in the doorway. Shaven now and clad in a neat blue coat, he looked just as prosperous as if he had not lost his ship. Hoare rose to greet him.

"You'll 'a' come for the clothing you lent me," Dunaway said.

"Not so, Mr. Dunaway," Hoare whispered. "I have quite a different purpose in mind. Two purposes, in fact: a warning and a question. Ale first. You look dry."

"Drier than I were when last we met," Dunaway said.

"And prosperous as well, if I may say so, for a Captain who has just lost his ship," Hoare said.

"My only real loss, sir, was the boy Jethro Slee," said Dunaway, taking up his mug. "Your good health, Captain, and thankee once again.

"Jethro were my partner's only boy, and he took the loss mortal hard. 'Twere my fault, me most grievous fault. I were a fule not to 'a' taken another 'and aboard, if not two.

"No, for the rest of it, I were mortal sad to lose me little *Fancy* lugger, for she'd been mine these ten years past, and me da's before me. But for a truth she was old and tired, and I'd insured 'er well. For more than 'er worth, fact is."

"Insured? At Lloyd's, Mr. Dunaway?" Hoare asked incredulously. "Do the names at Lloyd's offer coverage to smugglers, then? . . . If so, how about highwaymen? Or pirates? Or slavers, or wreckers, eh?"

"Now, Captain, be easy," Dunaway said reprovingly. "That 'wrecker' bit be nothin' more than a tale put about. No one on these shores beguiles the ships ashore. They's enough of 'em come ashore of a winter, without our help. Salvage, yes. Who's to say a poor man can't pick up what 'e may along the beach once 'e's wore out a-savin' of life, like you done for me, sir?"

"Beg pardon, Mr. Dunaway," Hoare said, and meant it.

"Nor 'ave them fine London gentlemen at Lloyd's aught to do with affairs down 'ere. 'Tis Sir Thomas Frobisher insures us . . . fishermen. Aye, and makes a tidy shillin' from the business, mostly.

"I'll say this for 'im: when I showed up on his doorstep the very day you set us ashore, 'e took the news like a game chicken. 'E went straight to his strongbox and counted out the notes an' the guineas then and there, an' 'anded 'em over without so much as blinking them goggle eyes of his. So I'll be at sea again within the week, mark my word."

Hoare was of no mind to reveal his astonishment at this news.

"I hope so," he said, "and may your new craft be as long-lived as your *Fancy* lugger was." He sighed. He felt oddly reluctant to broach the matter of Jamie and the pigeons with Dunaway.

"Now for the warning, Mr, Dunaway," he said at last. "As I said the other day, sir, I have no wish to pry into the details of your trade. But I must tell you I saw a flock of birds leave your lugger . . . just before I took you and your passenger aboard. Having seen . . . a similar flock elsewhere recently, I am quite certain that the birds were pigeons. Carrier pigeons, Mr. Dunaway, I would guess, being brought over from France.

"I have my doubts about your man Jamie and his bona fides. The jabber he talked to me was supposed to be London cant, but it was nothing but gibberish. I think he was no Englishman, Mr. Dunaway."

Hoare paused. Dunaway reddened and looked pensively out the window beside them. At length, he returned his gaze to Hoare.

"If 'twere not for the debt I owe you, sir, I'd as lief lie, to be square with you. But I'll not, for my life has been in your 'ands. An' the thing will never come to pass again, any gate.

"French 'e was, indeed, part of a package give me by a lass in Arromanches. Nay, I lie; she were no lass, but a comfortable armful. Besotted, I were, an' ready to do aught she asked of me. So, when she asked me to bring over that lad Jamie an' his coteful of pigeons, I thought nowt of it but took him aboard.

" 'Tweren't till we was well into mid-Channel that I found Master 'Jamie' was no more an Englishman than he was a blackamoor. Frenchman, more like, for all his London cant, or mebbe one of them Irish followers of Wolfe Tone. An' no sailor any gate, as me an' poor Jethro learned

74

to his cost. So I resolved to 'ave nowt to do with him an' his pigeons, more'n land 'im wherever I could, as soon as I could.

"Well, sir, as it coom out, 'twas you as landed 'im an' not me. I never saw 'im again, nor wanted to.

"I'd not do it again, Mr. Hoare. I'm a loyal Englishman, I am, and I'll have no trook wi' treason. God save King George! Poor loony that he is. That's what I say. That's me word, and me word's me bond."

To put an end to the topic, Dunaway hailed the White Hart's greasy potboy and ordered another round. Thinking on the smuggler's straightforward tale, Hoare felt compelled to believe it. In his judgment, there were honest criminals and dishonest ones, and he had known his share of both. For certain, Abel Dunaway was one of the former.

"I'll drink to your decision, Mr. Dunaway," he whispered, and kept his word.

Refreshed, Dunaway cocked an inquiring eye at Hoare.

"And the question you had for me?" he asked.

"About the Nine Stones Circle, Mr. Dunaway. Captain Popham of the excise cutter *Walpole* . . ."

Dunaway chuckled.

"The ol' rascal'll 'a' told you we be friends for donkey's years, 'e and I. 'E's won some; I've won some. More than 'e might know of, I'll warrant."

Hoare burst into one of his rare fits of silent laughter. He had once overheard a Portsmouth popinjay remark about Hoare's laugh that it "sounded like one hand clapping." The concept, especially coming from such a source, had left Hoare bemused for some days.

"He used almost the same words about you, if you'd like to know," Hoare said. "In any case, Popham tells me you know the Nine Stones Circle better than most."

"I'd warrant 'e's right, Captain. It makes for a good place to break up cargo, bein' out in the open as it is, where a man's not easy crept up on. Though it's been known.

" 'Appen Popham will 'a' told you 'ow 'e and his men nabbed me and mine, full fair."

"He told me he had done so, but not how."

"Well, 'twere this way. Look 'ere. These crumbs be the stones, see?"

With crumbs, forks, and a saltcellar, Dunaway took Hoare through the moonlit encounter, showing him where the excisemen had lain in wait; how, all unsuspecting, he had led a caravan of laden ponies into the Circle; how the other, smaller caravans he was to meet had arrived; and how, as the work was in full swing, Popham, who had hidden his excisemen in a fold of the down, had sprung the trap on him.

" 'E gathered in most of the goods that time, an' a good half of me boys to boot. 'E be a smart one all right, Popham be, an' he showed it that night. But he never would ha' twigged to us but for a dirty little man what got greedy an' blew the gaff."

Hoare was not certain he wanted to hear what happened to the greedy little man.

"Mislaid his bollocks, 'e did." Dunaway fixed Hoare with a meaningful eye. " 'Is dollymop, what led him astray in the first place, found 'em on 'er doorstep one mornin', stuck in his mouth.

"She weren't 'alf-surprised," he said in conclusion. "Picked up and run off to London, I 'ear."

The greasy potboy made to wipe the Nine Stones Circle away with a grubby cloth, but Hoare forestalled him. "Will you sketch that out for me?" he asked.

When Dunaway assented, Hoare had the boy bring paper and writing materials. Dunaway laboriously copied his work, his tongue writhing about as he drew, as if he were the child Jenny struggling with forming her letters.

"Tell me," Hoare asked, "do you know where I might conceal a party of my men on the way to the Circle—a dozen of them, say?"

Dunaway thought, but not for long.

"Why, yes," he said. "I've a barn—a smallish one an' poor, for I farm very little these days—t'other side of my land at Langton Herring. Yer welcome to shelter yer men there, so long as ye'll give me yer word they'll not be used against me or my lads."

"You have my word once again, Mr. Dunaway," Hoare replied. "I still care less than nothing for your men's doings, so long as they do not aid the King's enemies."

Hoare had Dunaway draw another map.

"When will ye be wantin' the place?"

"There's a difficulty there, sir, for I cannot now say. I may have no word of any doings in the Stone Circle before it's too late to pass you the word . . ."

Hoare took breath.

". . . What then? What if your lads and mine were to find each other there the same night?"

Dunaway chuckled. "That *would* make a fair do, wouldn't it, now?"

Again he ruminated, long enough, this time, to empty his tankard.

"Tell ye what. We've a signal. Since yer a master of odd noises, no offense meant, sir—"

"And none taken. So I am, I trust."

"Well, here 'tis." Pursing his lips, Dunaway made a rattling sound rather like the call of a corncrake. He made it again, in a higher register. Hoare noticed that the publican's ears seemed to prick up.

"Try it yerself."

On Hoare's third try, Dunaway deemed him proficient enough.

"Mind you," he said, "we change our signal every month or so, lest it leak out to the wrong folk. So ye'll need to pass this way at least that often, as long as yer likely to need it."

"It will be my pleasure," said Bartholomew Hoare.

At last, he let the potboy bring a stirrup cup and give rein to his unwonted sense of order by erasing the Circle of crumbs. The stirrup cup drained, the two dissimilar seamen parted with a firm seamanly handshake and what Hoare felt to be a mutual esteem.

Hoare and Thoday dined together, in almost complete companionable silence, at and on the Dish of Sprats. Thoday was unique in Hoare's experience. He was obviously well educated as well as arrogant. Hoare thought him most likely a Papist, which, of course, debarred him from commissioned rank in His Majesty's service. Why had he chosen to enlist? For it was most unlikely that a man of his education, and one of Sir John Fielding's men at that, would have been pressed. Family troubles, perhaps? In any case, Thoday's manner was not one that encouraged intimacy, and besides, it was none of Hoare's business.

Their two rooms at the top of the inn adjoined. Through the thin wall, just as he was composing himself for sleep, Hoare heard the plaintive sound of a violin, expertly and tenderly played. Listening, he drifted off. Tomorrow was Sunday; he would be in Eleanor Graves's company once again.

• • •

As Hoare descended the stairs the next morning, Titus Thoday was finishing his breakfast in the inn's common room. Hoare helped himself from the sideboard and joined his colleague.

"Was I dreaming last night, Thoday, or did I hear the sound of a violin coming from your room?"

To Hoare's astonishment, the man blushed, albeit faintly.

"You did, sir. I am sorry if my improvisations disturbed you."

"Not at all. They were something of a lullaby, in fact. But where did you . . ."

Thoday smiled, reached into his coattails, and extracted a kit fiddle and its half-sized bow, the sort that dancing masters carried. Tucking the tiny instrument under his chin, he tuned it quickly and, tapping his foot, launched into a hornpipe. At the conclusion, Hoare heard clapping hands from across the room.

"Bravo!" cried a merchantlike man at a table on the far side of the room. His portly wife smiled at her husband.

"Makes you want to caper a bit, does it not, Sam?" she asked.

"Reminds me of happy days," her husband replied.

"I shall be attending morning prayer at St. Ninian's," Hoare told Thoday. "If you'd care . . ."

"Thank you, sir, but no," the gunner replied, as Hoare had known he would. "I fear I do not subscribe to all the Thirty-nine Articles."

"Nor do I. But after all, the proprieties must be observed by someone. And if not by His Majesty's officers, then by whom?" With that, Hoare donned his hat, examined himself in the mirror that stood just inside the inn door, and—satisfied that he looked as seemly as he could, given the features the Almighty had given him—walked through the brisk air up the gentle cobbled slope to the Graves residence.

Eleanor Graves awaited her escort, Agnes at her side.

"You put yourself to unnecessary trouble, Bartholomew," Eleanor said when Hoare hove into sight. "I could well have walked to church without your protection. After all, Mr. Moreau's gang is long since dispersed, and I stand in no danger."

She forbore to say, Hoare noticed, that it was the activities of her late husband that had put her in danger when they first met, that those activities had ceased with Dr. Simon Graves's death, and that the danger had therefore disappeared. Hoare forbore to remind her. As far as he was concerned, the less reason she had to remember her dead husband and the manner of his going, the better.

"And how does Order behave herself this morning?" he asked as they walked back down the slope, followed by Agnes.

"As well as can be expected," she replied, "considering that Order is male. And, to answer your next question, his dam, Chaos, is also in good spirits, though as I felt her, she was unable to decide whether to attack my knitting or rest. And Jove was nodding. And I am quite well, as are Agnes—are you not, Agnes?—and my servant Tom. And the cook."

"But you seem somewhat out of sorts this morning," Hoare said.

"I am, Bartholomew, and you are indirectly the cause."

"Please?"

"After you left my house yesterday evening," she said, "Sir Thomas Frobisher was kind enough to call, despite the lateness of the hour. He had the effrontery to accuse me of misjudgment, if not worse, for having received you in my house so soon after Simon's death, if at all. He had heard the neighbors speaking of it. He spoke, of course, he said, as one who must view himself as being in loco parentis.

" 'In loco parentis,' indeed! He knows perfectly well that both my parents are perfectly well, considering their age. He's nearer their age than mine. Furthermore, he maintained that I was imperiling my soul."

She tossed her glossy brown head.

"My *soul,* for pity's sake! I have no more soul than the cat, Chaos! If I do, then where in my body it is located, pray tell me!"

Hoare remembered Dr. Graves's having confided to him that his wife doubted the existence of such things as souls.

"Furthermore," she said severely, "Sir Thomas reminded me that you are a married man."

"*Married?* I am no such thing! Like you, I am widowed, but long since. I had thought you knew."

"How should I have known, Bartholomew? You never saw fit to tell me. Shall you tell me now, as we walk?"

So Hoare told his companion how, when *Beetle* was on the North American station in the weary closing years of the American war, he and Antoinette LaPlace had fallen desperately in love and married, over the powerful objections of her devout family. How he had left her in Halifax early in '83, great with child, only to discover on his return after the peace that she had died in childbed. Her parents had swept up the babe, a daughter, and returned to disappear in the uplands of Quebec.

"So I have never even seen my daughter," he concluded, "but I dream of Antoinette very often."

"Of course, you do." Eleanor Graves pressed the arm she was holding. "And perhaps that explains your feelings for the child Jenny, of whom you speak so fondly."

"Fondly? Do I? Why, perhaps I do. Well . . . well, here we are, on our way to St. Ninian's," he said, "presumably for the betterment of our souls at Mr. Witherspoon's feet."

"*My* soul, if any, is a poor neglected thing in sad need of betterment. However, Bartholomew, I accepted your offer to escort me to church because of the damned— excuse me—*damned* neighbors. I wish to show them where I stand. Busybodies all, and Sir Thomas the busiest body of them all. He should be busying his body about those poor dead Captains you told me of. I can well take care of my own reputation and my own entirely hypothetical soul." She tossed her head again and snorted.

To himself, Hoare had long compared Eleanor Graves to a partridge, albeit a dauntless one. Now, with her snort, she resembled a moor pony, one like the beast he had seen her astride when, between them, they had put Edouard Moreau to death.

"Do you wish me to take Sir Thomas aside and reprove him?" he asked. He rather looked forward to the idea.

She stopped in midstreet and looked up at him. "You shall do no such thing, Bartholomew. I am a tub that stands on its own bottom, as well you know. He and you are sufficiently at odds already. It would do you no good were you to spring to my defense and would put poor pompous Sir Thomas into harm's way. No. We shall attend matins in peace, as we planned, and all the world may stare."

She tucked her arm in his; his heart leaped.

All the world stared, indeed, as the little party marched into St. Ninian's. The congregation's whispering made Hoare feel quite at home. Eleanor Graves was no person to hide herself. Chin high, her black-gloved hand resting lightly on the arm of her blue-and-gold escort, her progress followed by the staring faces of all Weymouth's best, she paraded up the aisle as if going up to dance.

The service having concluded and the Reverend Mr. Witherspoon duly congratulated on his endless sermon, the two left the porch of St. Ninian's only to come face-to-face with Sir Thomas Frobisher. No words passed between them, only stiff nods, though Hoare thought to hear the other breathe the word *bats*. Sir Thomas's footman opened the emblazoned door of his berlin, and he entered. As Hoare knew, he had all of four hundred yards' journey ahead of him.

Foursquare, high of cheekbones, with slanted eyes and a shock of unconventional coarse black hair, the knight's coachman had an oddly familiar look. Where had Hoare seen his like?

It came to him at last. During his station in Halifax, when he had courted his dear Antoinette, married her, and lost her, he had run across a family of wandering Esquimaux walrus hunters from the upper Labrador. Someone had told him that the first Sir Martin Frobisher, the famous one, had brought a family or two back with him to England, where they had become as much a nine days' wonder as would have been one of Dean Swift's Struldbrugs. Could this merry-looking manservant be one of their descendants?

Eleanor Graves's murmur returned Hoare to the autumn Sunday.

"The frog and the crane," she said.

"Sir Thomas and myself?" Hoare asked.

"Or you and myself," she said with a smile, and Hoare's heart leaped once again.

"You are no frog, my dear," he whispered.

They walked on in companionable silence for a while, arm in arm, trailed at a discreet distance by the girl Agnes. Then Eleanor looked up at him.

"That was pleasant, Bartholomew. To make the congregation stare so! *Oh!* I must dress only in this horrid black, which I know does not become me. I must remain at home for years, receive only my relatives and Simon's— or the widowed Sir Thomas Frobisher, who is hopping about, turning up every stone within fifty miles in his search for a new wife to cover. Yet I know what my beloved Simon would have wished for me."

"What would he have wished?"

"That as soon as possible I would commence to live the life of a normal woman. I want children, Bartholomew, and the time grows late."

Chapter V

O N MONDAY morning, as Hoare walked out of the Dish of Sprats for a constitutional before breakfast, he saw the clerk Rabbett striding toward him down the cobbled street, a bundle tied to a stick over one shoulder and his other hand wielding a stout staff. Rabbett, Hoare realized, had benefited by this venture out of his customary hole in Admiralty House, Portsmouth.

Heretofore, in Hoare's opinion, Rabbett had not only resembled the creature with which he shared a name; his actions had also been leporine. Lately, however, Rabbet even seemed taller. Was he standing straighter?

Fleetingly the thought entered Hoare's mind that he, Bartholomew Hoare, might have been thinking and acting in error throughout his life. Ever since he learned that his precious name was applied to Bad People, and female ones to boot, Hoare had been defending that name against mis-use as if against dishonor. To him, Rabbetts were timid, Wolfes predatory—and Hoares sinful. Others shared his obsession, he knew; he had once been acquainted with a fellow Orkneyman by descent who bore the even more unfortunate name of Bugga. Poor Mr. Bugga had defended his name on the field of honor no fewer than four times before falling at last, a brave Bugga to the end.

Some other Hoares, he knew—the eponymous bankers of Stourhead, for example—must certainly be happy Hoares as well as wealthy ones, and their bank could scarcely be mistaken for a bordello. Why, then, should he, Bartholomew . . .

"Sir," Rabbett said, "a message came to you in Dorchester last night. The man would not go beyond Dorchester, and I knew of no quicker way to bring you the message than to carry it myself. So I rose before dawn and set off for Weymouth without breaking my fast."

The clerk extended an envelope. Hoare broke its Admiralty seal, to find a note to which had been attached a slip of tissue.

The note read:

> Admiralty House, Portsmouth,
> 17 October
>
> Sir:
> The attached arrived momentarily by carrier pigeon, from your command.
> In the future, pray arrange for communications of this kind to be transmitted by a more direct route.
>
> Your humble, etc., etc.,
> G. Hardcastle

The enclosure bore a mere handful of lines in a minuscule handwriting:

Royal Duke,
17 October

Sir:

This by pigeon to Admiralty House Portsmouth, with request it be forwarded to you by courier.

I have broken the "Ahab-Jehu" cipher. I respectfully submit that it would be most desirable were you to return aboard forthwith, to examine the messages I will have decoded by your arrival.

> Your obedient servant, in haste,
> F. Taylor
> Master's Mate

"S. Taylor?" Who the devil was S. Taylor? Hoare cudgeled his mind, then remembered. S. Taylor was the big woman whom Mr. Clay had identified as *Royal Duke's* resident cryptographer and mathematician. She was Sarah Taylor, and she was, indeed, rated Master's Mate.

"Hell," Hoare whispered to himself. Here he was, in hot pursuit of the Captains' killers and his courtship, and this petticoat sailor had the audacity to virtually order him back aboard his own command. Really, between her and the nearly insolent Thoday, he began to wonder who commanded whom. It put him quite out of patience. Besides, why could she not have given him some clue as to what made the matter so urgent, so as to help him make up his mind whether to go or to stay?

He returned to the inn, Rabbett at his heels, and called upstairs for Thoday.

"Mr. Thoday," Hoare said when the man appeared, "what is your opinion of Taylor?"

"Sarah Taylor, sir?"

"Is she a levelheaded person or a flibbertigibbet?"

Thoday pondered. "A competent seaman—sea person, perhaps I should say, sir, and an arithmetician of distinction. I have even heard that, were she a man, she might be admitted to the Royal Society."

"That's all very well. But how is she for common sense?" Hoare showed Thoday the message.

"If she thinks you should return to Portsmouth, sir, you probably should—"

"Not, I hope, sir, before I hand you whatever crumbs of knowledge I have been able to gather up from beneath the tables of Dorchester."

"You may do so over breakfast, Rabbett," Hoare said. "Judging from the speed of your march, you must be hungry."

"I'll not deny it, sir," Rabbett said, and began. Indeed, he found it possible to take on a small mountain of steak-and-kidney pie without interrupting his report.

"The folk for miles about the Winterbournes," he said in a whining narrative drone, as if he had memorized it, "for there are twelve of them—Winterbourne Abbas, which you know already, sir, Winterbourne Monckton, Winterbourne Herringston, Winterbourne Steepleton, and eight others—are convinced that the deaths are connected with Satan worship. Or, if not, the worship of the Old Gods. And who is to say which of the two is the lesser evil?"

"Who, indeed?" Hoare breathed, letting his mind escape the clerk's recital. Rabbett's mention of "the lesser evil" reminded him of the jape invented by one of the more successful frigate Captains—Bolitho? Cochrane? He was wont to challenge a new acquaintance to a wager upon which of two beetle larvae, chosen at random from among those tapped from a piece of ship's biscuit, would be the first to reach the edge of the table. The unwitting newcomer naturally chose the larger grub. When it lost, as it always did, Captain Whoever would joyfully advise the stranger "always to select the lesser of two weevils" and nearly burst his breeches with laughter at his own paltry jest.

Aubrey. That was the joker's name. Lucky Jack Aubrey, they called him, from the wealth of prize money he had won at sea—and squandered ashore.

Hoare kicked himself back to what Rabbett was saying.

"For it is well known that our ancient ancestors did, indeed, hold their ceremonials there. The Circle antedates even the Druids, as I understand. Even now, shepherds and travelers report strange lights by night, and peculiar offerings have been found from time to time on the great flat stone in its middle—a bunch of mistletoe, for instance, a corn dolly in season, even a white cockerel."

Thinking back to yesterday's visit with Dunaway, Hoare was certain he could account for the strange lights. And Thoday had drawn what must be the right conclusion from the withered fragments of flower garlands. They were involved with Rabbett's "offerings."

"And what did you discover among the officials of the town?" Hoare asked.

Rabbett shook his head. "Nothing, sir. The gentry are closemouthed to such as I. But the other captain, Captain Spurrier, that is, is ill-regarded among us common folk. Feared, in fact. He was once preached against in the Church of All Angels—you remember, where they took the poor Captains' bodies. Captain Spurrier has done almost nothing to track down the murderers of the two Captains."

"And the inquest?"

"Has been indefinitely postponed, sir. Captain Spurrier departed Dorchester at speed on Saturday for an unknown destination, directly after your own departure for Weymouth."

Thoday, too, had drawn a blank. No one in Weymouth town had more than rumor to pass on about the deaths of the Captains Getchell. In fact, they had seemed reluctant to discuss the matter at all. More than one had suggested that Thoday apply to Sir Thomas Frobisher for information, but Sir Thomas was away.

" 'A-courting,' one of them told me, sir," Thoday said. " 'At his age.' "

"The frog he would a-wooing go," he added.

Hoare sighed. A block had been put in the way of his chase. He might as well face reality and return to duty.

"Our business here in Weymouth seems to be concluded for now," he said. "There is nothing to keep us here.

"You two, Rabbett and Thoday, return to Dorchester and keep the investigation moving from there. I shall accompany you in the chaise and continue on to Portsmouth. . . . Find the missing evidence—the head, the two drivers, the Admiralty chaise. Surely the chaise, at least, can be traced. Learn of any strangers, especially any with foreign accents. Keep me informed.

"In fact, I shall need to be kept informed on a frequent, regular basis. But none of us can afford the time to travel between Dorchester and Portsmouth. . . . So as to halve the time needed in travel, then," he whispered, "let us arrange regular meetings—weekly, say—at a point halfway between here . . . and Portsmouth. A place that we can reach easily by sea or by land.

"You, Thoday, can meet with Rabbett beforehand to collect whatever news he may have gathered, and bring the . . . consolidated information to—to where?"

He turned to Rabbett, whose knowledge of the land he was beginning to find invaluable.

"Christchurch, I'd suggest, sir," the clerk said. "As you

know, 'tis well south of the direct way from Portsmouth, but 'tis on the coast. By land, I believe it a long day's ride from either direction, perhaps forty miles all told. And you would know better than I, sir, about access by sea.

"The Crown would be your best base there, sir."

Hoare sighed again. Planning of this kind implied that the road to the solving of the two Captains' deaths would be a long one, and dreary.

Thoday had raised his eyebrows halfway through Hoare's orders, and they were still raised.

"You look dubious, Thoday. Spit it out, man."

"The plan is less than satisfactory, sir," he said. "There may be times when a lack of progress makes it injudicious to waste any time whatsoever on travel, and there may, I would hope, be times when the need to confer is urgent."

"True enough, Thoday," Hoare said. "But I can hardly change the geography of Britain to suit our convenience. Do you have a better proposal?" Mentally, he crossed his arms smugly and waited for the man to admit he did not.

"Hancock, sir. Yeoman of signals in *Royal Duke,* as I need not remind you. He gives me to understand that within a few days of their removal to a new location, weather permitting, his birds can be trained to return thence quite reliably. I think it requires several trips, each of which increases the distance they must travel. You could send Hancock here to Dorchester with a covey or flock, or batch, of them. He could train them to think of a local cote or pen or hutch as home, then return with them to *Royal Duke.* They can then be used to carry the news to us in Dorchester. And vice versa, of course, for messages to your ship."

"Interesting," Hoare whispered. "I shall inquire of Hancock. Meanwhile, I shall leave you two behind me in Dorchester, as I originally planned."

He ordered one of the inn's menservants to find the Admiralty's driver and tell him to prepare for their return to Portsmouth, via Dorchester. Hoare went upstairs, then, to pen a temporary farewell to Eleanor Graves.

Back in Dorchester, Hoare found Captain Spurrier, just returned from whereever he had gone in such secrecy and with such speed, all officious smiles.

"Come this way, if you will, sir," he said to Hoare, taking him by the arm in a brotherly way. "I have something to show you."

Spurrier led Hoare to the mortuary where the two Captains' corpses lay. Thoday followed them, uninvited, while the curious Rabbett trailed behind.

"There," he said, pointing.

Both bodies now had heads. Someone had carefully replaced the one that had gone adrift upon the shoulders where it belonged. It was much the worse for wear. The crows had taken its eyes, while they or other scavengers had enjoyed other easily accessible parts—ears and lips most noticeably. In both corpses, corruption had palpably advanced. Finding that an odor he might relish in connection with a properly hung grouse was less appealing in these circumstances, Rabbett made a smothered coughing noise and dashed for the door.

"Thank you, Mr. Spurrier," Hoare said icily. "You might wish to salt the remains down, pending the arrival of the dead men's next of kin."

"You need not teach me my duty, Hoare," Spurrier said.

"On the contrary, sir, I evidently do. You have much to learn." Hoare turned on his heel.

Outside, Hoare instructed Thoday and Rabbett to remain in Dorchester as he had previously ordered. They could put up at the Mitre, if they wished, or arrange for other accommodations.

"There is a daily Admiralty post between Portsmouth and Plymouth, is there not?"

"Yes, sir," Rabbett said. "In fact, I myself, when at Admiralty House, am charged with receiving the post for us and placing our signals in the postboy's hands. When not occupied with other duties, that is, sir."

"And would he not change mounts in Dorchester?" Hoare asked.

"Indeed, sir." He consulted a large silver watch. "In fact, the westward post should be stopping at the Mitre just about now, if he has not already departed."

"Then, as soon as I arrive in Portsmouth, I shall arrange for the postboys to leave there any messages I may have for you. Do you likewise leave with the innkeeper a daily report to be delivered to the eastward-bound messenger, addressed to me."

"A regular matter of that kind would soon come to the ears of others, sir," Thoday objected. "Instead, Rabbett's mother and father dwell on the highway just east of town. Their home is out of sight of here, and hence not under the eyes of prying strangers. His father, of course, is town clerk, so he must be at his desk in the town hall during the day, but his mother could receive and transmit our communications."

Hoare looked at the clerk to seek his reaction.

"She'd be happy to, I know, Mr. Hoare," he said. "Life is quite quiet for her now, since I left home and can no longer entertain her by recounting my adventures when I come home of nights."

"Very good, then. As soon as I arrive at Admiralty House, I shall arrange matters with . . . To whom do you delegate your duties, Rabbett, when you are absent from your post?"

Rabbett suppressed a snicker at Hoare's inadvertent play on words. "Witherspoon, sir. Jabez Witherspoon. Tell him I sent you."

"Be sure that I shall. Good-bye, then."

Before Hoare could board the chaise, he remembered and stopped.

"By the by, Rabbett," he said, "while I have you in my power."

Quickly he summarized the general concern about missing information, as epitomized by the lost word about those ciphers' being in French, which had irritated Sarah Taylor so.

"Are you aware of a lack of discretion on the part of any of your colleagues on the Admiral's staff?" he asked.

"Oh, no, sir!" Rabbett's reaction was one of shocked surprise. "Never!"

"Well, when you return to your post from this vacation of yours, pray remember to keep a weather eye out."

"Oh, yes, sir. I shall, you may be sure. I can . . ."

Rabbett's last words of reassurance were lost at the appearance of another vehicle coming down the street, a berlin. It drew up abreast of Hoare, and its occupant looked out the window, a lean, swarthy man, somberly dressed.

"Can you direct me, sir, to the Church of All Angels?"

"You can see its steeple from here, sir," Hoare said. "It is a mere minute away."

A thought struck him; he doffed his cocked hat.

"Do I address a relative of the late Captains Getchell, sir?"

"The father of Francis, sir, and the uncle of Benjamin."

"Please accept my deepest condolences, Mr. Getchell.

My name is Hoare. It is my duty to apprehend the person or persons responsible for their deaths."

The father's nostrils flared. "Count on me, sir, for any support you may require. Francis was the pride of my life, as Benjamin was that of his father."

The berlin drove off, leaving Hoare behind in the street, still bareheaded.

"Shove off, driver," he whispered, and climbed into the chaise.

Chapter VI

—⟫•◆•⟪—

O NCE BACK aboard *Royal Duke,* Hoare summoned
Taylor to his cabin.

"I hope your deciphering of the Jehu texts brings us
information that will justify your having summoned me
back to this ship," Hoare said. Having spoken, he regretted
the tone he had just employed and excused himself to her
on the grounds of weariness.

She donned her spectacles. "You can tell better than I,
sir," she said. "Once you told me they were probably in
French, the matter was easy. I unearthed a French Bible
and began with Kings. . . ."

"Very good, Taylor," Hoare replied. "I would be in-
terested to learn how you proceeded, but at a later date.
Right now, pray tell me what the messages say."

"Here are the clear, deciphered texts, sir. You can read
them at your leisure. Will that be all, sir? If so, I have other
pressing business."

Hoare was unused to having his people show such
marked independence. Thoday had shown it, and now Tay-

lor had as well. Hoare was not sure this custom in his command pleased him. Certainly, like most of the rest of *Royal Duke*'s peculiar culture, it was not Naval. But Taylor was right; he could read the decrypted texts perfectly well himself.

The decision was made for him.

"Message from Admiralty House, sir," said a voice at his cabin door. Hoare looked up from Taylor's papers before he could even begin, took the message, opened it, and cursed. He set aside the papers Taylor had left with him still without learning whether she had been correct about their urgency.

"Why the hell must Admiral Hardcastle command me to an Admiralty House reception *now?*" he asked of no one. "Doesn't he know I have five damned pots a-boiling?"

He chirruped his summons to Whitelaw. Once again, the silent servant had nothing to say but set out Hoare's shaving tackle. After bringing hot water from *Royal Duke*'s galley, he took out Hoare's best coat and began to furbish it. Hoare summoned Hancock, the foul-breathed pigeon master, and while adorning himself told him of Thoday's suggestion of the day before, that Hancock create a subsidiary home for his charges in Dorchester.

Hancock stood awhile in thought, then nodded.

"It can easily be done, sir," he said, "as far as delivering messages to *Royal Duke* is concerned. But to send messages to Christchurch, or to Dorchester or Weymouth, for that matter, that would be another thing again. The birds must accustom themselves to any new destination—it must be home for them, you know—and that takes as long as a week."

"Very good then, Hancock," Hoare said. "For the time being, we must satisfy ourselves with one-way service from

Dorchester to here. Take a half-dozen birds to Dorchester. You'll find your shipmate Thoday there, at the Mitre inn. Report to him, return, and begin working up another half-dozen to carry news the other way."

Once Hancock had left and Hoare could let himself breathe again, he tied his cravat in the simple knot he used for all occasions, stuffed Taylor's texts into a pocket, and called for his gig. Not a minute was to be lost.

The last time he had been commanded to an Admiralty House reception, one of *Vantage*'s Marine officers had run athwart Hoare's hawse, and Hoare had been obliged to shoot him the next morning. Hoare's shot had gone where he wanted it to, however, hitting Mr. Wallace in the buttock. A few days later, the Jolly had been blown to pieces in *Vantage* with all but a handful of her crew. Tonight, the Admiral's Flag Lieutenant, Francis Delancey, stopped him at the head of the stairs leading to the ballroom.

"You're to be presented, sir. I'll find you when the occasion arises. Kindly do not remain hidden."

Hoare knew Delancey had no love for him, holding both his name and his muteness in disregard and envying him his recent promotion, so he simply nodded and continued into the ballroom. Fortunately, he could already see more than one friend.

The room, torrid as usual from the flame of the tapers in the massive chandeliers, held as many scarlet coats as blue, for the reception was in honor of His Majesty's only true soldier son, Lieutenant General His Royal Highness Ernest, Duke of Cumberland, commanding the Southwestern District of the British army's home forces. While a small clot of intimates in blue and scarlet surrounded the

Admiral's royal guest, the other courtiers appeared none too eager to approach him very closely but surrounded him in a respectful ring.

Hoare had been presented to Cumberland's elder brother William, Admiral and Duke of Clarence, and found him kindly if stupid. It was common knowledge, in fact, that all of His Majesty's children were stupid. Most were more or less dissolute as well, some merely eccentric. Only Ernest, Duke of Cumberland, was positively vicious.

It was the first time Hoare had laid eyes on His Majesty's fifth son. He found the sight a dismaying one. To give the Duke his due, it was through bravery, not birth, that the left side of his florid Hanoverian face was fixed in a permanent snarl and his blinded left eye turned wildly outward. Those were scars of honor, Hoare knew. The Duke had received them from a shell burst at the battle of Tournai in '94, at the same time as his right arm was disabled and a mere week before the French bullet had deprived Hoare of his voice and his seagoing career.

But long before Tournai, rumors had floated that Cumberland was fond of tormenting others. If he could not gratify himself by inflicting physical pain, he would make do with causing the mental variety. His servants were known to be of two kinds: accomplices and victims. Some were both. According to further rumor, which could hardly be substantiated, his behavior toward his sisters went beyond mere cruelty.

Within the ring of guests that surrounded Cumberland himself stood four others. Three of them—the Admiral, his lady, and their decent, dumpy daughter, Felicia—were familiar; the fourth was not. A woman more than tall enough to look the Admiral in the eye, she was clad in a watered Tussore silk, of the same vivid blue as the Duke's

Garter ribbon. It brought out the color of her eyes. Raven-haired, ivory-skinned, she stood proud and slender in diamonds enough to buy the Navy a brig, if not a sloop-of-war. Her sapphire glance passed over Hoare casually, kindled him, left him. She shone.

Surely this was not H. R. H.'s Duchess, Hoare thought. He believed he remembered that, like his brothers, Cumberland had been laggard in marrying. If he *had* married, he would have surely been put out at stud to one of the blowsy beauties from Saxe-Hesse-Beanstalk or another of those toy German principalities whose principal exports were portly Princesses. This vision could be none of them.

Hoare took a glass of hock from one of the trays being passed by seamen in fancy dress and began to circulate, smiling. Since this occasion was his first appearance at a formal affair since he had put up his swab, he had to heave to frequently for a toast of congratulation.

"Ha! Captain Hoare! Fancy seeing you here! I had thought you fully occupied on *my* manor!" It was Captain Walter Spurrier, Sir Thomas's man in Dorchester, in his mysterious scarlet and gold.

Overlooking Hoare's obvious surprise at seeing him in this company, Spurrier grasped his arm as if they were the closest of boyhood friends.

"Hoare, let me make you known to my good friend, Frobisher. Martin, Commander Bartholomew Hoare of HMS—"

"*Royal Duke,* sir. Your servant, I'm sure," Hoare whispered, again caught by surprise. By his frog-shaped figure, actually stuffed into a bottle green satin uniform coat, and side-whiskered like Spurrier, the man could only be the son of his un-friend Sir Thomas, Spurrier's master. And the woman beside him would be—surely not the frog-soldier's wife . . . his sister. Yes. Hoare had once been left, loitering, to gather cobwebs in Sir Thomas's second-best salon while he awaited the knight-Baronet's pleasure. He had had the time then to learn the Frobisher features from a row of male and female ancestor portraits. The men were all frogs, their womenfolk lizards. The sister's wispy emerald green *faux-pucelle* gown displayed her light top-hamper and pronounced tumble-home to no advantage.

"Honored, sir," the frog said. "Heard of you, of course, from the guv'nor. Lydia, me dear, this is the, er, famous Captain, er, Hoare, who interests Pater so much."

Hoare bowed over the slabsided woman's languidly extended hand. From the lines on the hand and the face above him, she looked nearly Hoare's age, though she could hardly be thirty. No wedding ring on the hand. A Frobisher and still single? There was a mystery here. Since she must be worth a good thousand a year, it would be of no consequence to any brisk young fortune hunter that she herself could very well pass for forty-three, in the dusk with the light behind her. *A well-turned phrase, that,* Hoare told himself, and set it down in his mental commonplace book.

"And what happy circumstance brings this invasion by the Army?" Hoare could not believe his whispered words. He could not remember ever sounding so unctuous. It was catching.

"Oh . . . H. R. H., of course, sir." Miss Frobisher's high-pitched voice grated down his spine like a seagull's cry. "We three are pillars of the Duke's little coterie, you must know."

"How fortunate for the Duke, and how lucky for us coarse sailors that you accompanied him." Hoare felt his face take on a civil leer that he knew must match Captain Spurrier's.

"What progress have you made in the matter of the corpses and the carriage?" Hoare asked.

"La, sir, surely you can find a topic of conversation that is better suited to the occasion!" Miss Frobisher declared.

Spurrier disregarded the lady. His response was airy. "Oh, none, sir, none. H. R. H.'s demands take precedence, don't ye know?"

"Ah. Well, then, can you enlighten me about the unseemly rites that I hear take place in the Circle where the bodies were found?" Hoare was mindful of Thoday's observation about the peculiar sacerdotal garment he had seen in the Captain's quarters.

"Unseemly, sir?" Spurrier's expression froze. "You disparage things of which you know nothing. That is unwise, sir."

"Ah," Hoare continued in his whisper. He turned to the frog. "By the by, Mr. Frobisher," he said, "I am ashamed to admit that I do not recognize your uniform. It is an unusual color."

Frobisher's grin nearly split his face in two. "I am hardly surprised, sir. It is the uniform of the Dorsetshire Fencible Horse, sir. Our regiment is known only for having run away at Sedgemoor, its only engagement, before it was even ordered to charge Monmouth's rebels."

"Oh?" Hoare asked. The frog's candor was astonishing but engaging.

"Yes, Captain. That is one of the reasons why I chose the Fencibles—the Brown-Bottomed Bastards, I've heard us called. You see, I'm a coward."

"Ah, yes. 'The Fencibles, throughout the war, did nothing in particular, and did it very well,' " was Hoare's comment. Mentally, he wrote this phrase, too, into his commonplace book.

"That's just in the first place," Frobisher said. "In the second place, there's that matter of the crown of Ethelred."

"*Martin!*" His sister's voice was horrified. "You must

not speak of the Frobisher honor in such a connection!"

"I have heard something, Mr. Frobisher, about the royal blood of a Frobisher ancestor, but I confess that I know nothing of it. Pray enlighten me."

"Not here, Captain, if you don't mind." Frobisher's grin widened. "Don't you agree that it would be a bit of beyond to discuss my father's dubious claim to the Crown—"

"*Martin!*"

Martin Frobisher and his sister might be siblings; they were not friends, it seemed. The green gentleman dismissed her protest and pressed on. ". . . while preparing to be received by a son of the man who wears it today?"

"I suppose so," Hoare said. He was finding he could like this man. "I seem to recall your father's having told me . . . when he and I first met and before we so unfortunately became estranged, that you held a commission as an officer of the Foot Guards."

"*Me?*" Frobisher's laugh was suited to his figure; it was a peculiar batrachian croak.

"My dear man! I've already admitted to you that I'm a coward. How can you imagine the Foot Guards accepting a coward of any shape, let alone mine?"

"Your candor is refreshing, sir," Hoare said.

"Speaking of uniforms," he whispered with a spanking-new, oily smile, "I must also admit, Captain Spurrier, that the facings of *your* coat are also unfamiliar to me."

"Fourteenth Hussars, sir," Spurrier said coldly. "I would be happy to make you better acquainted with them."

Hoare was about to respond with a remark that might have been about turncoats and might lead to an encounter he was becoming inclined to seek from this bounding man.

But Delancey, the flag secretary, bustled up, followed almost immediately by Francis Bennett, legal counsel to the Admiralty in Portsmouth.

"Francis," Delancey said to Bennett, with a cool nod.

"Francis," Bennett replied. The two men shared not only the same Christian name but also the same ambition to be the aide closest to Admiral Hardcastle as well as—or so Hoare had heard it whispered—enjoying the favors of the same mistress. Bennett had served Hoare as second in his *rencontre* with the late Lieutenant Wallace of *Vantage*. Delancey, however, like Hoare's friend Peter Gladden of *Frolic,* was Miss Felicia Hardcastle's suitor. Hoare knew well whose side *he* was on. Delancey could go to the devil.

"I must take you away from your friends, *Captain*," Delancey drawled to Hoare with obvious pleasure. "I need hardly remind you of the purpose for which you were commanded here. Not invited, *commanded*."

None too subtly, Delancey ran his courtier's eye over Hoare, hoping, Hoare knew, to find a flaw in his dress that would make his presentation to Cumberland impossible, after all. Finding none, he let Hoare make his bows to Miss Lydia and her two attendants before he led him through the crowd, to and into the sacred circle about His Royal Highness. It made Hoare think of the Nine Stones Circle, with which he had already become all too familiar.

Perhaps the order of introduction to the royal party was dictated by Hanoverian protocol. Like everyone else, Hoare knew that Cumberland, if he failed to bounce his brothers, one after another, off the steps to the English throne, aspired to that of Hanover. Whatever the reason, fat Felicia Hardcastle, being lowest in order of precedence, was the first within the circle to whom Delancey presented his captive.

Unintentionally, perhaps, the girl put Mr. Delancey in

his place by asking hopefully if Hoare had any news of "dear Mr. Gladden" and by looking sorrowful when he said he could give her none.

"But did you know, Captain Hoare," she asked him with a happy sigh, "I am invited to his family, at Broadmead, just at the edge of the New Forest? I am *so* excited I can hardly speak! And I hear that you, too . . . But la! I must not tell!" She batted her little pinkish eyes at Hoare.

"Come along, Captain," Delancey said sourly, with a reproachful look at his Admiral's daughter, and stepped past her to make his bow to the woman with the sapphire eyes. Hoare followed suit.

"Mrs. Prettyman? May I introduce Captain Bartholomew Hoare? Captain Hoare is the—"

"Oh, I have heard of Captain Hoare. I am Selene, Captain Hoare. Selene Prettyman, wife of Colonel Ferdinand Prettyman," Mrs. Prettyman said.

Mr. Delancey took patronizing pity on Hoare. "Colonel Prettyman is one of H. R. H.'s equerries, Captain," he explained as Hoare lowered his head to her extended gloved hand. "Presently indisposed, sad to say," Delancey added.

Hoare rose from his bow to see those sapphire eyes fixing his own faded gray ones from beneath long lashes. As he had thought, they needed to look up only slightly. The lashes were black. They made the eyes enormous, searching.

"In fact, at least in part, Captain Hoare is why I am here," Selene Prettyman went on.

"Ma'am?" Hoare whispered. What had this lissome Cleopatra to do with him?

"You are surprised, sir," she said. "You are known to Mr. Goldthwait, who thinks well of you."

Then, seeing that Hoare had not twigged, she offered

him a tactful reminder. "Mr. John Goldthwait, of Chancery Lane."

Now Hoare remembered. Mr. Goldthwait, a small, lean, weary-looking, unremarkable man, had interrogated him extensively at the Navy Tavern when Hoare had delivered his explanation of the *Vantage* murder. In some way, Hoare recalled, he must be involved with Admiral Sir Hugh Abercrombie. He found it hard to remember that, though he had never seen the unknown Sir Hugh, since the latter never left London, he was his master and not his host Sir George Hardcastle here in Portsmouth. That, of course, was why *Royal Duke* flew the White Ensign. Sir Hugh was a Vice Admiral of the White, while Sir George was a mere Rear Admiral of the Blue.

Come to think of it, it had been then, too, that Hoare had been presented to Cumberland's brother, Admiral Duke William of Clarence. In some capacity, Goldthwait had been one of Clarence's train. Was Selene Prettyman likewise part of Cumberland's? If so, why?

"This puzzles you," Selene Prettyman said. "Never mind for now. Later, we shall talk. If not tonight, sir, then certainly before I return to London. I am to be found at the Three Suns. Until then . . ." She turned away with a gracious smile. Delancey disappeared, returning, Hoare suspected, to his Admiral's daughter, his hopes in that quarter evidently still unquenched. "While the cat's away," would be Delancey's maxim.

Hoare himself went on up the receiving line to Lady Hardcastle and her husband. In her figure and her fittings, Lady Hardcastle showed the world what her daughter would look like in thirty years. The prospect was not a pleasant one. But as Hoare knew, she was a kindhearted woman and a good wife and mother.

The Admiral acknowledged Hoare's bow for the entire

family, then said to the scarlet figure at his side, "Your Highness, it is my pleasure to present Commander Bartholomew Hoare, of, er, HMS *Royal Duke.*"

The Duke of Cumberland put his hands on his hips and stared fixedly at Hoare with his one good eye.

"*What what?* You call yourself *Commander* of a *royal Duke,* sir? I'll have you know that we royal Dukes are commanded by no man—except, of course, our father, the King."

Hoare held his breath. Was Cumberland jesting, or was he really displeased? He stood transfixed, awaiting his doom. The murmured voices within hearing fell silent.

"Haw! I've been waitin' to say that to somebody ever since Abercrombie told me about that yacht of yours. Then I remembered. Me brother Billy told me he'd put a *Hoare* into *Royal Duke.* Ought to be t'other way round, of course. Wouldn't be the first time *that's* happened, as me brother Wales would be the first to admit! Hee hee hee!"

The silent sycophants in the circle broke into their obliging laughter, and Hoare felt his face go red. He would have happily called another man out for that kind of remark, but . . . challenge Lieutenant General H. R. H. the Duke of Cumberland? He summoned up a weak laugh of his own.

The weak laugh was cut short by a sharp poke in the ribs from the royal fingers, extended daggerlike.

"Hee hee hee!" said Royalty again. "Just my little joke. Seriously, my man, I've a fancy to inspect your little ship. Never had a chance while she was lyin' in . . . in . . ."

"Chatham, Your Highness," the Admiral supplied.

"Yes, of course. Chatham. Tomorrow, then, what what?" With their *what-what's,* His Majesty's sons had acquired at least one of their father's idiosyncrasies.

"Aye aye, sir," Hoare whispered, aghast. He himself

had spent little more than twenty-four hours altogether aboard his new command. How was he to make her ready to show off to this royal villain in so short a time? He must shove off forthwith, Duke or no Duke. There was not a moment to lose.

Admiral Sir George Hardcastle had the well-deserved reputation of being a grim and a merciless man. Hoare had already discovered, however, that with respect to Hardcastle's portly daughter, he was neither grim nor merciless. Hoare now perceived the same exception in his Admiral's attitude toward royalty. Both departures from normal were understandable, Hoare thought. In the one case, it could be attributed to love; in the other, to fear. Thus, in the agonized day that was to follow, Admiral Hardcastle gave his subordinate no vestige of support.

"So, Captain Hoare," came a familiar voice at his elbow. "You are making your mark among the mighty, I see."

It was Eleanor Graves's friend, Miss Jane Austen, whom he had last encountered in Wells after both had happened to attend the ordination of Arthur Gladden, late Lieutenant of the late *Vantage* frigate.

"Well met, sir," she said. "Lady Hardcastle has been telling me more of your recent good fortune, of which I had known very little."

"You and Lady Hardcastle are acquaintances, then?" he asked.

"She is a connection of my close friend, Augusta Branson. I am her guest tonight. But tell me, sir: do you remember being introduced to Miss Anne Gladden on the happy occasion of her brother's ordination?"

"Indeed, I do, Miss Austen." Miss Anne was a classic

beauty, blond, blue-eyed, sunny of nature, about nineteen, and very, very small. She would be little taller than Hoare's ward, Jenny.

"A very charming person," he said noncommittally.

She nodded thoughtfully. "Infinite riches in a little room," she observed.

"Pray why do you ask?" Hoare inquired.

"The subject came up," she said, smiled graciously, and went her way.

Before the perplexed Hoare escaped from the reception, Delancey stopped him to inform him with ill-suppressed glee that he was to warp *Royal Duke* from her present mooring to a more convenient spot at the lesser naval pier. It would be more convenient, that is, for the boarding of an awkward, lubberly gaggle of landsmen such as Cumberland and his entourage. This movement would have been routine enough for any other of His Majesty's ships. There would be no need to set even one of the brig's beautifully harbor-furled sails.

For *Royal Duke,* however, her crew and her new Commander, the maneuver made for a morning of public humiliation and private pain.

The performance the day before of Joy, the boatswain, should have warned him. Clay had already warned him that but for one or two, Hoare's crew knew no more about ship handling than so many of Portsmouth's brutes, those red, stumpy women who earned their bread by servicing sailors. Now he was to learn that while Mr. Clay clearly knew what orders to give them, the ship's people, while willing enough, had not the slightest notion of how to obey them.

Not one but both boats put over the side to tow the yacht slipped from their slings as they were lowered. The coxswain of one had forgotten to insert the plug in its bottom, and it quickly filled. Once the tow lines had been passed and the red-faced coxswains had attempted to set a stroke, matters got no better. The oarsmen knew no more of their duty than a bevy of schoolgirls. First, one caught a crab, then another. An oar went adrift.

At last, the yacht began to creep across the short distance to her berth, towing in turn Hoare's own tiny craft, her new tender. If a boat could look mischievous, *Neglectful* did. The sight began to catch the attention of nearby vessels, and jeering remarks began to pass having to do with "washerwomen," "farmers," "whore's delights," and worse. Echoes of these appellations, Hoare assured himself bitterly, bade fair to spread throughout the fleet and never die.

Perhaps confused by the barrage of insults, the coxswain of the larboard boat ran it afoul of his mate's, breaking one oar and sending still another adrift. The contemptuous laughter grew. The hapless Hoare stood on his command's quarterdeck, watching her first public performance before the crack sailors of the Royal Navy.

By God's grace, Clay had had the foresight to station men in *Royal Duke*'s chains and at the tip of her bowspirit with fending poles. For just as she was gathering way, it became clear to Hoare at least that she was about to run aboard a smart brig, bow to bow.

"Sheer off!" came a cry from the brig. She was *Niobe*, 18. "Sheer off, ye gormless lubbers!"

Without audible orders, some of the other vessel's crew began to hang rolled hammocks over her side and pick up poles of their own. The two vessels neared each other like two knights tilting in a nightmare slow-motion tournament, their bowspirits aimed at each other like lances.

But, again by God's grace, *Royal Duke*'s meager tonnage wrought to her benefit. Between them, the two crews boomed their vessels apart. Even the larboard boat avoided being crushed between the two hulls like a walnut. Only his neglected *Alecto*—lately *Neglectful*—towing astern, rammed her bowsprit, as if resentfully, into *Royal Duke*'s stern sheets with a crunch and a shattering of Hoare's cabin window lights.

Once Hoare's wayward command had been laid at last alongside the pier, a gang of dockyard mateys took charge, mooring her and her disobedient tender in proper Navy fashion, and left her and her crew to sort themselves out as best they could. Hoare had to admit to himself that, cack-handed farmers though his people might be, they at least knew how to pretty their ship to a fare-thee-well. Obviously, he thought, that was all the seamanship the late Captain Oglethorpe had required of them.

Promptly at four bells of the forenoon watch, the Duke appeared at the entrance to the dock, accompanied by Admiral Sir George Hardcastle and a small glittering entourage. To his displeasure, Hoare saw that Captain Walter Spurrier was among them. In proper precedence, they crossed the brow connecting *Royal Duke* with the pier. That it was raining lightly would please no one in the inspecting party. Nor would the pitiful trill of the single boatswain's pipe they could summon up; Hoare could have done far better with his own instrument. The solitary sideboy was no boy at all but Lorimer, the wizened, smallest, and feeblest of *Royal Duke*'s clerks. Hoare knew well he, Hoare, would be blamed.

Cumberland made no pretense to being a Naval person, but a martinet is a martinet, and he showed that he, like his brother Kent, knew the martinet trade backward and forward. With a gesture, Cumberland halted the thin twittering of the pipe. He barely acknowledged the salutes of Hoare and Clay but stared at the little Lieutenant as though he were a bottled fetus and began his inspection.

At the sight of the brig's complement of green-uniformed Marines, the Duke stopped short.

"Who the hell are these? Or what?" Hoare had used the identical words when he first saw them, but where he could only summon a whisper, the Duke roared.

"Our Marine detachment, sir," Hoare replied.

"Marines wear *red* coats, you ass! By whose orders are these men out of uniform?"

"They are trained and equipped as riflemen, sir, and have been uniformed as such."

"*By whose orders,* I asked you! Are you deaf as well as dumb, sir?"

"Admiralty orders, may it please Your Royal Highness," Hoare said. This would be safe, he hoped.

"It does *not* please My Royal Highness," the Duke snarled. "That may be the way you sailors run your service, but, by God, you'd never get away with it in the army! Lobsters should be served *cooked,* not raw. Isn't that so, sir? What what? Isn't it, then?"

"Sir," Hoare said.

"Bah," said the Duke. "*Black* buttons, indeed. My word. They look like a batch of currants in a spoiled pudding."

Hoping the worst was over, Hoare accompanied H. R. H. down the even lines of *Royal Duke*'s crew. Cumberland halted before one trio and looked down his nose.

"And what are *these?*" he barked.

He was looking at three reddish gnomes. Hoare had never seen these members of his family himself. They had hidden, or been hidden, from his sight. They made him believe he was host to figures from some obscure Celtic myth.

But Cumberland was obviously waiting for an answer.

"Topmen, sir," Hoare whispered wildly. "Balthazar, Gaspar, and Melchior. Dutchmen, all. They also serve as sappers and miners as required."

"Hmph," the Duke said, and passed on. To Hoare's relief, the Duke did not even notice Taylor as he passed her, perhaps because she had wisely put on a smocked shirt belonging to a larger shipmate. The shirt was a loose fit and obscured her breasts. Since her thick queue was no longer than some of her male shipmates', she gave no clue to mark her sex.

Hancock, the pigeon fancier, had not yet had time to move his birds or disguise their ungainly habitat. The man himself hovered before the ramshackle construction as if trying to hide it from the inspecting party, surrounded by the miasma stench of his breath. Spurrier pretended to gag.

"Good God," the Duke said. "What have we here? Captain of the ship's shambles?"

"Pigeons, sir," Hoare whispered.

"*Pigeons?* What for, man, eh? For a pye?" At the idea of a feed, Cumberland's heavy-lidded eyes almost gleamed.

"Er . . . no, Your Highness. Messenger pigeons. But we have laid out a small collation below, sir."

Before he clambered below through the open scuttle that Hoare indicated to him with a bow, Cumberland turned, hands on hips, to look about *Royal Duke*'s deck.

"At least you have the decency to keep your guns polished," he admitted, but then, with a glance, resurveyed the crew he had just inspected.

"This pitiful little barge demeans her title. I shall recommend to me father that he have it renamed, if not sunk. *Honey-Barge* might suit, what what? Or *Dustbin*. Ya-as. 'H.M.S. *Dustbin*.' Hee hee hee."

Hoare knew the people in the neighboring vessels had missed no single word of this.

While the Admiral had not opened his mouth during the Duke's inspection, he had certainly been listening, for his face was purple. Silence did not come easily to flag officers, even in the presence of royalty.

"I shall speak with you later, Mr. Hoare," the Admiral grated as he passed.

Belowdecks with a few selected cronies—including Walter Spurrier, who commenced to snoop about Hoare's belongings—the Duke apparently found matters somewhat more to his liking. Among the dishes offered him as refreshment, he sighted a platter of sherried lobster meats, gleaming in the lamplight on the great cabin table before the stern windows.

"There. You see? *Someone* here knows the proper color for lobsters. Hee hee hee."

The Duke placed himself before the platter and began to feed. When he had emptied it completely, he turned to Hoare and grunted, "Well, man, at least you keep a good cook. Have him sent to me. I'll put him to use, by Jove. Ya–as."

He looked up from the empty platter through the hastily repaired stern window. Seeing *Neglectful* lying peacefully in the light rain behind *Royal Duke,* he grunted again, more forcefully.

"Like the looks of that little boat. Have her delivered to me in Plymouth. *With* yer cook. Ya–as."

With that, he belched and returned on deck. Spurrier lagged behind him.

"You go to sea in *this* little thing?" he asked. "Makes me want to spew just to think of it. Can't stand the water, y'know.

"Oh, and by the by, Hoare, stay away from the Nine Stones Circle, d'ye hear? If you should be found there at the wrong time, you'll get a welcome that might surprise you most unpleasantly."

With that, Spurrier turned and followed his master topside.

Ernest, Duke of Cumberland, departed *Royal Duke* without further ceremony, followed by his snickering entourage. He left her Commander alone on deck, shaken and sick at heart.

For Hoare, this first full day in command of a Naval vessel had dealt him a foul blow and one he had not anticipated. True, *Royal Duke*'s battery was trivial. But at least, he had thought, she could go to sea if permitted and serve as a dispatch ship, if nothing else. Now he knew that he would not dare take her off soundings, if even so far. Her crew would be too seasick to go aloft. Besides, they would have no idea what to do when they got there.

He must berate someone; he needed a cat to kick. There being no cat aboard as yet, Clay would have to do. He was handy, was unable to kick back, and was smaller than Hoare, as well.

"May I ask, Mr. Clay," Hoare whispered as soon as he could get the hapless man below, "how—beginning with this morning's bungled performance . . . between the mooring and the dock—you contrived to disgrace your ship, your Commander, and yourself so completely?"

Clay's face reddened. "Our hands are untrained, sir," he said. "They are proficient enough at their trades and at ship's housekeeping, but they are totally ignorant of seamanship."

"And whose fault is that, may I inquire?"

Clay could look anywhere, it seemed, except at his Captain. "Only a few Royal Dukes, sir—Iggleden, Joy, the woman Taylor—have ever been to sea at all. None of the standing officers."

"*What?* Surely . . ." Hoare could summon no words.

"I could not believe it myself, sir, when I first joined her. But when I discovered that the ships's people had no notion of how to cast off, let alone make sail, and when I began to take the standing officers to task for such neglect of their duty, they assured me that it was actually required of them. In fact, I was shown a document among the ship's papers in which Admiral Abercrombie explicitly forbade her Commander to take her to sea under any circumstances.

"Even worse, sir, I was forbidden to allow any of the crew aloft, even in harbor, unless they were fitted with lubber's harnesses. Virtually every man jack and woman jill might as well have been clerks in some city office. That's what several of them had been, sir, after all," he had the courage to add.

Hoare felt his sacrificial lamb beginning to elude him.

"Instead of using your undoubted creative powers, Mr. Clay," he rasped, "to dream up reasons for having disobeyed my orders . . . to prepare *Royal Duke* for an inspection, by royalty, at that, you might better have applied it to finding ways to carry them out."

He cleared his broken throat. He knew very well he was being most unfair, but he needed a cat to kick, and Clay had to be it.

"By the evidence of this morning, your excuse must certainly be true, although you can imagine how it reflects on your own performance . . . Nevertheless, it leads me to wonder how you managed to bring *Royal Duke* around from Chatham and down the Channel to Portsmouth."

Mr. Clay hung his head and stood mute. That was all any junior dared do.

"Well, Mr. Clay?"

"Our passengers, sir," Clay said at last.

"*What?*"

"Our passengers. A draft of men for *Niobe,* under a midshipman, with their own petty officers. The mid in charge of the draft showed me his orders."

"Which were?"

"To place himself and his men under my command, sir, for the duration of our passage to Portsmouth. I issued my orders to *them*, and the Niobes brought her here.

"Besides, most of our own people were incapacitated by seasickness as soon as we passed Greenwich, sir," Clay added.

"My God," Hoare said. "Do you mean to say that by ordering this poor mismanned barky to sea the Admiralty *deliberately* put her reputation at risk?"

"It appears so, sir," Mr. Clay said. "Of course, they could not have foreseen the Duke's contribution of this morning."

"What did Their Lordships think it would do to her— our—credibility in the fleet?"

"I can hardly say, sir."

Hoare lay long awake that night, lying snug in the swinging bed Captain Oglethorpe had left behind him and reviewing the painful course of the day and the blunders that had preceded it. How he himself had blundered again and again: swanning about that Channel gale in the then-named *Neglectful*—"Neglectful," indeed!—instead of standing ready to board *Royal Duke* immediately upon her being sighted off Spithead; paying court to Eleanor Graves when he should have been questioning the Weymouth watch; playing games with Abel Dunaway when he should have been pressing him for facts about his smuggling trade.

Above all, he should have fended off, somehow, Cumberland's ill-starred inspection. If he had kept at his duty and stayed in Dorchester himself to track down the Captains' killers, he would never have been commanded to the reception. Instead, he had let Taylor's message entice him back to Portsmouth, where Cumberland had his chance to torment him. *Damn Taylor; damn Cumberland.*

Come what might, he would never turn his own beloved little *Alecto* over to Ernest, Duke of Cumberland. Never. He would scuttle her first.

Admiral Abercrombie in London may have been justified in commanding that *Royal Duke* should never go to sea. Having had the courage to break all precedence in the Service and recruit her crew for its members' qualifications, regardless of age, seamanship, sex, or previous condition of servitude, he must surely have sought to ensure that the yacht, her peculiar people, and her treasury of secrets would remain safe, at least from the perils of the sea. Capture by the French, in particular. It would be a far, far better thing for Sir Hugh to scuttle her first, and himself with her. So, in the safe headquarters haven of Deptford, this constraint might have been acceptable. But now *Royal Duke* lay off Spithead, surrounded by fighting ships and fighting men. She was no toothless lighter; she was visibly designed to take the sea. She carried sail. Moreover, she carried guns, albeit tiny ones, which made her a fighting ship as well and not a mere handmaiden to wait upon her betters.

The effect this would have on the credibility of her secret work would be catastrophic. Judging from the jeers of the ships she had crawled past, and nearly into, this morning and the avidity with which their crews had overheard Cumberland's broadcast remarks, *Royal Duke's* mission of supplying the fleet with believable information about the French might already have failed. Unless Abercrombie let her loose to learn her maritime duty, she and her people would remain the laughingstock of the Navy and any information emanating from her would leave the Naval world a-sneer.

Hoare's stomach churned. He must speak with Admiral Sir George Hardcastle, since Sir George was his Administrative Commander as long as *Royal Duke* lay in Portsmouth. Thereafter, he must prepare a report to his true superior, Admiral Sir Hugh Abercrombie, in London. Hoare did not know which he dreaded the more: the Port Admiral's predictable outrage or the task of convincing the unknown Sir Hugh that he must reverse a mistaken command. And with permission or without it, he must somehow find a way to whip into shape an unfamiliar, untrained crew. Still viewing these dismal prospects, Hoare finally began to doze off.

God, he had forgotten the bloody ciphers. He had been intending to read them, and he had not. Instead, he had stuffed them casually into his uniform coat before he rushed off to last night's disastrous reception. *Please, Lord, let them still be there.* Wearily, he climbed out of bed, struck a light, lit a candle, recovered the decipherment with a relieved sigh, and ensconced himself in his night robe in Sir Hugh Abercrombie's enormous chair.

They might be en clair now, but they were still gibberish, written in imitation of James from one Old Testament character to another: Jehu, Ahab, Asa, Levi. Someone named Saul. Someone else named Jael, another named Sisera. Hoare wished he had paid more attention, of Sundays, to the ministering clergyman, back when father had hauled his Hoares off to be sanctified.

He must do some writing. He sighed again, decided he must make a night of it, and sat down again, this time at his writing table. He pulled out a little-used Bible and a sheet of foolscap and began to scribble.

By the time the gray of dawn began to light *Royal Duke*'s beautiful broad stern window and the miniature gallery behind it, he had assigned some of the names, somewhat uncertainly, to some of the persons who were—or might be—involved in a possible plot against the Crown. It was all very vague and quite unsatisfactory for a direct-minded sailor.

"Levi," he was quite sure, was Spurrier. "Jehu," the furious driver according to the handy concordance he had found in Holy Writ at about four bells, was probably the late Lieutenant Kingsley, hanged for the murder of Adam Hay, his Captain in *Vantage*. "Asa" was certainly a person of importance, the man whom Jenny Jagger's da had described as "Himself" and the Francophone Moreau as "*lui*"—Sir Thomas Frobisher leaped into his mind. And how about the Duke of Cumberland? How did *he* happen to turn up in his thinking?

Oh, dear, he told himself; this was getting him nowhere. He locked the packet of messages in his strongbox with the orders placing him in command of *Royal Duke* and turned in.

Chapter VII

S IR. SIR."Hoare was awake instantly, although it took him a noticeable time to recall that he was neither in his bedroom in the Swallowed Anchor nor aboard *Alecto.* Once he remembered he was in *Royal Duke,* he swung his feet to the deck.

"I'm awake," he whispered. "What is it? What's the time?"

"Just past four bells, sir," said the watch. "They're calling for you to come to Admiralty House. There's word Admiral Hardcastle's been shot."

His Admiral? Shot? Hoare whistled for Whitelaw. He would not wait to shave or be shaved. He threw on his uniform and in minutes was across the brow and ashore, ahead of the messenger, going at a near trot over the cobbles, through the sparsely lit sleeping port, to Admiralty House.

Admiralty House was lit as if for a second performance of last night's reception, its entrance full of comings and goings.

Hoare arrived panting. Outside the door, despite the lateness of the hour, a mixed crowd had gathered in the feeble lamplight. He had no breath to waste on apologies but simply elbowed his way through the hubbub and upstairs until he reached the Admiral's anteroom. This was crowded, murmurous. At the little desk normally occupied by the clerk Rabbett sat Patterson, the Admiral's secretary, fending off as best he could the questions and demands being fired at him by all and sundry. Beside Patterson stood the swarthy lantern-jawed figure of Oliver Leese, *Royal Duke*'s own Marine sergeant. Behind Leese stood another of her Marines. In their incorrect but practical Rifleman's green, the two were as different from the red-coated sentry at the Admiral's office door as Franciscans were from a cardinal. To one side of that sentry lay another, dumped in a heap like a pile of dirty clothes; whether this man was alive or dead, Hoare must wait to discover.

"Please, gentlemen, please!" Patterson cried as Hoare entered the anteroom. "I'm sure Captain Hoare—or somebody—will have news for us all momentarily! If you'll just . . . If . . . Oh, dear."

On sighting Hoare, Patterson interrupted himself long enough to turn and tell the redcoat at the door behind him to let the Commander past, then returned to his litany. The lobster came to attention, then opened the door for Hoare to enter.

The office might have been struck by a hurricane. A sea of papers lay strewn upon the floor and upon every other flat surface. In two places they were charred, where candles had fallen on them. Every chair, it seemed, had been overturned, half the pictures flung from the wall, the wall itself blood-boltered.

Hoare expected to find Sir George prone on a pallet, pallid, bleeding, dying, or dead. Bleeding he was, indeed, for a flabby medical person in a scratch wig was bent over his outstretched arm, relieving into a basin still more of the blood the Admiral must have already lost.

But, though pallid enough, the patient himself was quite alive, slumped behind his desk and roaring faintly. His uniform coat, heavy with bullion, had been cut away, and his fine lawn shirt as well. His white silk breeches, blood-spattered, were torn at the knees, as well as the skin beneath them. A bandage, already encarnadined, had been bound about the Admiral's white-furred chest and shoulder and another about his head. His mouth was swollen and bloody.

A second smaller, ragged mouth gaped in the muscle of his neck, but Hoare saw with relief that it had not reached through to the great blood vessels. If it had, of course, Hoare would have been reporting to a corpse. The knuckles of both Sir George's hands were bruised. Obviously, the Admiral had not been shot but assaulted, and he had gone down fighting.

So, too, had Francis Delancey, Flag Lieutenant. Delancey crouched over himself on a chair in a corner of the room, holding a reddened handkerchief against his nose and bleeding onto one of his Admiral's upholstered mahogany side chairs. Like his Admiral's, his knuckles bore signs of action.

The Admiral pointed to the full bleeding basin. "That will be enough, man! *Avast,* d'ye hear? Look lively there!" He mumbled a bit but was quite understandable.

"Now finish tying me up and be off with you! Report to Mrs . . . to Lady Hardcastle. Now!"

The medical man pursed his lips disapprovingly but secured one pad over the cut he had made and put another over the little extra mouth in the Admiral's neck. He picked up his fleam, inserted its keen blade into its little sheath, and was about to leave the room, basin of blood and all, when the Admiral forestalled him with another weak roar.

"Where d'ye think you're going with my blood, you thieving ghoul? Up to your Satanic tricks are ye, you slippery son of a bitch, you scoundrel, you squirming bum worm?"

Astounded, the surgeon gaped at him.

"Throw it out, man. Throw it out, where I can see you do it. Dispose of it. No, no," he added as the surgeon went to the window, "you worse than thoughtless thing, you; you'll dose someone with it. Into the grate with it."

Obviously stunned by his patient's commands, the surgeon tossed both blood and container into the fire, where it gave off the hiss of the Great Serpent and a vile sulfurous stink. Then he vanished, muttering about damned superstitious sailors—merciless Bedlamites—"call the savage out . . ."

Only the slam of the Admiral's door shut off the surgeon's lament.

"Have to watch those slimy bastards, Hoare," the Admiral said on catching sight of him. "They'll take a man's blood and then misuse it in the most ungodly ways, you know. Drink it, and probably worse."

"I am sorry to see you in such a state, sir," Hoare said. Only less than the surgeon was he astonished by Sir George's outburst. Had the event just past affected him in brain as well as in body?

"Well . . ." The Admiral had gotten rid of his temper now. "As you can see, some crew of murderous swabs tried to dispose of me, and of poor Delancey, too, while they were about it, which was more than he deserves. They'll have to try harder next time, what what . . . Damn, I seem to have caught that damned Duke's habit.

124

"Your damned green marines dealt with 'em at last; I'll give 'em credit for that. You know what you're to do, Hoare; get the bastards, and get 'em now. There's not a moment to be lost.

"First, get me brandy. That nincompoop surgeon took my decanter away. Delancey!"

Delancey sat up and began to struggle to his feet, but Hoare gestured to him to remain where he was.

"Mr. Delancey is unable to respond just now, sir," Hoare whispered. "No brandy. Port, to rebuild your blood, and to calm you down. Here."

"Damn you, man, I'm perfectly calm!"

"Port, sir. Here."

"Didn't you hear me the first time, Hoare, you dilatory dog? Brandy! And then be off about your duty!"

"I am about my duty *now*, sir," Hoare whispered. "Tell me, for a start, what happened."

At this, Sir George's rage dissipated like a summer tempest. As he recounted the affray, he became what he truly was: a white-haired man of sedentary habits who had just missed death by violence and who, while brave, was long unused to standing into harm's way.

"I worked late over these papers," he began. He pointed to some documents; the top layer was lightly spotted with crimson stains as if sealing wax had been spilled over it.

"I'd sent Delancey, here, off to his quarters. He's still young and needs his rest more than I do. Besides, I was dealing with some matters that are none of his business. Apparently, he chose to disobey my orders and stayed out in the anteroom. . . . Delancey?"

"Sir?" Again Delancey began to struggle erect.

"Thankee, Mr. Delancey . . . thankee. But never again disobey an order of your Admiral, d'ye understand?"

"Sir."

"I'm cold, Hoare. Bring my cape. There it is, in the hanging locker over there. Yes. Drape it over my shoulders. *Uh! Handsomely,* man! There; that's better. Now, a chamber pot, if you please. I don't choose to leave my chair just now.

"Ahhhh. Here."

He returned the pot to Hoare.

"Well, as I was saying . . . What was I saying?"

"You were working on some secret papers, sir," Hoare reminded him. "Are they still here?"

Supporting himself on both bruised arms, Sir George leaned forward to examine his desk. "How can I tell? Papers all over the place. Someone must . . . must . . ."

Sir George's upper body collapsed on the paper-strewn desk. Fresh scarlet began to spread out from the darkening stain on the bandage around his neck. Coming feebly to his feet, Delancey bent over his Admiral, while Hoare put his fingers to his mouth and uttered the piercing whistle that never failed to bring anyone in earshot. They came with a stretcher, this time, and took their Admiral away. Delancey followed, staggering slightly and still holding the kerchief to his nose. Hoare saw now that both the Lieutenant's eyes were blackened and his breeches torn. He, too, had put up a stubborn fight. *Popinjay he might be,* Hoare thought, *but no poltroon.*

Before following the cortege out of the sanctum, Hoare leaned over his Admiral's desk to see what he could see. At once, his eyes fixed on a small document covered with gibberish, five letters to the "word," in tidy lines identical to those on the papers that had featured so prominently in his last adventure. He pocketed it. He took a last look around the room, snuffed the candles behind him, took the key from inside the door, locked the door behind him, sighed, and quietly departed to take up this new burden.

Back in the anteroom, Hoare turned first to the Marine sentry.

"You will admit no one to this room, do you understand? *No one*, unless I order you to do so, whether in person or in writing. You *can* read, can't you?"

"No, sir."

"Sergeant Leese!" Hoare croaked, but when he realized that his loudest whisper would not override the tumult of voices in the room, he again gave his piercing "all hands" whistle for attention. At his beckoned summons, Sergeant Leese wove his way through the stilled crowd and came to attention before his Commander. He brought his ranker with him.

"Sir!"

Hoare had just repeated his special orders when a brisk, square, sandy-haired Captain pushed through the outer door and, to a repeated, "Make way there; make way!," strode up to him. He bore an epaulet on either shoulder, signifying more than three years' seniority.

"Who are you, sir?" he demanded. Hoare named himself.

"Oh. Sir George's pet ferret. Might have known you'd be about. I'm Trelawney, commanding *Devon,* 64—senior officer present, I understand. Sir George Hardcastle's duties devolve upon me until he can resume them, I fear. Pity. We just completed repairs and could have weighed anchor for Gibraltar tomorrow."

Hoare glanced at Patterson, the flag Secretary, for confirmation. Patterson looked relieved, as well he might.

"That's correct, Captain Hoare," he said.

"Correct, man? Of course, it's correct," Captain Trelawney snapped. "Said it, didn't I? Now, Hoare, tell me what this is all about."

"First, sir, I respectfully submit that there are many persons in the room who have no particular reason to be here. . . ."

"Yes. *Out,* all of you, all but you, Patterson. . . ."

Hoare whispered in Trelawney's ear.

"And you Marines."

When the anteroom had emptied, Trelawney turned to Hoare.

"Well, Captain Hoare?"

Hoare still felt a flutter of joy when a superior officer addressed him as "Captain." He now told Trelawney all he knew, omitting only his removal of the paper that rested in his bosom.

"But to tell you the truth, sir, I have yet to learn the details of the affair. From what I could see below . . . it was a running battle, beginning at the entrance to Admiralty House and continuing as Sir George and Mr. Delancey withdrew, into the building, up the stairs, and into this office."

"A fighting withdrawal, then, into the citadel." Captain Trelawney's voice was filled with approval. "Meeting resistance before him and assaulted from behind, the enemy broke up in disorder. I would have expected no less of Sir George. He's a hard and a merciless man, as you know."

"But Sergeant Leese here can tell us more, sir. As I said, Admiral Hardcastle mentioned that the Sergeant and his men drove off the attackers."

"Well, Sergeant?"

Leese assumed the parade rest position, hands clasped behind his back like a small boy reciting before the class, and began.

"I been patrollin' the port nightly since we come into Portsmouth, sir, with two of my men, so's to keep a weather eye out for trouble between our shipmates and hands from other ships what don't admire our seamanship in *Royal Duke*.

"We'd rounded the corner and was comin' up on Admiralty House 'ere—about three bells, it would 'a' been—when I saw the Jolly at the door was missin' an' 'eard what you might call a disturbance on the upper deck. An', well, me an' me lads was in there at the double, an' up the gangway before you could say, 'Jack Robinson.' When we got into thisyer room, I saw they was a gang of men—coulda been the Press but for where it was and but for most of 'em 'avin' knives instead of clubs. They was attackin' two officers. The officers was down but fightin', an' the gang was a-takin' turns a-givin' 'em the boot. They was some five or six 'ard coves a-workin' over the officers, sir, an' one more of 'em a-standin' back like 'e was a-givin' the orders.

"We run up to break up the fightin', an' I seen one of the officers was Admiral Hardcastle. Couldn't miss *'im,* 'ardly. So the three of us pitches in, drops two of the gang, and the others run off. I left one of me lads up 'ere an' give chase. Took three of 'em. That's all, sir."

"So you and your two men drove off a gang of six attackers, all bearing knives?" Trelawney asked.

"Well, sir, the two officers 'ad been a-puttin' up quite a fight, and the others, they didn't all 'ave knives. Some of 'em just 'ad clubs."

"Even so. . . . You have a formidable crew, it seems, Captain Hoare, even if they're no seamen."

"Not seamen yet, sir, perhaps, but they will be before long," Hoare whispered. "Leese, where's your other man?"

"Baker, sir? Left 'im below, sir, a-guardin' the prisoners. 'E'd got cut up a bit 'imself, and I wouldn't have 'im a-messin' up the floors 'ere in Admiralty House even worse than they be now."

"We might see what the prisoners look like, sir," Hoare whispered inquiringly to Trelawney.

"Damn, sir, don't *whisper*—beg pardon, Captain." Captain Trelawney must have recollected Hoare's muteness and, unlike many, had the courtesy to apologize for any discourtesy.

"Yes. Let's have a look at 'em, by all means," the Captain continued.

Sergeant Leese led the two officers below and out the Admiralty door into the torch-lit darkness, where a small crowd of mixed onlookers still loitered about. One at least was a gentlewoman, and an oddly familiar one at that, for Hoare heard an unmistakable seagull titter.

"Come away, damn you, Lyd!" It was the croaking voice of Martin Frobisher. "We've no business here!"

"But I want to see! Where's Walter? I want Walter! Let go of me!" There was a scuffle. Hoare had no time to crane about in search of the speakers, for Captain Trelawney, preceded by Leese, was thrusting through the crowd.

"There he is!" called a woman's voice.

"Wot's the green man, an American?" asked another.

"No, ye fule, 'e be one of t' Yeomen of t' Guard."

Guessing wildly at the tenor of the calls, Hoare concluded that one of the assaulted officers—Delancey, probably—upon his leaving as his Admiral had ordered had given the people a brief account of the fracas and the part Leese and his men had played.

"Where did you station Baker and your prisoners?" asked Trelawney.

Leese took them around the corner of Admiralty

House and into the mews that lay behind it.

Three disordered heaps lay against the back wall of Admiralty House, lit by the waning moon. Two were in civilian dress, still bound hand and foot, as Leese had left them. From their turned-out pockets, they had been thoroughly searched. Their throats had been cut.

The third body, badly cut about the arms, which still gripped its rifle, wore Rifleman's green. It had been stabbed deep in the back, and its head was missing.

"A formidable crew, perhaps," Captain Trelawney calmly observed to Hoare, "but not always unbeatable, it seems."

Chapter VIII

*G*O RIGHT in, Captain Hoare," Delancey said. "Sir George is expecting you."

Despite his fading black eyes, Admiral Hardcastle's Flag Lieutenant looked quite sprightly, in Hoare's opinion—even smug. Hoare remarked as much to him as he passed.

"Yes. He's given me the *Niobe* brig," Delancey said. "Eighteen guns. We're to join the Mediterranean fleet in three weeks' time."

Hoare wished him well in his new command.

The Admiral still wore his arm in a sling and the gauze about his wounded throat, but he, too, was clearly recovering apace.

"I'm pleased to see you looking so thrifty, sir," whispered Hoare. "The other night, when I saw you last, you looked like death . . . And Mr. Delancey is obviously none the worse for his experience, though he still looks as though he's gone forty rounds with Tom Cribb. I gather he stood by you manfully."

The Admiral began to nod, then winced and stopped himself as though the motion hurt his head.

"Indeed, he did, Hoare, and I'm seeing him recognized for it, by God. I've ordered him into *Niobe,* 18, as soon as she's rigged. But I imagine he's told you that; he's quite puffed. He'd been mopin' so much over losin' my Felicia to young Gladden, I'd already about decided to rid myself of him."

Hoare feared he would have to endure hearing that news of another officer's advancement for another three weeks. Once was quite enough, he told himself. But when he reminded himself that a brig like *Niobe* rated only a Lieutenant in command, while he carried a Commander's swab—brig or no brig—he felt much better. *Niobe,* he remembered, was the brig with which *Royal Duke* had barely escaped collision the other morning.

"Now tell me," the Admiral went on, "what have you done to find those impudent knaves who attacked me and Delancey? D'ye know, I do think the bastards were after our heads?"

He touched the cut in his neck with gingerly fingers.

"Bugger sewed me up," he explained. "Stitches itch like hell."

"I believe you're right, sir," Hoare said. "You know the man set on guard over the two prisoners was beheaded and the prisoners' throats slit?"

"I know. Trelawney told me. What are you doing about it?"

Hoare told Admiral Hardcastle how he had chosen Dabney, one of *Royal Duke*'s sharpest men, to examine the bodies and the mews where they had been found. He did not tell him he had done so on Mr. Clay's recommendation.

"The dead marine, Baker, was taken by surprise, with his back turned to his killer. That probably meant that it was a man he knew, or at least someone he trusted. . . . Whoever it was, he cut Baker's throat with one neat slice and then did the same for the Marine's prisoners.

"To keep their mouths shut, I suppose. He finished by completing his job on Baker and went off, taking the head with him. . . . Dabney was better than I would have been at deducing what happened in the mews. Almost as good, I think, as Thoday would have been."

"Today, yesterday, tomorrow," the Admiral burst out. "If Thoday's the better man, I want you to put *him* on the job, not some secondhand piece of baggy-wrinkle. Where *is* Thoday, anyhow?"

"In Dorchester, sir, on the trail of the people who beheaded the Getchell brothers."

"Get him *here,* you nincompoop."

"With respect, sir, I think . . . ," Hoare began.

"Damn you, you're not paid to think. Do as you're told."

"Again with respect, sir, I am."

"You are what?"

"Paid to think, sir. That's why Admiral Abercrombie chose me to command the Navy's thinking ship."

At this, Sir George did his best to turn purple and roar, but he was still too short of blood to succeed. Instead, he began to laugh. Again he must needs stop and clap his hands to his head.

"You're right, of course, Hoare. But I order you—*order* you, d'ye hear?—never, *never* to refer to *Royal Duke* or any other of His Majesty's ships as a 'thinking ship.' What with your silly voice, people will say you were a lisper as well as a whisper. And it would never do for an officer of the Navy to speak of his command as 'sinking,' eh?"

Hoare gulped and took his courage in both hands.

"Speaking of *Royal Duke,* sir . . . I have a request of you, sir, on behalf of her and her crew," Hoare whispered.

"Don't expect me to fall all over you for saving me life, I warn you," the Admiral said. "You didn't. Delancey did, and that fool doctor did, and your damned green lobsters. I don't owe you a bloody thing. Now, what is it you want?"

"Sir, after our recent performance in harbor, you can imagine the reputation *Royal Duke* has apparently already gotten among the crews of her . . . sister ships here in Portsmouth. I've already heard men from other ships, calling out remarks like, 'What ho, the Dustbins!' as our men row by. Or 'Shape up, ye whore's delights!' "

Did Hoare hear his Admiral suppress a splutter of laughter? *Never mind.*

"Understandably, sir," Sir George said, "and deservedly, considering the appalling performance your ship's company made of a simple maneuver like warpin' a brig a cable's length in to a pier. Oh, yes, sir, I was watching. And your command's hideous condition when the Duke of Cumberland himself condescended to inspect you. D'ye come whinin' to me like a schoolboy who comes to his master a-blubberin' that the other lads are callin' him names? You shan't get any coddlin' out of me, I'll have you know. That bedlam brig of yours deserves whatever name the Fleet tacks onto her."

"I must agree, sir," Hoare said. "We have fewer than five experienced men aboard, and one of *them*'s a woman, though how she got the experience I have yet to learn. Most of the rest have not even been aloft. . . .

". . . They moved her back to her original mooring this morning, sir, but their performance was still enough to make a man weep. . . . Those eight pretty, shiny little brass guns—the ones His Royal Highness admired so much the other day—have never . . . even been fired. *Never.* What I need, sir, is the loan of one or two more seamen—men who can teach my poor landsmen their trade. They're willing enough and smarter than your average landsmen . . . They should shape up handily.

"I had your men, Bold and Stone, in *Uninhabitable, Inconceivable, Alecto* now, I mean—in my own little yacht, anyhow—not so long ago. I'd like 'em back, sir."

Bold was a coxswain, competent to be boatswain in any vessel of twenty-eight guns or less, Stone a seasoned gunner. With them, Hoare could leave Thoday to his detection and send poor old Joy to some sinecure ashore.

Hoare had needed to interrupt himself repeatedly during this speech; now he ran out of breath entirely and stopped to cough. It was an awful sound.

Feeble though the Admiral still was, the level look he gave Hoare went through him like a knife through butter.

"I twig your game, sir. You want to take your command to sea," he said when Hoare had got his coughing under hatches and could hear him. "Well, you shall not. You're under standing orders from Admiral Abercrombie in London to stay inshore, and you know why. You have your copy of those orders, and I have mine."

"*Inshore* can mean more than lying tied up at a pier, sir," Hoare dared say, "or swinging round a mooring till we ground on our own beef bones. It can mean simply staying within sight of land."

"When *I* use a word," the Admiral said, "it bloody well means just what I choose it to mean—neither more nor less. *I* am in charge of my own bloody words."

That was a rather good line, Hoare thought. *Perhaps I should add it to my little commonplace book. Then, after I die, brother John or some other lucky being can use it himself or hand it on to someone who will.*

"Yes, sir," he said, "but . . ."

The Admiral must not yet be himself, because after prolonged haggling, he conceded that Hoare, or rather Clay under Hoare's direction, might take *Royal Duke* on brief training excursions that did not take her out of sight of the shoreline.

"And I don't mean 'sight of land,' either, sir, d'ye understand? I mean that you must be able to see the shoreline. From on deck. Tidewater, sir; not a fathom farther offshore," he added as he read Hoare's thoughts.

And, yes, he could have the loan of Bold and Stone, at least until Admiral Hardcastle was strong enough to go about in his barge, of whose crew the two seamen were essential members.

"Er, Hoare," the Admiral said as Hoare turned to leave the sickroom, "I've given in to your request, not because it is insolent and presumptuous—which it is—but because I owe you amends for having failed you."

"Failed me, sir?"

"Yes. In the Navy, loyalty should work both ways. I failed to protect you from bein' bullied by that Hanoverian poltroon. Go on, now; put your vessel into order. But only at your peril do you take your *Dustbin* beyond the bounds I've given you."

"Aye aye, sir."

As Hoare was on the point of leaving Admiralty House, Delancey—as if to rub salt in his wounds—condescendingly invited him to be present when he read himself in as *Niobe*'s Lieutenant in command. Delancey was to go to sea, while Hoare was still all but shorebound.

> " 'Mother, may I go to swim?'
> 'Yes, my darling daughter;

Hang your clothes on a hickory limb,
And don't go near the water,' "

Hoare muttered to himself as the gig's awkward, willing oarsmen took him back out to his own command. But now he could try to remedy *Royal Duke's* hopeless performance as a man-o'-war. To be sure, Hoare admitted to himself, if his cockleshell were to continue being an efficient sea-going office, she could never become a crack cockleshell. And the Admiral's prohibition against taking to the open sea, of course, violated every sailor's fear of being too close to shore. Every piece of land bore teeth. Nevertheless, he could hope she would at least cease being the Fleet's laughingstock.

With this thought, the idea that had eluded Hoare last night came home to roost. There might be a way to bring his own pinnace into play as well, thereby keeping her out of the clutch of Ernest, Duke of Cumberland.

So he could address his crew directly instead of through his Lieutenant, Hoare ordered Joy, the doddering one-eyed boatswain who had so maltreated *Alecto,* to muster all hands below decks, in their work space. Clay stood at his elbow—in case he faltered, he supposed—and Hoare's two new hands behind him. Hoare had cleared his feeble throat and was about to launch into his prepared speech when Joy stepped forward and forestalled him.

"Permission to speak to the Capting on be-be'alf of yer crew, sir," he said in a trembling voice.

"What is it, then, Joy? Speak up, but be quick about it, for *I* have much to say to *you*."

"The Royal Dukes wishes to make their shame an'

138

sorrer known to you, sir. We 'ave left undone those things what we ought to have done, an' we 'ave done those things that we ought not to 'ave done, an' there is no 'ealth in us." Joy's voice was a virtual chant.

Hoare found the man's words oddly familiar. "What on earth are you getting at, Joy?" he asked.

"We're bein' bad-mouthed about the Fleet fer our lack o' seamanship, sir, an' we don't like it, and we ain't goin' to 'ave it," Joy blurted.

"The Dustbins, they're calling us." The voice came from the midst of the gathering.

"That's what I understand," Hoare said. "How do you like it?"

There was a muttering and a shuffling of feet.

"Our David Davies took on three Niobes when they threw gash on 'is uniform," said a Marine. "Showed 'em what our lads can do, 'e did."

"Pipe down, Griffith," Sergeant Leese snapped.

"Well, men—er—and women," Hoare said, "once a ship gets a name, she's stuck with it. She'll never shake it loose, no matter what. What we have to do . . . is change what people think of us. That will be when we show them that our *Dustbin* may be small, but she's a fighting man-o'-war of the Royal Navy just the same.

"Now, I'm not going to make a speech to you, because that's not my way. It can't be . . . As you know, I can't talk very long. What I do want to say is this: if you're willing to put those sharp wits of yours to use at a trade that's new to most of you, and turn *Dustbin* into a . . . a name we're all proud to answer to with a laugh and a cheer, we sailormen are willing to show you how.

"In fact, Admiral Hardcastle himself has given us two good, tough, experienced sailormen to back up me and

Mr. Clay in whip—sorry, no whips aboard *this* barky—getting the old *Dustbin* into fighting shape.

"Bold, Stone . . . come forward. The scuttlebutt may have reached you that these are the men I had aboard . . . when we rammed the French schooner—on purpose that time, it was." There was a subdued, rueful chuckle.

"With their help and that of the old hands we already have aboard, Mr. Clay here and I will turn us into a man-o'-war we can all be proud of. We may be small, but we'll be swift, and we'll carry a sting. Are you with us?"

Hoare ended. He stopped to cough, and cough.

There were no cheers but an eerie animal growl that would have been appropriate coming from a hardened crew but which, coming from this strange assemblage of eccentrics, he had not anticipated.

"Then," Hoare said, "the first thing we'll do is warp back in to the pier and back out here again. I don't care how long it takes you, but you'll do it right before we're through if we have to do it all week. But first, Mr. Clay, we'll splice the main brace."

This spirited conclusion aroused a sound that was less a cheer than a general determined snarl.

Chapter IX

———⊱◈⊰———

"No, sir," Taylor told her Commander, looking up from her worksheets and taking off her spectacles. She had decoded the paper Hoare had pilfered from his Admiral's desk.

"It's a different cipher, sir, a standard Admiralty cipher. Besides, the others, the ones you gave me before, were in French, if you remember."

She stopped, as if she had now said all that was expected of her. Hoare waited.

"Well?" he whispered at last. "What's the message?"

"I can't say, sir."

"Can't you read it?"

"Of course, sir. I did."

"Well, then?"

"It is not addressed to you, sir, but to Admiral Hardcastle. It deals with Fleet movements. With all respect, sir," she added before Hoare could recover his wits or explode at her, "I respectfully submit that it be returned to the Admiral, unread."

She handed Hoare the paper, fitted her spectacles back over her ears, and returned to the document she had been studying there in the 'tween-decks work space, leaving Hoare to betake himself to his own cabin and seethe over *Royal Duke*'s administration.

What, the Admiralty asked querulously, were these repeated indents for "grain"? Grain was not to be found in the table of authorized supplies, except as a subcategory of gunpowder. He begged leave to inform Their Lordships that the grain was to be categorized as "pigeons, for the maintenance of." He was sure that further correspondence would follow on the matter, as did night the day.

He only regained his temper by persuading himself once more that when he was through with them, he ought, indeed, to have a fighting crew as well as a thinking one, and a ship to match. In fact, the sentry at his door today was no Marine at all but a small, nimble man—Blassingame, the former pickpocket. Sergeant Leese and his entire detachment had been set ashore and marched inland, where they would remain overnight, practicing surprise attacks on suspicious outlying byres. Like the two longboats that cluttered *Royal Duke*'s narrow deck, as many as were carried in a twenty-eight-gun frigate, his Johnnies had never been put to the use for which they had been sent aboard—making unobtrusive raids where they would have the most effect on the French. How, Hoare wondered, did Admiral Abercrombie imagine they would get into raiding position when he had forbidden *Royal Duke* ever to leave home? He had begun to dream of finding a useful stratagem for blooding them.

At last he had not only reconciled the gunpowder inventory and approved it but also replied to an Admiralty inquiry about the consumption of ink in his command. According to Whitehall, this would have sufficed to supply a flagship. Whitehall informed him that this simply would not do.

When he returned on deck, Hoare could see his own *Alecto* lying innocently astern, nameless for the moment, and looking like any other Navy-issue pinnace. He rather looked forward to the appearance of some blue-blooded booby of a Cumberland courtier, demanding to know where the yacht was that H. R. H. had commandeered.

"Lost at sea, sir, lost at sea," he would answer. "Totally dismasted."

On the day of decision a fortnight past, Hoare had put *Royal Duke*'s people on watches, as if she were at sea. On deck, two gangs were hard at work, both officially from the watch below. Under Bold's command, one of them was easing one of *Royal Duke*'s two longboats into her chocks. Bold's blue-black face stood out among his pupils' pale, unweathered ones like a cinder in a snowdrift.

"Handsomely, there, handsomely. Belay. You there, Lorimer. What did ye forget when they hoisted ye out of the water?"

A scrawny man, Lorimer could no more have handled an oar or served a gun than he could have taken *Royal Duke* to sea single-handed, yet at thirty he spurned the role of powder monkey. "A job for women or little boys," Hoare had heard him call it. Bold had noted those two longboats. Given the yacht's shortage of able seamen and oarsmen, he wanted to try a novel way of manning a boat and so had snapped Lorimer up and named him coxswain of the "red," larboard longboat.

Perched in the gently swaying longboat, the clerk-coxswain looked about him in dismay, then down at his feet.

"The plug!" he cried, and gave the thing a yank before Bold could stop him. The icy water in the longboat's bilges poured onto the crew at the hoisting tackles below, to the sound of bitter curses. Lorimer hurled the offending plug into the empty bilges, retrieved it, and shoved it home solidly once more.

"The 'green' boat's gone from 'stow' to 'stow' in three minutes already," Bold said, "and all squared away. Before I'm through with ye, ye'll both go into the water and come back aboard in half that. Hoist away again, lads."

The red boat's crew spit on their blistered hands and took a new purchase on their tackles.

A weird hooting call drew Hoare's attention to activity in the upper rigging of *Royal Duke*'s main topmast. It reminded Hoare of the howler monkeys he had once heard in the jungles of Guiana.

"Nay, nay, ye farmer!" Iggleden called. "If ye crosses yer 'ands that way in any kind of a blow, the sharks'll bite 'em off when ye falls off alongside. Or ye'll mash the Captain beneath ye. Better the sharks. Now, out to the yardarm again, and use yer 'ands the way I shown ye!"

Hoare nodded in agreement and went below again to finish today's paperwork.

Before eight bells sounded the beginning of the first dog watch, he went topside again to watch Clay watch Stone's efforts to teach his volunteer gun crews the rudiments of hauling a four-pounder inboard for loading. Despite the hands' obvious willingness to learn, it was a slow, slow business, and Clay as well as Stone champed visibly with frustration. It helped no one to have Clay and Hoare, too, watching. He summoned Clay to his side with a chirp of his boatswain's pipe.

"If we are ever to make this ship seaworthy, Mr. Clay," he said, "we must get those pigeonholes belowdecks. Where do you suggest we stow the creatures?"

Clay looked quizzical. He appeared to weigh, not the

question his Captain had just posed, but that Captain's most likely reaction to what he was about to say.

"Simply to put them under hatches would serve no purpose, sir," he said. "How would the birds get about? And I do not like to imagine the state in which our open 'tween-decks space would find itself before long. Pigeon shit all over the papers. No, sir, that would never do. I have already consulted Hancock on the subject."

Clay paused and gave Hoare what seemed like a final appraising look, then took the plunge.

"We concluded that the best solution is to erect a bulkhead a few feet forrard of your stern gallery, sir, and open up the gallery for access by the pigeons. As long as we are at anchor or making to windward, the birds can then approach by flying into the wind—a matter of importance to them, according to Hancock."

Clay paused again, as if preparing to withstand the explosion he anticipated from Hoare. The explosion came.

"*What?*" Hoare gasped. "Turn my very own new gallery into private quarters for a batch of filthy birds? And half my own quarters?"

As he had expected, he found the ceremony aboard *Niobe* lightly attended, for changes in command were so frequent in the Royal Navy as to arouse more yawns than cheers among those not directly involved. The new Lieutenant in command returned Hoare's salute to the quarterdeck with a patronizing flourish and left him to fend for himself. Hoare did not hesitate to advance across the deck to where a small flotilla of lady guests stood, managing their hats and skirts with varying degrees of skill.

Selene Prettyman was one of the more adept of these. She allowed no more sight of her person than she saw fit to grant. She was warmly dressed against the stiff autumn breeze, with a pelisse of finest wool, tinted a blue-gray that brought attention to her sapphire eyes. In reply to the leg Hoare made to her, she merely nodded.

"I am not used, sir, to gentlemen who do not see fit to respond to my invitations. Can you offer me any reason why I should excuse you?"

"Pressure of duty, ma'am," Hoare hastened to whisper. "I shall not bore you with the petty details. . . . They would be of interest only to another sailor, if to anyone at all."

"Then perhaps you would care to carry me ashore after this little ceremony. It promises to be *so* interesting."

Hoare thought Selene Prettyman's comment insincere, but not her request. Coming as it did from a Colonel's wife in the entourage of royalty, it was tantamount to a command.

"Delighted, ma'am," he said. He was prevented from a longer reply by the chirping call of "All Hands." To himself, he resolved to teach more of his hands the boatswain's pipe. His plans for *Royal Duke* did not include the senile Joy, and, of course, for Hoare himself as the brig's Commander to pipe his visitors aboard would hardly be the thing.

The ceremony took no more time than was necessary for Delancey to rattle through his orders, reading faster and faster as he went. And Delancey seemed almost eager to see the backs of his guests. He did, however, arrest the departure of Hoare and Selene Prettyman long enough to say, "Pity, Captain, that we shall have no chance to sail in company."

Hoare had no difficulty gauging the sincerity of *that* remark, at least. They both knew perfectly well that should the two ever meet at sea, the senior officer and therefore the one who ordered while the other obeyed would not be Francis Bennett but Bartholomew Hoare.

With that, a brainstorm struck him.

"Perhaps that can be arranged, Captain," he whispered. "I expect to put to sea myself within a fortnight. To give my people an airing, you know," he added, on seeing Delancey's stare of disbelief.

"An airing," the other said.

"Yes. And do you not sail for the Groyne about then?"

"Yes."

"Give us twenty-four hours' grace before you weigh anchor," Hoare said, "and *Royal Duke* will await you somewhere between the Needles and Portland Bill."

"Done, by God," Delancey said. "For a new hat?"

"Agreed. For a new hat," Hoare replied. He held out his arm to assist Selene Prettyman into *Royal Duke*'s gig.

"The cheer for Mr. Delancey demonstrated more uncertainty than goodwill, I thought," Mrs. Prettyman said.

"Delancey would be an unknown quantity for *Niobe*'s people," Hoare whispered. The Hard was to leeward, so he knew she would be able to hear him easily enough.

"But why did you address him as 'Captain' when he is a mere Lieutenant?" she asked.

"A custom of the Service. When an officer is in command of a vessel, as Delancey now is in *Niobe,* we address him as 'Captain.' "

"I vow I shall never understand you sailormen. Prettyman's a soldier, thank God."

Hoare coxed his own gig. He told his crew to stand by until he returned, unless eight bells struck earlier, in which case they could rejoin their ship for dinner. He offered his arm to Selene Prettyman, the cobbles of the Hard being somewhat uneven.

The walk to Mrs. Prettyman's lodgings at the Three

Suns took them past the Blue Posts, suitable for Midshipmen and Junior Lieutenants, and the Crown, where older Lieutenants and miscellaneous officers of the Army most commonly roosted. As Hoare and his companion passed the Crown, two flushed cavalry officers emerged, laughing loudly over their shoulders to companions within. One of them collided with Hoare, who recognized him as having been ejected from one of the Assemblies. Hoare had been one of the ejectors. The man had been troublesome then; he was troublesome now.

"Damn you, fellow, mind where you're goin'!" he exclaimed, and grasped Hoare by his free left arm. He looked at Hoare and at Selene Prettyman.

"By God, Dupree, look what we have here. *Two* whores a-prowlin'! And in the daylight, too! Bags I the blue-eyed 'un!"

"Take your friend away, sir," Hoare said to the second redcoat. "I'll overlook his remarks. He's drunk."

"Come along, Pargeter. He's right." The friend took Pargeter by the arm.

Pargeter, like Hoare, shook himself free. "Not too drunk to know whores when I see 'em," he said.

A small crowd had collected, so Hoare had no choice. Knowing what was about to happen, Selene Prettyman released his right arm, and he knocked the man down.

He swiftly ran through his own list of friends who might be ready to serve as his own second. At first, he thought of Mr. Clay, but his Lieutenant was still a stranger. Bennett had served as his second once before, and he would again, Hoare was sure.

"Have your man's friend call on Mr. Francis Bennett at Admiralty House, if he wishes to pursue this matter," he whispered to the redcoat still on his feet. Now he recognized the cherry-colored facings. They were officers of

Walter Spurrier's regiment, the Fourteenth Hussars.

Mrs. Prettyman took his arm again, and they continued on their way. Nothing was said between them about the encounter; to mention it until the matter had been resolved would not be at all the thing.

The Three Suns, with its eponymous hanging sign—the three coins of the Medici, borrowed without permission of that family—bore the reputation of housing only Britain's highest and their very good friends, when those friends were not such as to be announced to the world. Hoare's only previous visits there had been when he had Admiralty business with these personages. But after suppressing a raised eyebrow upon sighting him, the porter flung the door open with a flourish. He greeted Selene Prettyman properly and added, "Good *morning,* Captain 'Oare. And a fine, brisk morning it is, Captain 'Oare."

"Good morning, Pollard."

Pollard's eyes and ears were always open wide, and his mouth as well—at least for those who paid him to open them and for those, like Hoare, of whom he walked in dread. To Pollard and his cronies, Hoare was the Whispering Ferret.

Selene Prettyman led the way upstairs to the front suite. The place was already familiar to Hoare, who had been entertained there on two earlier occasions by two very different women.

Mrs. Prettyman excused herself for a moment, leaving him in the anteroom. In a few minutes, an ugly little maidservant appeared. After relieving him of his outer garments, she ushered him into the inn's second-best withdrawing room, the selfsame chamber in which Katerina Hay had received him. Earlier that year. His present hostess's gray-blue wool gown, like her pelisse, brought out the color of her eyes, while its fashionable high waist, set just under her admirable bosom, proclaimed it to just the right degree. Yet somehow the ensemble gave her a peculiarly sexless, countinghouse quality, as though she should be wearing *demi-lune* spectacles. She was not.

A tea service was already laid out behind her, the ugly little maidservant hovering alongside it. As he advanced into the salon, Hoare was struck by a paradoxical similarity between this hostess and the last one to receive him in this room. The resemblance was paradoxical since this woman was slim, ivory of skin, and raven-haired, while the other had been a rosy, opulent strawberry blonde. Both, however, were nearly his own height; both were blue-eyed. And, Hoare felt, the virtue of both might be negotiable. The previous occupant had required no recompense. In Selene Prettyman's case, however, the price would surely be beyond his means.

Selene Prettyman took her place on a chaise longue— the selfsame chaise longue where Katerina Hay had once entertained him so instructively.

"Pray be seated, sir." She patted the space beside her. "Tea for Captain Hoare and myself, Angelique." Angelique obediently offered tea, then biscuits and small sandwiches, and returned to her post behind her mistress.

"I have matters of state to discuss with you, Captain," Selene Prettyman went on without ado. In some surprise, Hoare glanced over his hostess's shoulder at Angelique.

"Angelique enjoys my fullest confidence," she said. "In fact, she is also in the fullest confidence—in the pay, I should say rather—of both H. R. H. the Duke of Cumberland and Colonel Prettyman. If I did not permit her to remain in the room, she would convey to either or both of her other employers the most interesting and destructive fables that you can imagine, about our encounter today. It is part of the understanding we have with each other. Since she has a vivid and highly improper imagination, she would almost certainly tell each of them a different one. She is a modern-day Schéhérazade.

"But she would die before she shared secrets with one of Bonaparte's agents. More to the point, the two or three of them who have tried to suborn her are now underground with their necks broken.

"Est-ce que j'ai raison, Angelique?" she asked over her shoulder.

Seeing that both Hoare and her mistress were looking at her, the maid gave a little bob but replied, "Pas tout à fait, madame. Souvenez-vous qu'il y reste Monsieur Charbonnier."

"Of course. We—Mr. Goldthwait and I—decided it was best to keep Charbonnier alive and well, by feeding him tidbits to report to Joseph Fouché of the Sureté. As you would expect, Captain, the true ones are trivial, while the others are false. In return, M. Charbonnier feeds Angelique with gold and . . . other favors. N'est-ce pas, Angelique?"

"Oui, madame."

"That way, I am not out of pocket. Now to business. I know that you find speech uncomfortable, so I shall not take offense if you use gestures instead."

"Not quite so, ma'am," Hoare whispered. "In quiet surroundings such as these, I can generally make myself understood quite well."

"All the better," the lady said. "Now: You have never met Mr. Goldthwait, I believe, Captain."

"On the contrary, ma'am, I have, but only once—here in Portsmouth last summer, in the company of the Duke of Clarence."

"Of course. Tell me, did you find his excessive weight disturbing?"

"When I saw him, Mr. Goldthwait was underweight, if anything," Hoare said. "Perhaps, ma'am, you are thinking of Sir Hugh Abercrombie. Or else your claim to know Mr. Goldthwait is, er, exaggerated."

"Not at all, Captain Hoare. I merely wished to learn whether you were telling the truth and whether Mr. Goldthwait was doing so. I learned that both of you were, which is not always the case with Mr. Goldthwait. With him, the truth is only one of many cards in his hand, to be played or discarded as he judges best for his purposes. Do not play cards with Mr. Goldthwait, sir. But I wander.

"What I wish to convey, Captain Hoare, is that you may not know you are dealing these days with several unusual persons. Each of them, or all of them, may be what they seem, or more, or less, or all three. In that, they are much like Angelique here."

"Merci, madame," the maid said in a subdued voice.

Selene Prettyman did not reply to Angelique in words but nodded to her. At the nod, the maid ducked into the adjoining room. Her mistress continued to address Hoare.

"I speak, sir, of Sir Thomas Frobisher, of his children Martin and Lydia and his minion Walter Spurrier, indeed, I sometimes fear, of Mr. Goldthwait himself—even, perhaps, of his Royal Highness Ernest, Duke of Cumberland. It is far from certain that these persons and their cronies of either sex are friends of the Crown."

"How am I to know, ma'am, that you yourself are a 'friend of the Crown'?"

Angelique reentered, carrying a folded document that she handed to Mrs. Prettyman.

"I would have been disappointed in you, Captain Hoare, had you made any other reply. This may reassure you, sir. You recognize the seal?"

"Let me look at it more closely, if you please," Hoare said.

The document told "all persons having interest" that the bearer was, indeed, Selene Prettyman and that her instructions to persons under Naval discipline were to be obeyed as if they emanated from the Admiralty Board itself. It bore three signatures and the Admiralty seal.

"It looks very much like the Admiralty seal," he said at last.

"And the signatures?"

Hoare knew two of them. One, that of John Barrow, Second Secretary to the Admiralty Board, also appeared below the orders that Mr. Clay had read out for Hoare on the deck of *Royal Duke,* thus placing him in command of the yacht. The second was Sir Hugh Abercrombie's. Both could be gifted forgeries—as, of course, the Admiralty seal could be—but Hoare thought it unlikely. The paper bore the Admiralty watermark. Besides, what was he to do: question every piece of paper that came his way, and every statement? At the end of that corridor lay madness. A mad King was bad enough, but a mad Naval officer in the wrong place could put the entire nation in jeopardy.

The third signature on the document, in the same bold hand as the note by which she had summoned him, was Selene Prettyman's own. He stepped to the little boule desk, moistened a pen, and handed it to the lady. Briskly she signed. The signatures were the same.

So much for his glowing suspicions of Selene Prettyman; they must be doused. She must be as safe as the other signers, or as Britannia herself.

"I'll keep this paper, if I may," he said.

She smiled at him.

"Of course, you may not. Don't be silly," she answered, holding out her hand for it. "How else can I assure myself that I am, indeed, Selene Prettyman, née Claiborne, and not some impostor?"

"And a friend of the Crown?"

"And a friend of the Crown. In any case, I have been engaged to ascertain whether the Duke is such a friend and, if he is not, what he is up to. That, of course, necessitates almost constant attendance upon his person."

"How have you managed that, if I may ask?" Hoare whispered.

"To be blunt, Captain Hoare, I must share his bed from time to time; it gives one no pleasure, by the by. That is why Colonel Prettyman is 'indisposed' at present. You will agree, I think, that having a cuckolded husband drifting about in the background is no small inconvenience to the consummation of adultery. So the poor man stays in London when I leave town and attends to his regiment of militia—in Cumberland, of all places—when I return. He really has very little to do."

"Very interesting," Hoare said, and waited for Selene Prettyman to come to the point of her summons.

"I invited you to call on me, Captain Hoare," she went on, "because I cannot juggle more balls than I now have in hand. Cumberland and his crowd of hangers-on are quite enough for one person to keep under observation. I must ask you to keep watch over the Frobisher coterie for me. The puzzling activities of Mr. Goldthwait of Chancery Lane must be delegated to another, and I must return to London posthaste to attend to that matter."

"Am I to understand then, Mrs. Prettyman, that you wish me to determine . . . if the 'Frobisher coterie,' as you called it, is engaged in occasional treason and—if so—when and how?"

"And to frustrate their knavish tricks, if they do so engage."

"I'll be happy to do so. Am I to do this alone, or may I call upon the talents of *Royal Duke*'s crew? And why should the Frobisher group not be put out of the way in any case, whether they are committing treason or not?"

Selene Prettyman held up two fingers of one slender hand and touched one.

"To answer your first question: By all means, draw upon your crew. From what little I have heard—from Cumberland, for instance, who gave me a most entertaining report of his inspection of *Royal Duke*—your ship has unusual characteristics."

"Indeed," Hoare said.

She touched the second finger.

"To answer your second question: We do not *know* that Sir Thomas is a traitor. As it is, moreover, he and his friends command several important votes in the Commons and are not without influence in the upper house as well. The Admiralty and the Prime Minister are in agreement that the evidence must be overpowering before action is taken against them—if, indeed, action is to be taken at all. They may simply be a cluster of harmless eccentrics, like Francis Dashwood's Hell-Fire Club, for example. Or both."

"I understand," Hoare said. "Then I shall add this to *Royal Duke*'s tasks. Frankly, I would find it a personal pleasure to put Sir Thomas in his place. . . . We have never seen eye to eye. And, in any case, the task may not be so far afield from my current interests."

"How is that?" Selene Prettyman asked.

Hoare gave her an outline of his encounters with the Frobishers, including the suggestion that Sir Thomas and

155

he were on a collision course with respect to a certain widow in Weymouth.

"Aha!" Mrs. Prettyman said on hearing this. "This makes amusing news. For I was thinking it might be well for you to visit Broadmead. Now I know you should. Sir Thomas will be there, if I do not mistake myself, on a mission that I deem quite unsuitable for a widower of his age and reputation. You know of Broadmead?"

"Miss Felicia Hardcastle mentioned the place the other evening, if my memory serves me. The Gladden estate, is it not?"

"Yes. And are you acquainted with the daughter, Miss Anne?"

"I met her once. It was last autumn, on the occasion of her brother's ordination."

"Of course," Mrs. Prettyman said. "The young man whom you saved from being hanged. Now, the girl's parents, and the girl herself, are in an interesting and difficult situation."

"Indeed?" Hoare wondered what the Gladdens had to do with the previous subject of conversation. Miss Gladden was lovely as a Dresden figurine and very little taller. He suspected that Sir Ralph and Lady Caroline Gladden were desperate to find a husband for their daughter. If this was the line Selene Prettyman was taking, it would not do.

"I fear that for a number of reasons I am not an appropriate suitor for the young lady's hand, Mrs. Prettyman."

"That is of no consequence," she said. "In any case, I shall mention you to Miss Felicia as a possible escort for her when she visits Broadmead. Before I leave for London, I shall make the necessary arrangements with her father. In fact, I shall commence now. There is not a moment to be lost."

She rose to her feet, indicating that their tête-à-tête was at an end.

"Before we part, Captain Hoare, let me give you a warning. Do not be surprised if you see me again in unexpected circumstances. If you do, please do not acknowledge me in any way unless I give you a sign. Let me see . . . yes. Unless I say something about 'friend of the Crown.' Understood?"

"Understood, ma'am. 'Friend of the Crown.' Until then." With that, Hoare made his farewell bow and let Angelique hold the door for him.

Hoare had vowed to himself that he would keep an engagement with his ward, Jenny Jaggery, at his former quarters at the Swallowed Anchor, to review her progress in writing her alphabet and to enjoy a cuddle. As he strolled eastward, then, he had to confess to himself that he regretted not having leavened the practical content of the meeting just concluded with at least a cuddle or two with a partner more mature than skinny little Jenny. Selene Prettyman was glorious to look upon, as others, including H. R. H. of Clarence, evidently agreed.

But then, who was he to meddle in royal amours? *Better not*, he thought. In any case, the lady had not shown the least sign of being attracted to him. Then, too, he had an unexpected duel to fight, and he must warn Bennett of the role he had assigned to him.

Chapter X

———⟫·◇·⟪———

*J*ENNY PROVED to have mastered the letter *K* and therefore to have earned her kitten. Hoare promised to bring it to her with his next visit. He then penned a request to Sir George as Port Admiral that he be permitted to sleep away from his command tonight and also wrote the necessary warning to Bennett. Hoare invited his prospective second to address a chop that evening.

"You need not have sent me the warning," Bennett told him immediately upon his arrival at the Swallowed Anchor. "A Mr. Dupree of the twenty-ninth Foot waited upon me this afternoon. We agreed on tomorrow, at the usual hour. Dupree insisted on swords, and I had no recourse but to accept. I'm told that your opponent, Pargeter, is a formidable swordsman—at least when he's sober."

Bennett looked at Hoare questioningly and perhaps a trifle apprehensively. As far as his friend knew, Hoare suspected, he had never before faced a swordsman on the field of honor. It had always been pistols.

"I'd have preferred fists," he whispered. "Drunk or sober, the son of a bitch misused my name and grossly insulted the lady who happened to be in my protection at the time. I wonder if he knows she's a Colonel's wife and the very good friend of the Duke of Cumberland."

Bennett whistled. "Flying a bit high these days, ain't you, Hoare? I'm surprised at you. You've been lying pretty low lately, since you began making those visits to Weymouth."

"Believe me, my friend, Mrs. Colonel Prettyman is a business acquaintance, nothing more."

Bennett was a sea lawyer—a genuine one, one in the service of the Admiralty, and not one of those semiliterate lower-deck troublemakers who went by that name in the Navy. He knew when to keep his mouth shut, but Hoare could read his mind.

"*Business,* eh?" Bennett's voice was skeptical.

"Your good health, Bennett," Hoare whispered, raising his glass of claret.

On their previous excursion of this kind, Hoare and Bennett, with their opposite numbers and the surgeon referee, had had to wait their turn on the convenient strip of greensward over the town while a pair of boys settled their grievance. Today's deep blue dawning saw the party in sole possession of the field. Mr. Hawley, the surgeon, who had experienced even more of these affrays than Hoare, oriented the line along which the combat would open so that neither opponent would have the sun in his eyes when it rose. Subsequently, as usual, the engagement would take its own course.

From a long mahogany case, Hawley removed a pair of swords, taking a third for himself. Even in the gloaming,

Hoare recognized them. He had used them or their like as fencing sabers, for they had been borrowed from the atelier of the *emigré ci-devant* Vicomte Marc-Antoine de Chatillon de Barsac. Their buttons, however, had been removed and their points brought to a razor sharpness.

"My opponent ought to be told that I'm used to these weapons," Hoare said, ostensibly to Bennett, but in a whisper loud enough to reach the two soldiers.

"I don't give a damn whether he was raised with them in his cradle," Pargeter said.

Each of the duelists doffed his uniform coat and handed it to his second. Each stepped up to Hawley, the referee, to select his weapon and tested it between his hands before taking his place as instructed. During the referee's instructions, Pargeter let his gaze wander about the glade while Hoare listened intensely. Pargeter, he saw out of the corner of his eye, moved well. He would be a tough opponent. Hoare thought he would be lucky not to be struck first: First blood was to conclude the affair. The two saluted each other and crossed blades across the referee's.

Hawley raised his referee's sword sharply, to clear the fighters' blades. A tap, a clink, and the dance was on.

Pargeter's wrist was firm, his eyes level in the growing light. They circled once, back, feeling each other out while holding themselves in reserve. Hoare parried Pargeter's first lunge, threw it aside, lunged himself, was stopped, and the two came chest-to-chest in a bind. With a shove, Pargeter made to thrust Hoare back, out of balance, but Hoare was prepared and would not be toppled. It was Pargeter who rocked back.

The point of Hoare's blade pressed up, none too gently, into the soft flesh under Pargeter's chin.

"Did Spurrier put you up to this?" Hoare whispered

harshly in Pargeter's ear as the seconds cried, "First blood!" in unison.

Hawley whipped his sword up, disengaging the combatants.

"Lower your weapons, gentlemen," he commanded.

He had no need to inspect Pargeter. A trickle of blood, detectably red in the sunrise, stained the soldier's cravat.

"Show me your palms, sir," Hawley said, turning to Hoare.

Hoare spread his hands, as if in appeal. They were whole.

"I see blood on only one of you gentlemen," Hawley said. "I declare honor satisfied."

"Do you need medical attention, sir?" he asked Pargeter.

"For *this* pinprick? Don't be an ass," Pargeter snarled. His blood was up. So was Hoare's.

"Henceforth, mind your tongue, sir," Hoare rasped.

"Henceforth, fellow, mind your back," was Pargeter's reply.

Neither showed ready to shake hands with his adversary. The three noncombatant members of the party stood at a loss. At last, both groups drifted away, in clouds, almost palpable, of business left unfinished.

Chapter XI

⊰◆⊱

$\mathcal{H}$ OW IT happened Hoare could never be sure. Perhaps it was through Selene Prettyman's mysterious
authority, perhaps by Admiral Hardcastle's less mysterious
command. Whoever and whatever lay behind the invitation to Broadmead, Admiral Hardcastle had been adamant.
Hoare was to accept it, despite his protests that, if he did
so, his other undertakings for the Admiral would languish
and priceless evidence dissipate like dew in the morning
sun.

Hoare's best efforts to get Admiral Hardcastle to change
his mind had been futile. Besides, the Admiral had let drop
a hint that Sir Thomas Frobisher was to be a guest as well.
The two knights being un-friends, Hoare knew that Sir
George would not mind at all if Hoare were to put a spoke
in Sir Thomas's wheel. So here was Hoare, less than forty-
eight hours later, trotting smartly on a sorrel hack along
the Portsmouth–Bath turnpike beside the berlin carrying
Felicia Hardcastle, her former nurse and present abigail, and
an elderly female cousin.

They had broken their journey at a roadside inn outside Salisbury and overnighted at Wylye. Only at these points had Hoare to endure Miss Hardcastle's company, for which he was grateful. Felicia Hardcastle was a kindly lass, but she *talked*. Most of her talk was about the virtues of Lieutenant Peter Gladden, to whom, she confided to an unsurprised Hoare, she was now secretly betrothed. At Wylye she had digressed briefly to extol the scenic quality of Stonehenge.

"Just think, Captain Hoare; it would be only a few miles out of our way! And just think of the letter I could write to dear Peter about its awesome, eerie presence! Oh, do let us break our journey there, sir!"

Hoare was having quite enough to do with one prehistoric henge monument these days, he felt, without being required to view another. Moreover, he wanted to get the trip over with. He despised horses and hated riding them. He found them disorderly, disobedient, unpredictable, and happy to tittup and fart about wherever they pleased, leaving their excrement underfoot to be trodden in by their betters. He could never understand why country gentlemen were any more enthralled by a horse than they were by a medlar tree. Certainly the latter's leavings were more useful. So he had stood firm despite Miss Hardcastle's pleadings and pouts.

The party drew up the long curving drive that led to Broadmead. From his station on the berlin's larboard quarter, he could hear his charge's squeals of anticipation. Even though her lover was at sea—he was newly promoted first in *Frolic,* 22—she was agog to meet his family. Here Hoare had the advantage over her. The entire Gladden family believed he had saved their elder son, Arthur, from a hanging and now behaved toward him as though he were a saint, if not the Savior Himself. Felicia Hardcastle, as he had become tired of experiencing, was only slightly less full of worship.

Hoare was pleased to see that Sir Ralph and Lady Caroline successfully hid any distress at their first sight of their daughter-in-law elect. They and the Reverend Arthur all greeted Hoare with great warmth. As was only proper, Miss Anne Gladden's welcome was more reserved, but the expression of her periwinkle blue eyes, as they looked up into his from so far below them, was as sweet as he remembered and her smile as endearing.

Hoare was not particularly surprised to see Miss Jane Austen among his fellow guests. When they had encountered each other at the reception for the Duke of Cumberland, she had said nothing to him about being engaged here. But, after all, the two of them were not precisely bosom beaux, and she had had no reason to confide in him. As she returned his bow, he thought her look somewhat calculating.

Hoare was also happy that Admiral Hardcastle and Selene Prettyman had dropped him their hints about Sir Thomas Frobisher. For there the knight-Baronet himself stood, in the greater reception room, among the other guests who had gathered to inspect the new arrivals. Unlike Hoare, Sir Thomas was clearly astonished at the encounter, for his eyes goggled. He had no word for Bartholomew Hoare. Sir Thomas was not amused.

Hoare had long since discovered that his whisper, with its implication of confidentiality, led many persons to believe him a man with whom their deepest secrets would be safe—an illogical belief, he considered, yet understandable and often useful. The late Janus Jaggery, Jenny's da, had been one of these persons, and Mrs. Selene Prettyman apparently was another. Now, the next morning, as he and Miss Gladden strolled through a gentle mist among the late-blooming flowers in Broadmead's cutting garden, he found that she, too, was ready to trust him as if by instinct.

"May I speak with you frankly, Captain Hoare?" she asked. "And in the certainty that my words will go no further?"

"You may. You have my word," Hoare whispered, "unless, of course, what you tell me endangers our country." He could say so in good conscience, since he was quite certain her coming confidence would have no bearing, for good or evil, on the national welfare.

"As you may know, sir, Sir Thomas Frobisher is a powerful man in the region, and a widower, as you may also know. He has seen fit to speak to Papa—"

"*What?* Sir Thomas a suitor for your hand?" Forewarned Hoare may have been, but his reacquaintance with Anne Gladden, his earlier glimpse of Sir Thomas, and the idea of her diminutive form . . . Out of revulsion, he could say no more.

She nodded. "You may imagine that my parents wish him neither to marry me nor to take offense at being sent empty away. I should tell you that they hope you will consider rescuing me from his attentions by offering for me yourself."

With a speaking look, Miss Anne Gladden blushed under her bonnet and added, "The notion was put into their minds, I think, by Miss Austen."

Miss Austen again, Hoare thought. *Damn the interfering bitch, she interferes in matters that . . . she does not understand.*

"I . . . ," he began, but Miss Gladden had now taken her courage in both hands and must conclude before it eluded her again.

"The arrangement need not be a genuine one, Mr.

Hoare. I would cry off whenever you asked me to free you—"

"But—"

She raised one hand against his interruption and continued her recital. It was obviously rehearsed.

"On the other hand, sir, while I am small of stature, I would be amply dowered. In fact, Papa suspects that the three thousand a year he must settle on me upon my marriage has more than a little to do with Sir Thomas's ardor. And I cannot abide the man!" she burst out. "He could be my father, or even my grandfather! Why, his *daughter* is older than I! I would rather be wed to a frog!" She was on the verge, Hoare saw, of breaking into tears.

She regained control of herself with a gulp. "I mean the reptile, Captain Hoare, not the Frenchman. The latter might be tolerable, but Sir Thomas . . .

"And truly, sir, I believe you and I might suit, after all."

"I am quite certain we should suit, Miss Gladden," Hoare said, "but it cannot be."

"Oh," came a small voice from the small person beside him. There was a silence. Then, "She was despised . . . rejected," she sang softly, sweetly, and sadly, to the tune of Handel's plaintive aria.

"No, Miss Gladden, never despised," Hoare said. "But, you see, I am not at liberty. My heart is not my own."

"Who is the fortunate person who owns it?" she asked.

"I tell you in confidence, Miss Gladden, for the lady has yet to accept my proposal."

"You gave me your word, sir; you have mine in return," Anne Gladden replied stoutly.

"She is Mrs. Eleanor Graves," he continued, "the widow of Dr. Simon Graves in Weymouth." *As I believe Miss Austen well knows,* he continued to himself.

"I could wish myself as fortunate," she said.

"To be widowed? Hardly."

"Of course not, sir. To have one's hand sought in marriage."

A long, awkward silence followed. As she passed it, Anne Gladden plucked a daisy and picked its petals, one by one.

"If your own heart is still at liberty, Miss Gladden," Hoare said at last, "and if you will permit me, I may be able to help you and another person to happiness. Let us be seated, and I will explain my thought."

When he had finished, Anne Gladden literally clapped her little mittened hands with joy.

"Perfect!" she cried. "Let us go in now and address Papa!"

Leaving the garden, the happy couple, linked hands swinging, returned to the house to bring the glad tidings to the elder Gladdens.

At dinner that evening, Sir Ralph—perhaps in preparation for the announcement he intended to make—encouraged Hoare to expound on his adventures. Hoare felt himself carried away, inspired. As he spoke, he remembered the jape he had inflicted upon Sir Thomas Frobisher when they first met; he had discoursed to the knight-Baronet about bats. Hoare really did not like Sir Thomas.

"I am not sure," he said, "that it has come to the attention of our natural philosophers, but the icebergs of the North Atlantic harbor a special population of creatures that are to be found nowhere else."

"Polar bears," came a voice as he caught his breath.

"Walruses," came another.

"Yes, those," Hoare said. "But the most interesting, I think, are the petsters."

"*Pesters,* Hoare?" That was Sir Thomas. *Ha!* The fish had struck.

"No, Sir Thomas, *petsters.* The iceberg environment is so cold, you see, that even the lobsters must grow coats of fur in order to survive. . . . The ladies of the Halifax ton seek them out and tame them. Of a summer evening, they parade about on the walls of the fortress, leading the creatures on leashes. . . . They claim that a well-trained petster is a necessity to defend them from encroaching boors fresh from the old country."

After a puzzled pause, one of the guests gave a crack of laughter. A few others followed suit. The jape, as Hoare had known it would, had fallen flat.

Sir Ralph now called for the company's glasses to be filled and made his announcement. His beloved daughter Anne, he told the table, was to be wed to Captain Bartholomew Hoare. On Sir Ralph's words, congratulatory applause burst out. Miss Austen smiled like the Serpent of Eden. Sir Thomas Frobisher, however, turned black with rage, leaped from his chair, and marched out of the room without a word, slamming the great door behind him. What must have enhanced his wrath was the fact that the door was too weighty and well fitted to slam properly. Instead, it swung closed with a gentle hiss.

"What I do not understand, Miss Gladden—"

Sir Thomas had not tarried to break his fast at Broadmead but had taken an early, hungry departure. Hoare was making his farewells to his hosts and, especially, to his "betrothed."

"Anne, please, Captain . . . Bartholomew. After all, if we are engaged to marry, we must behave accordingly."

"Anne let it be, then. Terms of affection . . . ," Hoare began, but then stopped, feeling unutterably pompous. ". . . would be in bad taste, wouldn't they? Although I do hold you in high esteem."

Miss Gladden's easy blush came and went.

"But, as I was about to say," Hoare continued, "I do not understand why your father did not take this whole matter up with me, instead of leaving it to you."

She hung her head.

"I fear, Bartholomew, that Fate gave all the courage in our family to my brother, Peter."

"Not so, Miss . . . Anne. She gave a large packet of it to Peter's sister, Anne, as well."

Hoare rode into Dorchester on the heels of another high wind. He had left Miss Felicia Hardcastle under the trustworthy supervision of her abigail, aunt, and coachman. All *his* work with her was ended; joyfully he sang, soundlessly, to himself. He knew that, by having undertaken this side jaunt among the ton and its intrigues, he had neglected his principal duty, so he was quite ready for the effect Thoday and Rabbett had on his inflamed conscience.

His two investigators, he learned, had made much of their stay in Dorchester. Thoday would not deliver his report in the comfort of the inn but insisted upon their proceeding to an open field nearby for their conference.

"The entire town is alive with listeners, sir," he explained. "It was wise of me to make that arrangement with Rabbett's mother."

Not only had the missing head been recovered—the event that had so disturbed Rabbett's digestion. A swineherd had also discovered their Admiralty chaise overturned in a coppice near the hamlet of Abbotsbury, just inshore and only a few miles away. Its seat was heavily blood-stained, as Thoday had predicted.

"And," Thoday continued, "Mr. Spurrier, who disappeared for two days last week, informed me upon his return that his people had found two additional bodies which he thought might be those of the drivers. He offered to show them to us.

"They were in poor repair, I must say. Both were naked. One, like Captain Francis Getchell, had had his throat cut. The other had died of the entry of a pistol ball into the right side of his chest. His right arm must have been extended when the bullet struck him. That, of course, further confirms my deductions at the scene of the crime."

Thoday's voice sounded self-satisfied.

"And I suppose you have identified them?"

"*I* did, sir," Rabbett said with some pride. "I knew the one with the throat myself. It was Jones, whom Mr. Patterson at Admiralty House retains—retained, I should say—to keep him and his chaise at the Admiralty's disposal."

Evidently, Rabbett had learned to overcome his squeamishness.

"As to the other, sir," he went on, "a cousin of my father's sister-in-law had been bewailing the disappearance of Amos Swithin, her betrothed. 'Twas no great loss, from all I have heard, for the man had no good reputation in the neighborhood.

"I persuaded her to view the deceased, and she did not hesitate at all to identify him. By certain marks upon his privities," he added with some relish. "They had been preserved."

"That is not amusing, Rabbett," Hoare whispered coldly.

The clerk shrank into himself.

"What conclusions have you two drawn from these discoveries?" Hoare asked the two.

Rabbett looked blank, but Thoday's eyes brightened. "From the chaise and Jones's body, sir, nothing," Thoday said. "Their condition was what I—we—expected. From Swithin's body, little was to be learned, although his identification made stronger the likelihood that the crime was planned, or at least executed, locally."

"Because Swithin was a local man?" Hoare asked.

"Precisely. Very good."

This tone would not do.

"Step this way, Thoday," Hoare said. "No, Rabbett, remain where you are."

When he judged them out of Rabbett's sharp hearing, Hoare turned on Thoday.

"You were a schoolmaster at one time, I observe," he said.

As Hoare had intended, his observation took Titus Thoday aback.

"Why, yes," he said. "How did you know?"

"Because of the supercilious and patronizing tone you habitually take to your interlocutors, including me—your commanding officer."

Hoare drew breath and went on, using his command voice, feeble though it was.

"Mr. Thoday," he grated, "I am senior to you in years as well as in rank, and you shall not address me as though I were merely a promising pupil."

His command whisper took all his strength. He paused again for breath, then continued at a tolerable level.

"This is not the first time I have had to caution you. I shall consider continued . . . disrespect of this kind as nothing short of insolence. If it does continue, I assure you, I shall not hesitate to deal with you accordingly. Do you understand?"

Thoday grew white about the lips.

"Answer me, man. Do you understand me?"

"Sir."

"Again."

"Aye aye, sir."

"Very good. Now, let us proceed."

"I believe, sir," Thoday said as they strolled back to the waiting clerk, "that Rabbett and I must focus more closely on the doings of Captain Spurrier."

"Why?"

Hoare had to give Thoday credit. He did not sulk at his Commander's reprimand but instead adopted an attitude toward him that suggested he viewed Bartholomew Hoare as an equal instead of his promising pupil. Hoare hoped the change would be permanent, for the vision of having this dignified, proud, gentlemanly, clever, meticulous King's bad bargain of a sailor flogged at a grating aboard *Royal Duke* was simply absurd.

"Because Mr. Spurrier lords it in Dorchester," Thoday said. "Not a leaf blows in the wind, I discover, but Walter Spurrier knows of it. I could even suspect him of believing he gave the leaf permission to blow, if not having made it blow himself. In that, he is much like his master. The question, however, is not, sir, one of Spurrier's power in the district, but of his *true* master. For from whom does his power derive?"

"Why, from Sir Thomas Frobisher, of course," Hoare whispered. "Who else?"

"That is what must be determined, sir. You see, I hear nothing of Sir Thomas, nor does Rabbett."

"That's so, sir," said Rabbett. "It used to be that folk

hereabouts walked in fear of Sir Thomas. Why, in the inns of an evening, it was a common thing for a man to start a complaint—oh, about the latest enclosure of part of the commons hereabouts or about someone else's midnight catch of rabbits, for example—and then stop himself with a glance around the company and make some remark to the effect that one of Sir Thomas's people might be listening.

"And it might well have been so, too. I know of two men transported because they talked out of turn and someone carried the word back to Sir Thomas. But now, sir, if the common folk still walk in fear of Sir Thomas, they do so in silence. I hear nothing of him these days. *His* doings are quite another thing, perhaps.

"No, sir, the word may still pass to Mr. Spurrier, but it may go no further. Or it may go to another, as Mr. Thoday suggests."

"This needs some thinking, then," Hoare said, and at last, "I agree. Your aim must be the disclosure of Spurrier's true master—Sir Thomas or another."

Hoare paced up and down the field for a few more minutes, collecting his thoughts. If Spurrier was such a "power in the district," it would be disastrous if he were to discover that Hoare's men were on his scent. Thoday and Rabbett were, after all, mere seamen in a toy man-o'-war. In a turn-up, Spurrier could squash them like a pair of black beetles. In fact, Hoare felt doubts that he himself would have the weight to overbear the man in his own district.

"This is what I suggest," Hoare said at last. "Redirect your inquiries toward Spurrier, but under some pretext. You might revisit the Nine Stones Circle, for instance, letting it be known that you are on the track of a smuggling gang . . . No, that hardly rings true. The excisemen would be here instead of you. Think of a better excuse for remaining hereabouts, and proceed. For the present, that is the best advice I can give you."

Advice? From a Commander to his men? Not "orders"? Hoare wondered at his own choice of words. He caught his breath, made his excuses to his two men, clambered into the saddle, and departed for his ship.

Chapter XII

"ARE YOU married, Mr. Clay?" Hoare asked his Lieu-tenant as the two dried themselves off after their morning bout.

Until de Barsac, the emigré swordsman, had taken command of the *Vendée* frigate, Hoare had frequented the *salon d'escrime* of the Chevalier Marc-Antoine de Chatillon de Barsac. But then the Vicomte's wife had taken over as manager. As such, she was competent, but she could hardly teach swordsmanship herself. Moreover, the hirelings she had offered as opponents had been depressingly inept, and Hoare had largely abandoned the place. Now he was more than displeased at his lackluster performance as a swords-man in the recent duel, and every morning when he fas-tened the waistband of his breeches, he knew himself to be going flabby. So when, some days ago, he had learned that Clay prided himself on his swordsmanship, even though on his small frame the officer's sword resembled a two-handed broadsword, he had suggested they indulge themselves in a bout. The first passage at arms had taken place the next morning, the deck being clear and most of the crew at work below.

Clay had stripped well, though pale-skinned, displaying the wiry muscles of a gymnast. His performance had not belied his physique. It had been raining lightly in that gray dawning. After the two had exchanged salutes, Clay had stalked into the eyes of *Royal Duke* and Hoare to her taff-rail. At Hoare's piercing whistle, the two ran at each other, meeting with a sharp *clack* of weapons to one side of the mainmast, between it and the upturned longboat.

When Clay charged, he moved in an irregular, unpredictable forward dance, his blade flickering before him, his footwork unimpeded by the slippery deck. For Hoare to predict where the Lieutenant would be at any fraction of a second was beyond him. Bewildered, he felt that he might as well never have spent those hours.

Up and down the length of *Royal Duke* they had ranged, leaping and parrying, up to the cat-head, back to the binnacle, first one taking the offensive and then the other. Clay bounded like a ball. In his lunges, his muscular arm seemed to double in length, as though he had borrowed it magically from the gibbon-topman, Iggleden. Coming on deck, Iggleden himself and Stone had stood agape, as idle as the rest of the gathering watch on deck, until Clay feigned a slip in a spot the watch's mops had missed, let Hoare overstretch, disarmed him with a powerful flip of his blade, and took his surrender.

Every possible morning thereafter, they had met again, whatever the weather. It saved Hoare time and money spent ashore in the de Barsac salon and was quite as effective. Now, day by day, he felt his wind improve; day by day, it took Clay longer to make his touch.

Today, for only the second time, Hoare was the first to score upon his opponent, with a crippling cut to Clay's left leg. It was this success that emboldened Hoare to pose his impertinent question.

"Married, sir? Hardly," Clay answered, rubbing the stricken leg. "I shall be black-and-blue in the morning. No, with my lack of stature, the only ladies who would have me have remained single themselves for good and generally obvious reasons. I do not consider myself overparticular, but if you were to see the kinds of antidote—even crone— that have set their caps at me on account of my fortune, you would shudder.

"Why, even that friendly, pink Susan Hackins at the Swallowed Anchor as much as told me I could have her, but only in exchange for my name. I respect her for her candor as well as her virtue, but . . . to be brief, what I lack in inches I fear I more than make up in pride. No, sir, I am quite unattached. May I ask why you inquire?"

"I would not wish to interfere in your personal affairs, Mr. Clay, were it not that I recently made the acquaintance of Miss Anne Gladden, daughter of Sir Ralph Gladden of Broadmead, near Frome, in the Mendips."

Hoare paused to await Clay's reaction. There was none.

"She is a charming young lady of poise and presence who impresses me as both sensible and gifted," Hoare continued.

Silence.

"However, she does not go into society as a general rule."

Silence. Clay's expression was closed.

"She is also exceedingly small."

This is hard going, Hoare thought. *I would far rather be Heracles to Admiral Hardcastle's Eurystheus than Cupid, or Pandarus, between Miss Anne Gladden and this cool little officer.*

"Come to my cabin when you have refreshed yourself,

Mr. Clay," Hoare concluded, "and I will lay out my thought for your consideration." *This* would dish Miss Jane Austen, he thought viciously, and her own schemes for interfering in his pursuit of his own particular partridge.

Soon Hoare was to discover that he might well attend to the affairs of his own heart, not those of his Lieutenant. Only through the scuttlebutt did word reach him that Eleanor Graves had arrived in Portsmouth. Indeed, scuttlebutt whispered in his ear that she had put up at the Swallowed Anchor, his erstwhile quarters ashore. Why had she not let him know she was coming? Nonetheless, he would hasten ashore to find out, salving his conscience by telling it that he was simply picking up the day's post. He forbore to remember that an Admiralty wherry had already delivered it.

Besides the anticipated refusal of the Admiralty to increase *Royal Duke's* ink allowance, today's daily message from Dorchester came heavy today. It comprised several pages of clerkly script and a number of enclosures in the same hand.

The Mitre, Dorchester
Wednesday

Sir:

Last night I succeeded in making use (*primo*) of Mr. Spurrier's absence from the town and (*secundo*) of the skills taught me by our shipmate, James Bly, to go a-burgling. I picked the lock of Mr. S.'s office door with ease and conducted an extensive search of the place.

This search disclosed the following items of interest:

A. In a carved blackwood cabinet:
   1. The cope which I called to your attention after our first encounter with Mr. S. Its decorations were as obscene and sacrilegious as I had thought to observe at that time.
   2. A book, in which what appeared to be several rituals were set forth in fine calligraphy. The book was bound in a fine soft leather, which my oversensible imagination suggested was human skin.
   3. A chalice of bronze, into which human and animal figures had been chased. Their activities are best left to the imagination.
   4. Several black candles.
B. In the right-hand lower drawer of the escritoire:
   1. Two sets of Admiralty orders, one addressed to Captain Francis Getchell and the other to Captain Benjamin Getchell.
   2. Two gold watches, identical in appearance except for the monograms engraved into their covers. I did not take the time to decipher the monograms, but one might assume they belonged to the Captains Getchell.
   3. Two empty purses.
C. On the top of the escritoire:
   1. Numerous items of correspondence, of a personal nature.
   2. Several ribbons and similar gewgaws.
   3. The usual writing paraphernalia.
D. In a readily detected secret drawer behind the middle drawer of the escritoire:
   1. A folder bound in red tape, containing at least a dozen pairs of documents. Of each

pair, one bore the distinctive appearance of the "Ahab" ciphers already in our possession, while the other, in pencil, heavily crossed out and corrected, bore casual marginal graffiti, mostly erotic in nature.

2. A Bible, in French, between two leaves of which S. had left three papers. The left-hand leaf commenced with 1 Isaiah, v. 4, while the right-hand leaf ended with 2 Isaiah, v. 21.

S. had evidently been interrupted just after translating, and beginning to encipher, a message of his own. He had completed only two lines. Although I deem S. unlikely to be of a character who would keep count of his papers, I did not dare to abstract any of these, lest my judgment be in error. I considered it essential that he remain ignorant of my surreptitious intrusion onto his premises. I used my remaining time—which I could sense was growing short—to make a hasty but complete copy of the original English-language message and the first lines of his French translation. (S., I could not help but observe in passing, may pride himself on his ability to speak French, but his mastery of the written language is negligible.) Even more hastily, I scribbled down the first lines of the enciphered message.

I enclose the copies I made of these three documents. I trust that these fragments will enable Taylor to master the "Ahab-Jehu" code even more completely than she already has.

Before I had finished copying the Captain's scrawls, Mr. Rabbett, who was standing watch outside the window, alerted me to the unwelcome sound of horsemen coming down the High Street from the direction of Plymouth. It being close on dawning, I concluded that the arrivals were Mr. Spurrier and some of his men, so I placed the papers back as I had found them and decamped.

I was fortunate to have done so, for my suspicion was well founded. S. had arrived betimes.

To conclude: S. makes a poor agent in my opinion, being far too careless about the security of his private papers and overinclined to intermix his personal sins with his official ones. (We are fortunate in that respect, at least.)

Despite its apparent strength, the evidence we now have against S. is only circumstantial, and, besides, I have had to leave it where I found it. He may, in fact, be merely a deluded believer in some religion related to Satanism, paganism, or witchcraft and not an agent at all. A way must be found of catching him in flagrante.

The courier from Plymouth should arrive momentarily, so Rabbett must carry it, in all haste, to his mother's house. The courier must snatch it up en passant.

> Your humble and ob't sv't,
> T Thoday
> Master's Mate

Spurrier's plaintext message, which Thoday had copied, was brief.

Ahab:

Now Asa wisheth the priest his servant to sacrifice at the altar of Baal. This will further make the reins of the Philistines to tremble. I shall send unto thee a bird of the air as harbinger.

The greater and the lesser servants of the Captain

of the Philistines drink wine in our vineyard and, pray, and are idle.

Levi

"Levi," Hoare concluded, was probably Spurrier himself. Hoare had thought so. Spurrier's efforts to write in the style of the King James Bible might make his translation and encryption tasks easier, Hoare thought, but they sounded puerile. Someone unknown, bearing the code name "Asa," intended to make some sort of sacrifice. As Hoare had also thought, "Asa" was certainly a person of importance. "The altar of Baal" might be the Nine Stones Circle and the Philistines the Royal Navy.

Since "the greater and the lesser servants" almost certainly referred to Thoday and Rabbett, Spurrier might have promoted Hoare to Captain. In this, of course, Hoare hoped Spurrier was a reliable "harbinger," though if so, he was surely premature in his prophecy, since Hoare's swab had yet to dry from its first wetting.

Or the entire cast of characters might be quite different. The whole business was obscure, like so much of the Bible, suggestive, ominous.

One thing was certain: further mischief appeared to be cooking at the Nine Stones Circle, and it behooved Hoare to make ready to foil it.

More seriously still: Spurrier was evidently aware that Hoare and his hounds were on his traces.

Chapter XIII

—◆—

MR. HACKINS of the Swallowed Anchor had an
additional packet of correspondence for Hoare,
routine correspondence about *Royal Duke*'s high costs, so
the lie he had told his conscience had been unnecessary.

He found Eleanor Graves standing in the inn's sun-
drenched parlor window, foursquare as always, roundabout
and appealing. There was an empty basket on her arm, and
she was smiling gently at a jubilant Jenny. Dignified, the
kitten Order lay in the child's arms, making the sound of
a very small tumbrel. Mrs. Graves's friend, Miss Jane Austen, sat across the room by the fireside, her slightly angular,
slightly faded face observant now as always. He acknowledged her presence with a polite bow, which she returned
from where she sat.

When Mrs. Graves saw Hoare, her smile disappeared.
She merely nodded at him before returning her attention
to the little girl.

"Look, look, Mr. Hoare! The nice lady brought me a
kitten! Please, sir, may I keep 'er—her?"

"I promised you that when you had learned to write all the letters in the alphabet you should have a kitten, and Susan told me you have done so," Hoare said. "But if I remember correctly, it is a boy kitten."

"Yes, I 'ave—have, sir, and now she's teaching me to 'broider them. Soon as I've comforted my kitten, I'll show you, shall I?"

"Do so, Jenny. But you are Order's Captain now, you know, and must make sure he is fed whenever he goes on watch. . . . And you must teach him to be a sober cat and true, and attentive to his duty."

"Oh, I will, sir; I will! Susan, Susan! See what the lady's brought me!" Jenny spun on her toes, pale hair flying, and was about to dart off when Hoare brought her up all standing.

"Manners, Jenny. You must remember to thank Mrs. Graves."

Jenny turned again, made an awkward bob to Eleanor Graves and said, "Thank you, ma'am," quite properly, and sped into the kitchen with her Order in her arms.

Eleanor Graves had not yet spoken to Hoare. Now she did.

"I learn, Captain Hoare," she said, "that I am to wish you happy in your forthcoming marriage to Miss Anne Gladden of Broadmead. I do so, of course." Her voice was not that of one who extended the wish in all sincerity. Did it even sound a little forlorn? He gulped. He had not yet had the chance to explain the charade to Eleanor.

"The news will have come from Miss Austen," he declared.

"Indeed. And confirmed by Sir Thomas Frobisher."

Sir Thomas must have rushed back to Weymouth in all haste, to announce Hoare's perfidy to all the world—

especially, and foolishly, to Eleanor Graves. But Hoare had not yet clawed off this lee shore.

"Not so, Eleanor," he said. "What neither of your . . . eager informants could know, and therefore could not tell you, is that the betrothal is a farrago, a fraud, a piece of make-believe."

Miss Austen's expression did not change, not by a jot. *This woman,* Hoare thought, *is formidable, indeed.* But why had she taken him in such distaste, almost from the beginning? She had spoken then of her and Eleanor having "dowded it together" in Bath before Eleanor married her crippled physician of a husband and left Jane to dowd it alone. Could she have feelings for her old friend Eleanor Graves that were of a Sapphic nature? He had heard of such things.

"Oh?" Eleanor Graves asked. "That is hardly what I expected you to say, sir. Are you telling me that you have offered for the poor girl for reasons of your own—reasons that are hardly likely to be gentlemanly, since you openly state your intention to jilt her? A knavish trick indeed, sir. I had thought you more of a gentleman."

"The case is quite different, Eleanor," Hoare whispered. "Will you not be seated while I explain it?"

"Not at present, sir. I prefer to remain standing. But begin, if you wish."

Hoare began. Soon Eleanor Graves took the seat Hoare had offered her. Shortly thereafter, the welcome crinkles reappeared at the corners of her mouth. At last she burst into a throaty gurgle of laughter. Miss Austen's expression was carefully null.

"My, Bartholomew. You have, indeed, embroiled yourself. But I must say, you have embroiled poor Sir Thomas even more deeply. You have forked him, in fact."

Hoare was not at all sure he had heard the lady correctly. "Ma'am?" he asked.

"Oh. I recall now; you do not play chess, do you? We shall have to remedy that in due course. Well, Bartholomew, the 'fork' is a move in chess—a truly wicked move—to a spot from whence a player can take either of two of his opponent's major pieces without risking more than the loss of his threatening lesser piece. Often a knight will threaten a queen and a castle or even put the other player's king into an ignominious check.

"You have done that to Sir Thomas. With one inspired move, you have deprived the poor knight, at one time, of two possible captures—wives, that is. For when he rushed to tell me how you had snatched little Miss Gladden out from under his nose, he did not think of how I would react to his disclosure that, while vowing undying love for *me*, he had been hot after another. Well done, Bartholomew, well done!" Her chortle broke into a full-throated, unladylike belly laugh.

Miss Austen, who did not laugh, had a sudden headache, begged to be excused, and withdrew.

"But you would not have accepted Sir Thomas in any case, would you?" Hoare asked anxiously.

"*Sir Thomas?* At this point, I should play the flirt, if only in revenge for the shock you gave me," she said. "But—no, Bartholomew, no. I would not. I am no Princess, so I need kiss me no frogs. Besides, my heart is bestowed elsewhere.

"Now, Miss Austen and I have calls to make and a visit to pay to Madame LaFarge, the mantua maker in the High Street. So go, and examine Miss Jenny's prowess with her pen. Come, Jane!" she called upstairs, merciless as Admiral Sir George Hardcastle.

Once Jenny Jaggery had proudly displayed her sampler

and her calligraphy to Hoare, returned into her mouth the tongue that had helped her perform, and obtained Hoare's confirmation that she was properly and permanently entitled to the kitten, Order, she demanded to accompany him to *Royal Duke*'s gig.

"Can you find your own way back to the inn?" Hoare asked.

"Oh, yes, sir." Jenny's voice was earnest. "Susan lets me go everywhere with her. She even lets me carry her market basket sometimes."

"Good. Come along, then. You may carry my packet."

Having bade farewell to Order and told him to keep a sharp lookout for the Frogs, Jenny took Hoare's packet of correspondence in her little paw. She put her other hand in his and stepped off at his side, swinging their linked hands and skipping occasionally to keep up with her guardian as he strode.

"The fat lady who gave me my kitten. She's nice. Is she your doxy, then?" Jenny looked up at him with wide black eyes. They widened still farther when she felt Hoare's reaction. He stopped in the middle of Weymouth's esplanade and glared down at her in a way he had never thought to use upon her before.

"*Fat* lady? *Doxy?* Are you speaking of Mrs. Eleanor Graves, you young vixen?"

"Me famble, sir!" Jenny squeaked, slipping back into the cant she had heard her father use. "Yer 'urtin' me dab!"

Realizing he was crushing the hand he had been holding so gently before she spoke, Hoare brought himself under control. He crouched down so as to look the child in the eyes. They were full of tears.

"I'm s-sorry, sir! Did I say summat what made ye parky? I'll never do it again, sir, truly. But she *is* fat, sir; ain't she?" Jenny asked timidly.

"The more for us to love, lass, if so. But I would be far more pleased if you were to speak of her as 'well endowed.' "

"Well endowed then, sir. But . . . what about t'other?"

"The other, Jenny?"

"Wot I called her."

"Oh. No, Mrs. Graves isn't my doxy. I hope she will do me the honor of becoming my wife."

"Ooh," Jenny said.

Looking down at the little person beside him, Hoare realized she was a person, indeed, a cheerful, determined person who deserved far more attention—love, in fact— than a toy or a pet casually picked up in some foreign port like a monkey. "Cause me to remember thy loving kindness in the morning," he said, dredging the words from some part of his unconscious.

"And . . . if we are both good," he added, "your stepmother. And Order, the kitten's, as well. Now, come along. We mustn't keep *Royal Duke* waiting, must we? There isn't a moment to lose."

"Ooh," Jenny said again. In her astonishment, all her new, precarious, proper pronunciation fled once more. "I never really 'ad, *had*, a muvver, *mother*, before. Orta be nice."

On deck in the light October mizzle, Hoare placed himself where, without interfering, he could observe the attempts of *Royal Duke's* starboard gun crews to complete the mock reloading of their pieces. While they were still agonizingly maladroit, the men no longer tripped each other up as a matter of course. Nonetheless, if the Royal Dukes did not soon better their current four minutes between broadsides, Mr. Clay and Stone would join in an apoplexy. Two minutes would rate as only fair for a broadside of eighteen-pounders, so one minute should have sufficed for *Royal Duke*'s popguns.

Stone, the borrowed gunner, was at least visibly suppressing the stream of oaths with which he would have accompanied his teaching had he been dealing with experienced hands. Instead, Hoare was glad to see, Stone had the judgment to know that these people, inept though they might still be, had come to their task more than willing already. They needed no tongue-lashing to do their best.

Meanwhile, Mr. Clay was exercising another gun crew.

"Hand me your handspike for a minute, Burkitt," he said. "Now, watch the way I use it to move the piece."

With the handspike, Clay shifted the aim of the piece, from as far aft as the port allowed to a point well forward of the beam.

"Now try doing it my way," he said, handing the implement back to the burly Burkitt. "It took *me* two hands. With your size, you should even be able to do it with one hand and handle the outhaul with the other."

Burkitt did so. "I'll be swiggled," he said.

Coming alongside, a waterman hailed *Royal Duke*'s quarterdeck. He had to reach up to grasp the brig's rail with only one hand while extending an envelope with the other.

"For Captain 'Oare," he said to the ship at large. "There'll be a shillin' for me, messenger sez."

The man snatched the envelope out of reach as Hoare reached for it.

"Not till I sees the color of yer money, mister. No shillin', no letter."

Hoare dug into his pocket for the ransom. It was outrageous, but, after all, the man had rowed out to the yacht just to deliver one letter, a trip that was no shorter than it would have been had he been bringing Hoare himself aboard.

"Thanky, guv'nor," the wherry man said, and shoved off. Hoare examined the letter where he stood. The seal's sapphire blue wax marked its sender for him instantly; of his acquaintance, only Selene Prettyman had the audacity to use such a color. He broke the seal without further thought, however, and tore open the envelope.

The communication within was brief, but it brought all Hoare's senses to the alert.

Plymouth,
23 October

Mr. Hoare:

I return from Dorchester, where H. R. H. and his cronies—including your humble servant—have been rehearsing a Black Mass or similar pagan rite of an orgiastic nature. The ceremony itself, I am told, is to take place on the night of 31 October, at that Nine Stones Circle, which is of such interest to you. I am to play a major part in it, such as Hecate, Baubo, or some other equally naughty deity.

I have taken the liberty of informing Sir George to that effect. You will know what to do about it, if anything.

Yr. obedient, etc.
SP

Now, perhaps, Hoare's training of the seamen and Marines in *Royal Duke* would bear fruit. He ducked below into his shrunken cabin, lit now only by the skylight, to write ashore on a slip of tissue for permission from Admiralty House for a cruise to the westward. Then he wrote a second message, this one to Rabbett and Thoday in Dorchester. A faint acrid scent of pigeon guano seeped from behind the ugly new bulkhead that blocked the brig's beautiful little stern window from view.

His messages written, Hoare summoned Hancock, the pigeon man, to send them off. Now, by God, was the time to put his plans for *Royal Duke* into effect. If only *Niobe,* too, were about to weigh anchor! He hoisted signal to Admiralty House: "Preparing for sea," and directed the same signal to the attention of *Niobe.* He vowed one of the ship's pigeons to Aeolus as a thank-you offering for the mild northerly breeze. Perhaps, given the gentle seas that would result, enough of *Royal Duke*'s people would be able to keep their bellies in order to handle the brig. Hoare was lucky that his Marines were back aboard, for while they had pigeons with them that could bring him their news, he could send nothing by that means. The birds would be unable to find a moving destination like his live green Lobsters.

The Admiral must have been in good spirits, for it was less than ten minutes before *Royal Duke*'s number rose to the signal mast at Admiralty House, followed by the expected: "Why have you not weighed anchor?"

Hoare whistled for Mr. Clay.

"Sir?" Clay could read the signal as well as Hancock or Hoare. He was already at Hoare's side, breathing fire.

Hoare, too, stood straighter as his Lieutenant brought *Royal Duke* to life at last. It all came back to him.

"Set sail, Mr. Clay. Set her course for Weymouth."

Mr. Clay nearly goggled at his Commander. Then he grinned and turned.

"All hands to unmoor!" he cried in a voice that would have roused a sleeping seventy-four. "This is no drill!"

More calmly, as the astonished Royal Dukes set about obeying in earnest, he added, "Let fall the topsails!"

In so small a vessel, topsails were commonly set before unmooring. Led aloft by the hooting Iggleden, the assigned topmen swarmed out onto the two topsail yards. His heart in his mouth lest one of his Jack Newcomes lose his footing and drop, Hoare craned his neck to watch them. The snowy virgin topsails dropped, flapping gently in the light air.

Clay had recovered his self-control. "Tacks and sheets; cast for the starboard tack."

The topsails, still flapping, were brought under control. *Royal Duke* jibbed like a filly, straining to go westerly but still restrained by her mooring.

"Ready there, forrard?"

"Aye!" came from the forepeak.

"Cast off, then!"

As the slip rope came aboard, *Royal Duke* gathered stern way momentarily, but when Clay called for tacks and sheets to be trimmed, the topsails gave a soft, brief thunder, took on their graceful sheer, and thrust the brig forward. Now the hands set topsails, fore-staysail, and spanker. For the first time in her career, *Royal Duke* was under sail in the charge of her own crew, proud and eager.

"Brace up forward. Make a course for Yarmouth, Mr. Clay," Hoare ordered.

Hoare realized that he had hardly breathed during the entire simple maneuver. *Royal Duke* had run athwart no one's hawse; nothing had carried away; no one had gone overboard. Though woefully slow by Navy standards, her crew had unmoored as well as the average merchantman could, and a good deal more tidily.

"No jeers from our neighbors this morning, Mr. Clay," Hoare said.

"No, sir."

Royal Duke steadied on her course. Under easy sail, she threw only a small bow wave against the blue waters of the Solent. Now she heeled a strake or two. Her tender, Hoare's *Alecto,* chuckled along in her wake like a filly foal behind her dam.

A light leftover sea from ahead threw a sprinkle of foam over her bows; she gave a minute heave. In response, one or two smothered groans of distress arose forrard.

"To leeward, damn you, to leeward!" Clay bawled.

Stone picked up one sufferer bodily and heaved him to the larboard rail just in time to spew over the side. Other hands set to without orders to pretty up all lines once again—the one skill the Royal Dukes had learned during those endless months when their ship had lain in the Thames estuary, in danger of grounding on her own beef bones.

"Now, then, steady as he goes, Taylor," said Lovable Bold, the borrowed bosun, as he turned the helm over to the cryptographer. "Time you earned yer rating."

Seeing that Taylor's lips were clenched in her teeth, Bold waited within reach until she had begun to learn the brig's ways before starting forward.

"How does she steer?" Hoare asked.

"She gripes a bit, sir," Taylor said.

"Better than a lee helm."

"Aye. Especially with this crew," Clay interjected. "But if we want to make her easier, all we need do is move a handful of pigeon feed forrard."

Hoare suppressed a snort of laughter. That had been the first witty remark he had heard his Lieutenant make. Perhaps getting under way at last was putting him at his ease; certainly it was unknotting Hoare.

The two now hastily put together a schedule of training that would break in the Royal Dukes between Spithead and their arrival off Weymouth.

"Perhaps, sir, we shall even be able to fire the great guns. It would surely encourage the crew were we to do so. The noise, you know." Mr. Clay sounded eager. Since there was no longer any point in Hoare's keeping his plans from the other officer, he revealed them. Clay was visibly jubilant.

"Let us complete the day by saluting the sunset, then," Hoare concluded. "But first, let us put her through her paces."

So, once they had cleared the Needles and were out of sight of the nearly empty anchorage, Clay set all hands to lowering *Royal Duke*'s topmasts and topgallants and sweating them up again, stretching out onto her yards and back again, over and over, until their palms bled and they could barely stagger. Even then, they needed no urging. At the last, Clay even had them set the brig's stun-sails and her kerchiefs of royals. Under these, the little yacht swept seaward until Hoare recollected his orders and made his Lieutenant take in the little scraps so they could beat back into protected waters. All this while, *Alecto* towed obediently behind.

Finally, Hoare permitted Clay to drop off a beflagged cask. After working her up to windward, he shortened sail and put *Royal Duke* in position to sweep down again upon the cask, gliding westward a cable's length north of the target.

"Proceed, Mr. Clay," Hoare said.

"Silence, fore and aft."

The command was not necessary, for *Royal Duke* was only whispering across the water. Silence was already complete, expectant. Up flew the four larboard gun ports.

"Cast loose your guns," Clay ordered. "Out tompions."

At each side-tackle, a man heaved, to roll the four-pounders inboard so the tompions could be removed from their muzzles. Long since, Mr. Clay had had the charges drawn and replaced. There had been a rat's nest in one of the guns, though how the rat had gotten inside the gun in the first place passed Hoare's imagination.

"Run out your guns." Out trundled her gleaming miniature broadside.

"Level your guns."

"Prime." Each Captain broke the fresh cartridge at the bottom of his gun's bore, using the priming iron hung from a lanyard around his neck. The Captain of Number Two gun, however, fumbled at his throat and looked at his Lieutenant in agony.

Stone reached out with a spare. "Ere, Gridley. But yer grog's stopped tonight."

After using Stone's iron, Gridley returned it.

"Now get on with it, man. Catch up with the others; they're a-waitin'."

"You may fire when ready, Gridley," Clay said.

Hastily, Gridley poured a handful of powder into his gun's vent and stood to attention.

"Point your guns." The four Captains leaned over to peer along their guns' barrels and heaved on the pry-bars they used to train their pieces. *Royal Duke* rolled a trifle.

"Fire as you bear."

The sharp little hiss of the burning fine powder in the first gun to bear was the only one of its kind not drowned by the subsequent bursts. As Clay had said they would, the gun crews broke into spontaneous cheers at the noise, the orange-red bursts of fire, and exhilarating backdraft of pungent powder smoke.

Three little waterspouts rose, all well distant from the target keg. More cheers. Number Two gun, last to bear and to fire, now had all hands' attention. The cask flew apart in a shower of staves.

"I'll be go to hell," said Stone. Then, under Clay's shout of, "Stop your vents!" he added, "You've just earned yer grog back, Gridley."

"Sponge your guns!" Clay called.

Then, "Load with cartridge."

The four powder boys—none under twenty, actually, and one a woman—ran up with the grub-shaped charges, handed them firmly to the spongers. One sponger fumbled his catch, dropped his rammer, and tripped over it.

"Pick up the cartridge, Williams," Stone quietly told the powder boy. Then, seeing that the sponger had recovered his rammer, Stone said, "Now. Hand the cartridge to Miller. There. Carry on."

When he saw that all four cartridges had been loaded, Clay gave his next command. "Shot your guns."

Now the cycle was complete; all four larboard guns were ready to fire again.

"What time do you make it, Mr. Clay?" Hoare asked. He could not believe his own findings.

"Four and a half minutes, sir," Clay answered.

"Appalling," Hoare said.

"Yes, sir."

"Tack ship, Mr. Clay," Hoare whispered. "Larboard guns, cease fire; prepare for action starboard."

The four crews must now leave the weapons they had just fired and switch sides. This time, no cartridges were dropped, and Stone could stand fast to watch the crews do their utmost to prepare the starboard battery while Mr. Clay gave the commands that brought the brig about. To Hoare's relief, she did not hang in stays but went about like a lamb—though slowly, slowly. Another keg was dropped.

This keg survived, though the fall of shot threw spray on all sides of it. *Royal Duke* eased away and left it behind in the gathering twilight. The starboard broadside had achieved even worse time. At least, though, Hoare mused, he had let the brig fulfill Clay's desire to exercise the great guns in reality.

Royal Duke's gun ports once closed and her guns bowsed solid against them, the watch below could rest from its labors. Hoare's own labors, however, had just begun. During the morning, while the yacht was still short of the Needles, he had summoned Sergeant Leese to choose his landing party.

Hoare knew perfectly well that Leese knew far more than he himself ever would about the Dustmen's individual fighting and sneaking talents, so he had told the lantern-jawed Sergeant what he wanted and left the landing party's selection up to him. Bold and Stone had pressed themselves upon Hoare and Leese but were firmly rejected.

"You're needed aboard *Royal Duke*," Hoare told them.

"But I'm black, sir!" Bold said. "Black, and sneaky, too."

"No, Bold. You and Stone remain aboard. You're both too important to the ship's handling."

Leese's own five surviving Lobsters had threatened mutiny unless he gave them all the chance to avenge their beheaded messmate. To them he had added Butcher, master-at-arms and gymnast; the apelike Iggleden; blackman, carpenter's mate and all-in wrestler; Jellyboy, black Indian strangler; and Mary Green, cook. Green had enlisted from among the "brutes" of Portsmouth. With forearms the size of many men's thighs and a projecting jaw under cropped hair, the very look of her gave Hoare a grue.

As if she were not daunting enough in her own person, she carried her favorite cleaver.

Now, Hoare gathered the entire landing party around his lamp-lit cabin table for a briefing.

"We're going ashore tomorrow night," he told them. "Let me tell you why. You already know about how someone who doesn't like the Navy chopped off two Captains' heads—"

"An' cut poor Baker's froat, tu," came a voice. From the accent, it was Blackman, the wrestler. There was a general growl of agreement with Blackman's implication.

"Probably," Hoare said. He should have remembered that; it was only natural that the Royal Dukes would care more about their murdered shipmate than about the decapitation of two Post Captains whom they had never seen. It would go hard with any foe who got within these people's reach.

"Our objective," Hoare went on, "is to capture the leader or leaders of the band. I want to question him. If we cannot capture him, he must be killed. The leader may be in some kind of fancy dress. He could be either . . ."

Hoare described Spurrier and Sir Thomas Frobisher as best he could. He could not be certain that either would actually be the leader, but most signs pointed to it. He could not bring himself to point the finger at royalty as well, although he feared a second encounter with Ernest, Duke of Cumberland, more than he could say.

"He, or they, will probably speak like gentry and—I imagine—will do most of the talking, or preaching."

" 'Spect so, sir. The gentry ginerally do," said a voice from the group. Soft laughter followed. Even if he had wanted to, Hoare could not have helped joining in.

"Take the leader at all costs, and then as many of the

others as you can, but don't chase any who get away," he continued.

" 'Ow many of 'em do yer expect us to be takin' on, sir?" Green growled.

"There's no telling, Green. Probably between five and fifteen. Some of them will be women," he added on a hunch.

Leese at his side, Hoare now showed them by map the terrain between their landing spot and Langton Herring and thence to Winterbourne Abbas.

"Any questions so far?"

"Where are we to lay up, sir?" Green asked.

"I'm coming to that," Hoare said, and told them the arrangement he had made with Mr. Dunaway for their accommodation.

"There's a chance there'll be others ahead of us in the barn," he said, "on business of their own. If so, you are to treat them as neutrals—neither friend nor enemy. Before any of us gets close, I'll signal to alert them. That'll show we're on their side."

" 'Appen they'll 'ave an anker of brandy fer us, then," Blackman said.

"If they do, we'll have to wait to broach it till our job is finished," Hoare said. "Now, listen carefully." I shall repeat this tomorrow evening, before we go ashore and again before we shove off from the barn. . . . By then, though, I'll expect each and every one of you to be able to tell it to the rest of us. In fact, I may have one of you do just that, so be prepared.

"All of you save Leese and myself will shift to landsmen's clothing before going ashore. . . . Blackman and Green, for example, can easily pass for tinkers, Iggleden and Butcher for itinerant acrobats."

"That's wot I was, sir," Butcher declared.

"All the better," Hoare said. "Gather around, now.

"Here's a sketch map of the place where the enemy will be meeting. I got it from a man who's familiar with it in the line of business. . . .

". . . Get the map firmly in mind and take bearings. Do that now, for you won't have the map by you on the day. Leese will pass out compasses. Any of you who can't read a compass?"

Silence.

"Sergeant learned us t'other day, sir," Ledyard explained.

"Very good," Hoare whispered. "Now, at the barn, we shall divide into groups of two. Each pair . . . stays together, at all costs. We shall have the day to filter up to the Nine Stones Circle, each pair going its own way. Do not seem to be in haste, for you do not want to attract attention. . . .

". . . Besides, we have all day in which to make the Circle. In fact, any of you who are within sight and hearing of the Stones in daylight must heave to until dusk, keeping watch. In case the venture goes awry or you lose your way, *Royal Duke* should be lying off Weymouth by then. If she isn't, the rendezvous will be the cutter *Walpole*."

"If any of ye *do* go adrift, I'll 'ave yer guts fer garters," Leese interrupted as Hoare drew breath.

"After it's nearly dark, Sergeant Leese will signal you to take your places in the Circle. Leese, can you make some sort of country noise?" Hoare asked.

"Mm-ooooo-ooo-uh," Leese said lowly.

"Now, Leese will show you on the map where you are to place yourselves. Imagine it is dark, remember; and *remember the map!*"

Leese pointed out to each pair a spot in the Circle

where it would be out of the other groups' way yet would have clear lines of sight to the place where he and Hoare would establish themselves. The Sergeant went over these posts with his people, with and without the map, until he could turn to the waiting Hoare and declare himself satisfied.

"When I judge that it's time to move on the enemy," Hoare now said, "I'll sound my whistle. *Not before!* On your life!"

With those words, not thinking of the likely consequences, Hoare demonstrated his whistle. A mounting thunder of footsteps ensued, from all parts of *Royal Duke*. First to burst through the door of Hoare's cabin was Mr. Clay, but the little Lieutenant was crowded out of the doorway and all but trampled underfoot by the press of his shipmates as they rallied to their Captain's summons. This ended the rehearsal.

"We shall have to cool that hot blood of yours, Mr. Clay," Hoare said, "before you shove off for Broadmead."

Chapter XIV

━━▶◆◀━━

B Y ONLY two bells of the forenoon watch, *Royal Duke* lay hove to a mile off Abbotsbury, midway down the long strand of Chesil Beach. After dark, she would close the shore and drop off the landing party. Having done so, she would double back and retrace her course to Weymouth, there to await their return—"with your shields or on them," as little Lorimer, the clerk-coxswain, put it. Like an astonishing number of his shipmates, he was classically inclined.

The weather was gray, overcast, with a steady westerly breeze and a light chop over the long Atlantic rollers that marched ashore.

"Ye'll be well washed down, lads, before you come aboard this barky again," Stone said. His voice oozed envy. He and another seasoned seaman would cox the two longboats in, for Hoare and Clay agreed that part-time tars like Lorimer would never get the boats ashore without their broaching to in the surf, light though it was likely to be.

Meanwhile, the two officers decided, after putting their

202

heads together, that they would use the time to continue their exercises of yesterday—first aloft, then at the guns. Throughout most of the day, then, the Royal Dukes' vital paperwork was securely stowed while the clerical tars, stiff from yesterday's drills, turned to again.

By the time the gray day drew closed with spits of cold rain, Hoare found himself less despondent about *Royal Duke's* performance than he had been the previous afternoon. Sail handling had been adequate, though their performance when tacking ship had been enough to make any real seaman weep. However, the crew of the second pair of guns had bettered four minutes not once, but twice, and were cock-a-hoop over it.

After all, Hoare thought, the Royal Dukes *were* picked men, and women, picked for intelligence and initiative. They were catching on far faster than your average plowman or bankrupt tailor.

As a final fillip, Hoare had informed his people, he and one of the crew would embark in *Alecto* and the two lilliputian men-o'-war would stage a mock duel. He selected Taylor to accompany him, for he wanted to see whether a woman could make any kind of ship handler. He cautioned himself to make sure they were never below in *Alecto* at the same time. It would never do for the scuttlebutt to run that their captain was having at one of his crew.

Ever since rescuing it from the ballast of an ancient condemned fifty-gun ship of the line, Hoare had been eager to fire *Alecto's* own great gun, a solitary one-pounder swivel. It had been an antique when he found it then. It might once have graced the maintop of a Tripolitanian pirate. Or it might have fought at the Hague over a century ago before being dismissed from the service and left to rust as kentledge in new construction. It was better off with Hoare, as he and the port's master parker had agreed. The only change he had made to it was to affix a reliable flint-lock firing mechanism over the simple touchhole that had satisfied the long-gone original gunner.

While still under tow, then, he and Taylor rousted the awkward piece out of *Alecto*'s forward bilges, where it had rested ever since being brought aboard. When they had set it in its larboard socket, Hoare tested and greased the crude slide that took up its pitiful recoil. The two then hoisted *Alecto*'s two tall, graceful, simple sails, and they were ready for battle. Hoare signaled *Royal Duke* to cast them off.

"We're a French privateer, men," Taylor called out, relaying Hoare's whispered command, "loaded with captured bullion and brandy. Come take us, if you can!"

At the helm of the pinnace, Hoare sheered away, out of *Royal Duke*'s wake, and undertook to show the woman how the peculiar little vessel worked to windward. The tender pointed well above the bigger midget's best, scorning *Royal Duke*'s efforts to bring her under her lee.

"Broadside!" Clay bellowed to his Captain in lieu of actually firing. Hoare sneered; *Alecto* was well forward of her opponent's larboard bow, and Clay could never have trained his guns that far forward.

"Call 'Miss'!" Hoare ordered Taylor, and she did so. In the chill October wind, Hoare thought, and excited by the battle, the woman really looked quite attractive. He must beware.

Royal Duke wore, presented her starboard battery, and "fired." This time, Hoare decided, he must encourage the others.

"Signal 'one hit, larboard chains,' " he said, and made to go forward to the swivel for his turn to fire.

"Excuse me, sir," Taylor said. "What is that brig up to?"

Hoare was about to reprove her for a meaningless question about their own *Royal Duke* brig when he realized she was looking in the exactly opposite direction.

The stranger was *Niobe,* Hoare saw. As he had hoped, Francis Delancey had read between the lines of Hoare's signal back in Portsmouth and was standing out to do battle. She was half again the size of Hoare's little gem and would carry a broadside of eight-pounders, nine to a side. Her broadside, then, would throw several times what *Royal Duke* could deliver. But she was still only a Lieutenant's command, so Hoare could wish Delancey well.

"May we join the dance, girls?" came the hail from *Niobe's* quarterdeck. Hoare saw that her crew was lining her nearer side.

Since *Niobe* was newly put in service, Delancey's crew would be new to her and to one another, but Sir George Hardcastle would surely have seen to it that they were experienced hands all.

Hoare was about to welcome her to the exercise when he realized that Delancey's crew was jeering them.

"What ho, the Hoare's Delights!" came clear from her deck. "Ahoy, the Dustmen!"

Looking more closely, he saw Delancey himself on her quarterdeck, squatting under her spanker boom, mouth agape with laughter.

Hoare's temper was seldom far from the surface; now, he lost it.

"Signal 'Catch me if you can'!" he ordered.

Taylor relayed his words in a voice weighted with challenge. To Hoare, she sounded like one of those female Norse divinities that carried away the battle-dead—veeries? Barkalees? Yes, he must, indeed, take care.

With that, he began the dance. He pirouetted around *Niobe* like a midge around a bullock, leading her away from *Royal Duke* until the two brigs were lost to sight of each other in the gathering dusk, the pinnace forming the wide third point of an obtuse triangle. Then he swept up under *Niobe*'s counter and past her. Handing the tiller to Taylor, he went forward to the swivel.

He raised one hand long enough to catch Taylor's attention.

"Steady as you go now, Taylor," he whispered futilely and grabbed hold of *Alecto*'s forestay before he could go overboard. With his free hand, he aimed the swivel well over Delancey's head, less than a cable away. He backed off and pulled the lanyard of the flintlock. The piece went off beside his ear, leaving it a-ringing. *Alecto* would be *Alecto* no more, by God; from now on, she would be *Nemesis* forever.

The small cloud of powder smoke went off to leeward swiftly enough. Hoare heard Taylor cough. By God's good grace, his shot went precisely where he had wanted it to go—through *Niobe*'s spanker, a foot above her Captain's head. Delancey, Hoare was delighted to see, had ducked so quickly as to lose his hat over the side.

Hoare waved his own, made his way aft to *Nemesis's* tiny cockpit. There he took over the helm and turned the little yacht about while *Niobe* disappeared in the gloaming. On his way back to *Royal Duke,* he managed to reach over the side and recover Delancey's hat from where it bobbed cheerfully in the Channel, upside down.

As *Nemesis* retraced her tracks, Hoare indulged himself in a happy waking dream. In the presence of an enraged Delancey, he was addressing Admiral Sir George Hardcastle.

"I truly regret having alarmed Mr. Delancey, sir," Hoare imagined himself saying, in the loud, clear voice he remembered so well. "I fear I mistook him for a Frenchman."

"How could you possibly have done that?" he had the imaginary Delancey bluster. "Did you not see my colors? You must have known you were firing on a King's ship."

"Yes, indeed, Mr. Delancey. But I have also known one of His Majesty's ships to hoist French colors in order to amuse the enemy. Why should not a Frenchman do likewise to amuse me?"

In this dream, Hoare had no need to pause for breath but continued.

"For my maneuvers between *Nemesis* and *Royal Duke* so evidently amused you that your manners led me to assume that you could not be English. What else could you have been, then, but French? Or Brother Jonathan, perhaps?

"Oh, and by the way, Mr. Delancey," Hoare said in this waking dream, "you dropped your hat. Here it is."

Shaking himself back to reality, he returned to duty and the deck of *Royal Duke*.

Chapter XV

———⟩•◇•⟨———

*U*NDER JIB, main topsail, and spanker, *Royal Duke* eased past Portland Bill through the night, towing *Nemesis* faithfully behind her. When the ruins of Abbotsbury Abbey bore northeast, Clay brought her as close inshore as he dared and anchored. The wind had shifted to just north of west, sweeping the length of Chesil Beach.

Sergeant Leese mustered the landing party in the dark, for Hoare had ordered "darken ship." Except for Leese and Hoare himself, who wore their proper uniforms, they looked no better than a troupe of mountebanks in the varied pieces of landsmen's garb they had drawn from the yacht's capacious slop chest. As he had looked over Blackman's shoulder to watch him make his selection from among the garments, Hoare had felt he could be looking at a theatrical company's store of properties. He had even seen a hobbyhorse in it, a tawdry crown, and what could only be the scaly lower half of a mermaid. Surely no other slop chest in the Navy was so stocked.

Every member of the party bore some sort of visible

weapon in the form of a stout cudgel or staff, and Hoare was certain that other similar objects were hidden in their raiment. Green fondled her cleaver, a weapon with which, Leese warranted to Hoare, she could lop off both legs of an opponent in one wicked swipe. Once again, the sight of her made Hoare shudder. He himself carried a brace of horse pistols under his cloak and had tucked a sap into his belt.

The longboats lowered, one to a side, their passengers clambered aboard them without incident. With *Royal Duke*'s low freeboard, it was no drop at all.

"Cast off." Stone's voice was echoed from the green boat to starboard.

"Good luck, Captain, and a happy return!" Clay called after them. Hoare waved an invisible arm. Invisible in the darkness, the gesture was no more futile, he thought, than trying to make his whisper heard over the wash.

"Ready all . . . row."

The red boat's oarsmen bent to their work. Astonishingly soon, *Royal Duke* had disappeared in the gloom, leaving the longboats to toss alone in line abreast, in what might as well be mid-Channel.

In minutes, however, Hoare could hear the slow, heavy breathing of the light three-foot surf as it ran along Chesil Beach ahead. A wave broke.

"The bar," Stone said conversationally. With these paltry seas, there would be no need, even with the green hands at the sweeps, to turn about and back the boat into the sand.

"Easy all; paddle."

Now Hoare could see the breakers curling on the beach. It would be half-tide. Once the landing party was ashore, the boats could readily withdraw.

"Now when I say, 'Row,' put yer backs inter it."

Stone waited for the surge of a seventh wave, then, "Row!"

A heave, and the longboat was under way again. Another, and it was surging forward. Another wave broke, its crest slopping over the side. Two more heavy strokes, and they were clear in the backwash; another brought them scraping onto the beach. The starboard longboat pulled up beside them.

"Off ye go, men!" Stone said. He forgot himself and slapped Hoare on the back to urge him on. Over Hoare went with his half of the party, filling his boots with salt water as he plunged ahead with the others. Once above tidewater, he paused to empty the boots before he sought out the tall figure of Leese.

"This way," Hoare said, and gestured, knowing he could not expect to be heard over the breakers, low though they were. They left the beach behind and plowed up over small dunes covered with beach grass.

There was a roar of wings from a startled flock of shorebirds—snipe, perhaps, or whimbrels, from their whining protests—driven from their rest in the lagoon to starboard. Hoare felt his boots strike a firmer surface: the road, a mere pair of ruts in hardened shell and sand, leading eastward from Abbotsford toward Langston Abbas. It would be a mile and a touch from here to Abel Dunaway's barn. The party formed two straggling lines, one in each rut, with Hoare and Leese in the lead, shoved along gently by the lightening breeze. Once or twice, the moon, all but full, broke clear and showed a desolate landscape to their left, the lagoon and then the endless beach to the right, stretching on eternally.

"There'll be fog inland tomorrow night," Leese said quietly. Their feet crunched on the shelly surface.

The barn should lie . . . Yes, there it was, black against

black on the skyline. The building was dark, soundless, but that meant nothing. Any of Dunaway's people, if they were there, would not be men who would reveal their presence by lights, and the barn was still to leeward of Hoare's party, so that no roistering sounds would come their way. Signing the others to stop where they were, Hoare left his rut. He walked softly through the grassy sand until he was no more than forty yards from the barn. He uttered the corncrake rattle Dunaway had taught him, then stood fast to listen. Nothing was to be heard except a *creak, creak,* perhaps of a loose door swinging on its hinges. It was certainly neither a corncrake nor a man.

Hoare crouched to the ground and crept to the end of the building. There ought to be a door or two there. There it was, swinging idly, giving off its avian creaks, shutting darkness in and darkness out. Hoare crept within; still no sign of life. The scent of musty hay filled his nose. He smothered a sneeze. A runny nose and watering eyes were, he remembered from boyhood, two of those endless miseries of a rural life that had made him welcome the sea.

He left the barn, stood up, and walked out onto the road where his party could see him against the horizon, and gave them a beckoning signal. In no time, they surrounded him and trooped with him into the barn, where Leese struck a light.

"Take over, Sergeant," Hoare whispered.

"Aye aye, sir."

While Leese called the roll, Hoare looked about him in a more leisurely manner. The moldy hay was there for certain, in quantity. It lay loose in old stalls and in windrows along the walls. He let loose his stifled sneeze. By the flickering light of Leese's dark lantern, the barn seemed as huge as some Gothic cathedral and just as cold.

"Yer all 'ere, I'm pleased to see," Leese said as he drew

Dunaway's chart from beneath his forest-green jacket. "I 'opes I'll see ye the same when we're back aboard.

"Now draw round me. You've seen thisyer map of the Captain's before, so I'll 'ave each of ye show me where yer supposed to lie up when ye make the Stones Circle. You first, Adams."

One after another, the members of the party stepped up and pointed out their respective hiding places. Only two had to be corrected, to Leese's audible scorn.

"Now, you an' me, sir. *You* show me, if you please, sir."

Hoare obliged.

"Very good, sir." So saying, Leese folded the map and returned it to his bosom.

"Now, one more thing," he said. "In the morning, ye'll drift off in yer pairs. Not all at once, and not all the same way. Take yer time, for I won't 'ave yer gettin' to the Ring afore dusk. Some of yer—you two, Green and Adams, and you, Dwight an' Cattermole—*you* go right past the Circle, out of sight of it, an' lay up till dusk. The Captain an' I, we'll lay up 'ere an' twiddle our thumbs till dusk, an' then we'll up an' join ye at the Circle.

"Remember, lads, there's like to be all kinds of weird doin's among the enemy as they 'eave inter sight. Maybe you'll go over that part for us, Captain, sir?"

"As I told you last night, these people will be pretending they are members of a crazy heathen religion," Hoare began. "Or perhaps not pretending; it's hard to say. In any case, they're likely to play weird instruments and sing weird chants . . . and I expect the leader to stand at that big stone in the center of the Circle as if he were a priest and go. It's about then that you can expect me to give the signal for attack. Remember what the signal is?"

"Mm-ooooo-ooo-uh," someone said.

"No, ye idjit." Leese's voice crawled with disgust. "That's *my* signal when I wants yer to rally into the Circle at dusk. No, it's the Captain's whistle. You 'eard it when 'e took command, and last night, too."

"I shan't make the noise again now; it's too loud," Hoare said. "You'll remember it when you hear it. Now, make yourselves as comfortable as you can till morning. Be sensible about your rations, for they're the last you'll get till we're back aboard *Royal Duke*. Smoking lamp's out, and no talking any louder than my whisper."

He lowered his natural whisper. "That's all," he breathed. "Stand down, the landing party."

Hoare had not bedded down in forage since his early boyhood, and this straw was not of the best. His sleep—what there was of it—was fitful and disturbed by feverlike dreams and shortness of breath. In one dream, he was very small, being chased through a labyrinth by a woman with no face. She metamorphosed into Titus Thoday, bearing a switch. Hoare's feet, in turn, took wings, and he could outrun his pursuer with great bounds.

Hoare was awakened by a steady cold drip onto his neck from a persistent leak in the barn roof under which he had positioned himself when finding his own nest of hay in the dark. The leak had not only explored his neck intimately but also penetrated to his ill-packed satchel of hard bread and salt beef. The morning had brought intermittent showers with it; the slow journey inland would be a soggy one. He and Leese, unlike the others of the party, must stay out of casual observation until as late as possible, for they would find it difficult to explain their presence, wandering about the South Dorset countryside, afoot, in His Majesty's uniforms. Given the sad, weeping skies outside, Hoare regretted this not at all. He shifted position and left his friendly drip behind.

He nodded at Leese.

"Off ye go, then," the Sergeant said. "Green and Butcher, you first."

Leese and Hoare waited in the doorway until the first pair had plodded out of sight in the morning mist, then called for the next, and the next. Now Leese and Hoare were left alone.

Leese's green Marines knew their business, Hoare mused. They moved with quiet confidence, unlike the rest of Hoare's rattletrap crew. He said as much to Leese.

"Well, sir," Leese said, "we been together some years, and after all, this is our job. 'Tisn't like the rest of this lot—more clerk than seaman, all of 'em. An' I've had a chance to whip 'em into shape. We've done exercises out in the country, an' in town, too, thanks to your good self, sir.

"Reckon that's why I won't mind at all scraggin' 'oever 'twas cut Baker's throat," he added after a pause. " 'E were one of ours, like.

"There's plenty of time now fer a kip, sir, if ye don't mind."

"Carry on, Leese," Hoare said. "I'll stand watch and knock you up about noontime."

Leese found a dry spot, pulled an armful of hay over himself, and within minutes was audibly asleep. Hoare squatted in the doorway of the barn to watch it rain.

The sky was visibly lighter, and the rain had eased up when Hoare heard the rattle of a corncrake behind the barn. He replied with a rattle of his own.

"I thought I might find ye here, Captain," Abel Dunaway said with a grin, appearing from around the corner of the barn.

"Take a pew, Captain," Hoare whispered. "What brought you to that conclusion, pray?"

Behind him, Sergeant Leese stirred. Without looking, Hoare knew a pistol was aimed at Dunaway's middle.

In instinctive imitation of Hoare, Dunaway's reply was whispered at first.

"News from Dorchester, Captain." Then, in a normal voice, he added, "The town's half-full of madmen, I'm told. And madwomen with 'em, too. Most of 'em gentry. Even royalty, 'tis said."

Hoare remembered all too well Spurrier's warning upon leaving *Royal Duke* after that awful inspection.

"Stay away from the Nine Stones Circle, d'ye hear?" the hussar had told him. "If you should be found there at the wrong time, you'll get a welcome that might surprise you most unpleasantly."

The threat was dire enough. Worse still, Hoare was at a total loss to know what to do with Ernest, Duke of Cumberland, if he were to be caught tonight in the trap Hoare was about to set. As royalty himself, it would hardly do for Cumberland to be brought before some ecclesiastical court on a charge of witchcraft or Satan worship. And if a ritual murder were planned, as was Hoare's worst fear, he could not see Cumberland in the dock, charged as being at least an accomplice.

Hoare sighed and summoned up, as best he could, the pretense of good spirits.

"Oh, Leese, this gentleman is our host, Captain Abel Dunaway, of these parts."

Leese rose to his feet. "Pleased to meet ye, yer honor."

"I thought I'd bring ye along a spot of the needful," Dunaway said. "Bloaters and beer."

"Ahhhh," Hoare said. "Good."

Over stone bottles of that brew of the White Hart that Hoare had liked so well, a round loaf, and a pair of smoked herrings, the three reviewed the implications of Dunaway's tidings.

"Would ye want reinforcements, Captain?" Dunaway asked. Hoare could swear he sounded bashful.

Hoare's first thought was that with the numbers the smuggler could surely muster, he could be assured of capturing the whole group, whether the latter consisted of sincere members of Spurrier's cult—whatever it was—his political minions, or both. But then Hoare bethought himself of the confusion that would ensue. There would certainly be random collisions between Hoare's twosomes and Dunaway's people, with results no one could control. Once the encounter at the Stones Circle took place, the confusion could only peak. Hoare thanked Dunaway but declined, explaining his reasons.

The older man nodded in understanding.

"Reasonable enough," he said. "But it might help your folk if I was to pass the word to mine to be easy-like on any pairs of strangers they might come across a-wanderin' the highways and byways hereabouts."

Hoare saw the merits of this offer and accepted it.

"I'll be off, then," Dunaway said. "Good luck to the both of ye."

Patches of ground fog drifted eastward across the moor surrounding the Nine Stones Circle, keeping station on each other as if they were a gleaming ghostly Great Armada on its way to defeat among the shoals off Zeeland. The full moon played hide-and-seek with the low clouds that paced them, now bringing the Stones Circle's nine menhirs into full dramatic view, now obscuring them in dank darkness.

Face blackened like those of the rest of his command, Sergeant Leese oozed from point to point, establishing that each pair of his party was in place. Hoare had disappeared into his own dark gorse bush at the foot of one megalith, where, at length, Leese joined him. Their wait began; time stopped.

The fog and the clouds above them continued to float down the wind, leaving the stones naked to the moonlight at one moment, shrouded in gray the next. *Quite Gothick,* Hoare thought; all the scene needed was the mournful shriek of an owl. And bats. The notion of the little flittering things reminded him of how easily his half-hysterical mocking had made a permanent enemy of Sir Thomas Frobisher.

Hoare's thought might have been a cue. Until now, the Circle had been quiet, the fog even muffling the faint ever-present background of animal chirps and rustling foliage. Now, the fog lifted briefly, and the animal noises ceased. Hoare realized that for some time he had been hearing, eastward toward Dorchester, the sounds of human movement.

Gradually, figures, mostly singletons but some in couples, began to appear out of the mist and slip into the ring of stones. Most appeared to be countrywomen, on the elderly side, but there was a scattering of farmerish men as well, some couples who might be petty tradesmen and their wives, a few younger pairs, and even two or three children. Most of the women carried baskets, some sheaves or garlands of late flowers.

When he was a lad, Hoare remembered, he and his family had unaccountably arrived early for the harvest festival at the village church in Cuckney, below the property Captain Joel Hoare had purchased not so long before. Seated between brother John and little Cassandra, the three of them guarded by father on the one side and mother on the other, Bartholomew had watched the Cuckney folk gather in their ones and twos, bearing their varied thank offerings. Just so were these worshipers assembling.

The sight of them disoriented Hoare. He had steeled himself for some ancient pagan rite, one that would culminate in another ritual killing; hence his having launched the landing party in the first place. The offerings of the rural folk who were gathering in the Nine Stones Circle tonight simply would not do. These people would be as misplaced at a Black Mass as so many nuns in a brothel. Had he misjudged what was to take place here tonight? Had he, then, made an utter fool of himself? From Leese's restless movement beside him, he sensed that the Sergeant, too, was uneasy.

Like those of a herd of startled deer, the heads of the scattered audience or congregation lifted and turned eastward. Hoare's own ears pricked. In the distance, he heard a strange wild, jangling rattle, then the strained bleat of a pipe and the rhythmic thump of muffled drums. As the players, still invisible, advanced, their music swelled. A reddish light flickered in the eastward distance.

The fog pounced again. One minute, Hoare could note each of his party's hiding places and see all of the attending worshipers in the Circle; the next, the surrounding Stones were again no more than hints of black against gray nothingness. The black began to take on ruddy overtones; the discordant music sounded louder and louder.

The fog lifted unevenly, as if it were the curtain of a provincial theater. The congregation drew apart; Hoare saw one anxious woman dart out and snatch her child from the path of the procession itself as it straggled into sight.

Out of the fog appeared two men carrying torches. As they approached, Hoare saw that the torches were oddly carved; they guttered in the light wind. Stripped to the waist, the bearers wore thick hairy breeches as if they were to be taken for satyrs. They came on with slow, majestic steps and looked about them anxiously. Perhaps, Hoare thought, they were afraid their torches would blow out and leave them alone in the dark.

Six musicians, male and female, followed on their heels. The first pair of women shook lyre-shaped rattles and chanted as they came. The second pair, cheeks puffed out like those of wind cherubs on an antique chart, squalled desperately on double pipes that might have been taken off one of those Grecian vases. The last two whistled on pan-pipes.

Like the bearers of the ithyphallic torches, the band of musicians was also naked to the waist, the men clad in the same hairy breeches and the women in long full skirts. The figures thus exposed were far from classic and looked very chilly. Hoare shivered in sympathy. A foggy Hallowe'en night was no proper time for an orgy.

With the torchbearers, the awkward orchestra now drew up in a double inward-facing line, as if taking its positions for some macabre fancy-dress contradance, and played on. One by one, the folk in the congregation drew near the altar and deposited their modest offerings around it and returned murmurously to the outskirts of the gathering.

Four small boys now came into sight, their treble voices raised in a meaningless song as they thumped away on little drums for all they were worth. Though they, too, were naked except for hairy buskins—perhaps, Hoare thought, they were supposed to be fauns—the brave noise they made and the exercise of beating the drums must keep them, at least, warm. And possibly the mere fact that they were engaged in mischief kept them in temper. In fact, like all boys so occupied, they kept glancing at one another and stifling snickers; Hoare heard them in his lair and nearly snickered himself. Whatever the reason, the imps were the only persons in the gathering who looked to be enjoying themselves at all.

A second pair of torchbearers followed them, ithyphallic torches in hand.

Into the circle of dolmens, behind the urchins, came a solitary squat figure in a viridian robe, carrying a T-shaped standard as he chanted and staring up, as he marched, at several small furry carcasses that dangled from its crossbar. It was Martin Frobisher, so soon—according to his father— to receive the traditional Frobisher knighthood. He looked bored, even embarrassed.

Hoare knew the two women, bearing a covered wicker cage between them, who were the next to enter from the night outside the Circle. One, quite flat-chested and broad of hips, he had last seen at the reception in Admiralty House. But he had heard her seagull voice in the crowd outside that same house the next night, after the assault on Admiral Hardcastle. It was Sir Thomas's daughter, Lydia, Martin's sister, and her face was that of a woman on the verge of hysterics. She was not singing now, not at all.

Her companion, also half-dressed like the other women in the procession, displayed to better satisfaction. Gleaming in the torchlight, Selene Prettyman's glossy black rope of hair swayed behind her; her firm ivory breasts swayed before. She wore an archaic proud, contemptuous smile, but her eyes roamed, taking in her surroundings as if in search of something. Hoare and his party, perhaps? The two women drew to one side, with their covered cage.

The first of the two men who brought the procession to a close was Captain Walter Spurrier. A heavy cloaklike garment concealed most of his frame. Hoare was certain he had seen it before. In one hand, Spurrier carried a single-edged, wide-bladed weapon, a short sword or falchion like a huntsman's that ended in a peculiar backward hook. Hoare had seen a similar weapon being wielded by a classical bronze hero; he could not remember which one.

The white-cloaked pouting man beside Spurrier, Hoare saw with dismay, was one who must already be quite familiar with processions, if not—Hoare hoped devoutly—of this sort. His left eye glared fixedly to his larboard side. In his good hand, Ernest, Duke of Cumberland, bore a footed dish. It was a krater, a bowl or chalice. It might be, Hoare thought, the very chalice Titus Thoday had included in his inventory of Spurrier's peculiar possessions. Hoare wondered what the Duke was making of this bucolic bacchanal.

Beside Hoare, Sergeant Leese startled. Yes, he, too, had been subjected to Cumberland's sneering inspection on board *Royal Duke*.

Spurrier and Cumberland reached the altar, Selene Prettyman and the Frobisher woman following on their heels, the wicker cage between them. With a final ragged bleat, jangle, and thump, the musicians fell silent.

So far, except for the time and the open-air venue, this could be Sunday morning service in Dorchester's Church of All Angels, and, except for the decorously exposed bosoms, the congregation could be the ton of the town.

Turning to face his flock, Spurrier raised his arms skyward.

"Let us invite and invoke our prepotent masters and mistresses," he intoned. A confused mumble followed. From it Hoare thought to hear names he was sure he had heard elsewhere: "Isis" . . . "Asmodeus" . . . "Ashtaroth." "Baal" was certainly familiar. Hadn't the Phoenicians or the Carthaginians or the Philistines sacrificed babies to

Baal? For his part, Hoare hoped that Selene Prettyman and Lydia Frobisher were not lugging someone's missing child about in that covered container and that he was not about to witness a ritual infanticide.

Hoare could not doubt it. Plautus might have been written the whole ceremony into one of his broadest comedies. But from the intent expression of Captain Walter Spurrier, whatever deity he was addressing was a real one to him, and a dreadful one.

Spurrier turned to Selene Prettyman and Lydia Frobisher. From the wicker cage he withdrew—not a baby, Hoare was relieved to see, but a great black cock nearly the size of a turkey. Holding the struggling bird by the neck with one hand, Spurrier raised it in the direction of the moon in dedication, as though he were elevating the Host, intoning more gibberish as he did. He murmured an instruction to Ernest, Duke of Cumberland.

Cumberland appeared as if he devoutly wished himself elsewhere. These people, Hoare could tell already, were too simple for the Duke's tastes—and too sincere. So was the ceremony. But he was the son of a King, after all, and *noblesse oblige*. With his sound left hand, the Duke extended the chalice and set it on the ashlar.

Spurrier grunted, caught the cock's neck with his weapon's strange hook, twisted the bird onto the altar, and beheaded it with one clean backhand blow. The headless creature fluttered to the altar and, as any chicken will when its head is chopped off, staggered about the broad stone surface for several seconds, spattering its blood about before Spurrier caught it and held it over the chalice as firmly as he could. In the deathly silence of the Circle, the blood trickled audibly into the chalice.

Like acolytes, two of the faun-boys came up, looking pale. One bore a brass jar and the other a torch. After rendering an unseemly backward-facing obeisance with evident gusto, the lad with the jar emptied part of its contents into the chalice and part onto the headless cock. It was rum, as Hoare knew from its odor, and powerful rum at that.

Taking the torch from the second boy, Spurrier thrust it onto the rum-soaked flapping cock. A puff of bluish flame, and the pungent, acrid reek of burnt feathers drifted into Hoare's nose. He must struggle against a coughing spell. Spurrier resumed his unintelligible chant. "Gaah," said the Duke, and backed away with a disgusted look to join the two bare-breasted ladies.

Perhaps Spurrier sensed that his royal auditor was becoming discontented, for, using plain English now, he called into the darkness, "The sacrifice has been accepted. Draw nigh, ye worshipers, and receive your token of our sacrifice; then go ye hence, to foregather at the Hall of Feasting!"

With this, Spurrier plucked a branch of heather and dipped it into the mixture of cock's blood and rum that filled the chalice. Selene Prettyman took one of the Duke's arms and Lydia Frobisher the other and led him to the altar, where Spurrier stood ready to dash the branch across the three clenched faces.

The Duke shook himself free.

"That will be enough, Spurrier. Call this a rite?" he grated. "Why, it's the most farcical piece of fustian I've ever had to witness. You had the gall to bring me all the way from Plymouth for *this?* Compared to Dashwood and his crowd, you're a choirboy. And if you call this a 'pagan orgy,' you can call me an abbess. By the time I was fourteen, I'd seen more, and done more, than you could dream up in a hundred opium dreams. Be damned to you, indeed."

He spun to address Selene Prettyman.

"And as for you, madam, I shall have words with you at my later convenience."

The lady sank into the deepest of curtseys; the Frobisher woman followed suit with far less grace.

The Duke marched off into the dark in the direction from which he had come. The ladies lifted up their heavy skirts and followed. After an embarrassed pause, Spurrier resumed his summoning of the congregation.

In response, the common folk approached timidly to receive their aspersion, then drifted away as silently as they had arrived, leaving the celebrant to stand alone, facing his altar and his stinking headless bird as if rendering a closing prayer. Perhaps, Hoare thought, Spurrier would now dodge round to the entrance of the Stone Circle as if by magic, like the vicar at Sunday service, to greet his parting flock and be congratulated on his powerful sermon.

At Hoare's side, Leese stirred restlessly and gave his Commander an inquiring look. *Call it off?* he mouthed.

Hoare put out a hand and pressed it onto the Sergeant's shoulder. *Wait,* his gesture said.

Spurrier still brooded at the altar, cope and all. As Selene Prettyman returned into the ring of megaliths, he looked up, visibly hauling himself back to the mundane world from whatever bourne he had been sojourning in.

"What are *you* doing here now?" Spurrier asked. "You're supposed to be shepherding Cumberland back to Dorchester."

Spurrier sounded depressed, it seemed to Hoare, as well he might, considering that his ceremony had been a fiasco and that he had just lost one powerful backer.

"Don't worry, Spurrier," she said. "I gave him into the protection of the Frobisher children, who have him under their wings. I kissed him good-bye. Perhaps he'll linger at those odd quarters of yours. If so, you can make your excuses to him yourself."

"That's all very well. But you have no business here now," Spurrier said.

"You should know by now that I go where I choose to go," Selene Prettyman said briskly. "Now be about your own business, for if I'm not mistaken, your business is about to come to you." As she shrugged, her breasts bounced. Under other circumstances, Hoare thought, their motion would have been enticing.

"Very well," Spurrier said. "Keep out of my way, then, d'ye hear? Now then, let's be about it."

He bent, retrieved a torch, struck fire to it, and waved it in an unmistakable signal. There was a scuffle outside the Circle.

"Come along, you," came a hoarse voice from the dark. "Don't give us no trouble, now."

Two captives were half-hauled, half-carried into the torchlight, each gripped by a pair of hard-looking men. The prisoners were hoodwinked, their arms bound, their shoeless legs hobbled.

"Take off their hoods, you men. We'll start with the little one," Spurrier said.

Hoare suppressed a grunt of dismay. The prisoners were Hoare's own men, Rabbett and Thoday.

It must have long been obvious to Spurrier, Hoare could see now, that Hoare's two aides were on his trail. What, then, since they were lonely intruders into his territory, could have been simpler or more logical than to ensnare them and dispatch them like a brace of hares? By making them his true sacrifice, the one that the death of the cock had merely simulated, Spurrier would be accomplishing three things at once. He would clear his own trail, he would add to the Royal Navy's alarm and despondency, and, if his worship was genuine—a possibility that, after the proceedings just ended, Hoare could not dismiss—make a sacrifice to his deity or deities compared to which that of the big black cock was petty. Again Hoare pressed Leese's shoulder. He must make ready to signal the rest of the hidden landing party.

The leather gags across their mouths kept the two captives from uttering more than half-smothered mumbles. But it was obvious that they could see and they could struggle, which they did as best they could. A blow to the belly doubled Rabbett up.

"Over here," Spurrier ordered. "Stretch him over the stone, now. No, you idiots, face up. There. Now hold him. Yes, just like that."

"Are you sure you want to go through with this, Spurrier?" Selene Prettyman asked in a cool voice.

"Be silent, woman."

Spurrier took a firm hold of the odd, impractical-looking knife once again, raised it into the foggy night air, and looked fixedly at the moon. Then he leaned over Rabbett.

At Hoare's piercing whistle, he froze.

Leese at his heels, Hoare threw himself across the few feet toward the altar. The rest of his party sprang from their hiding places and grappled with the guards. Dropping their prisoner, Rabbett's guards turned to defend themselves.

Spurrier leaped for the gap between two menhirs, the cope flying behind him, the drawknife in his hand. Hoare fell headlong over the clerk, reached out for Spurrier, clutched the fleeing foot, twisted, and began clawing up the other's leg. Spurrier dropped his weapon but gripped Hoare by the hair.

In no time, Hoare had both hands on Spurrier's leg and was almost within reach of his privities. Hoare would grip them as soon as he could and crush them in his fist till Spurrier surrendered.

"Take him from behind, woman!" Spurrier shouted.

Hoare looked over his shoulder. Selene Prettyman, raven hair flying as wild as any maenad's, lunged toward him, the hook of Spurrier's blade in her hand. She flipped it deftly end for end, catching hold of the hilt. Hoare winced and awaited the blow that would finish him. Instead, flinging herself full-length across Hoare's prone body, Selene Prettyman swung the flat of the weapon squarely into Spurrier's upturned face, and the man went sprawling.

In a single series of smooth, practiced-looking motions, Selene Prettyman cut the fastenings of Spurrier's cope, pulled it from his shoulders, and modestly draped it over her own.

"That's better," she said. Her palm was bleeding where it had clutched Spurrier's blade. She ripped a length from the hem of the cope, looked at it, gave an *ach!* of disgust, wrapped the silk around her hand, and knotted it with the other hand and her even white teeth.

Two of the landing party made to seize her.

"Let the lady go," Hoare said. "She's a friend of the Crown."

"Good for you, Captain Hoare," she said. "This affair has gone quite far enough, I think." She drew the cope more closely about her.

Rabbett had collapsed to the ground but now propped himself against the altar. His eyes, strangely small without their accustomed spectacles, looked up at Hoare in entreaty. Hoare bent down and cut away Rabbett's gag and his bonds. He turned away from the clerk's stuttering thanks to do the same for Thoday.

"Your arrival was timely, sir," Thoday said. "This is

227

evidently the place to which one should take recourse if one wishes to lose one's head."

Leese came up to the group. "Sorry, sir," he said. "Two of the wretches got clear away. I'll 'ave summat to say to my people when we're back aboard, that I will. Eight smart sailormen an' all that preparation, just for four no-good rascals. Not to speak of losin' them antic folk what opened the show. I'll 'ave their 'eads."

Shaking his own head, Leese took the three extinguished torches, lit them from the one Spurrier had rekindled, and jabbed them into the ground. In the light they cast, Leese inspected them with mingled disgust and respect.

"Looks like great big pricks," he said. "Beg pardon, ma'am."

"We got the only man we needed, Leese," Hoare said. "Perhaps it's for the better that the others got away."

"You speak no less than the truth," Selene Prettyman said. Her voice was low but heartfelt.

"Well, sir!" came Abel Dunaway's voice from the dark outside the Stones Circle. "I think my lads 'ave bagged ye some pretty little coneys! Come along, lads, and show the Captain what ye found!"

"Oh, my God," Hoare whispered. They had managed to see Cumberland off unscathed. Had the smuggler, thinking to help, brought him back?

One at a time, hustled along by Dunaway's men, fugitive celebrants began to appear. The smugglers' bag numbered five of the women, three of the men. The captives' ecstasy had worn off; the women clutched themselves from modesty or cold, or both, while the men simply looked hangdog. The two Frobishers, the rest of the men, and the four faun-urchins had evidently eluded the new arrivals.

So, Hoare saw with relief, had Ernest, Duke of Cumberland.

"If your men will take over our bag now, sir," Mr. Dunaway said, "we'll be off. It's as well your men don't get too good a look at mine."

"Of course, Captain," Hoare replied. "Where the Navy failed, your people succeeded. Well done, and my thanks to you all."

He swept his eyes over as many of Dunaway's men as would meet his glance before they all drifted away into the night. Dunaway waved cheerfully as he disappeared.

"It's just as well, Hoare," said Selene Prettyman, "that the Frobishers got away and took our noble friend with them. They were off before the real mischief started, after all. And while Sir Thomas may be objectionable and more than a little mad, he is still a power in the region and in parliament. He is better disarmed than destroyed.

"And in case of need, both you and I—and your crew, of course—saw his son and daughter taking part in that silly performance. No, with a tale like that hanging over his head, we have no more need to disturb ourselves with Sir Thomas.

"Mr. Spurrier's other master now, whoever he is . . . that's another thing. We must interrogate the good Captain—intensively, if need be. For that, best we take him to Dorchester."

Hoare felt an unaccountable reluctance, first, to do Selene Prettyman's bidding and, second, to relinquish Spurrier to her.

"To *Royal Duke,* I think, ma'am," he said.

"Why?"

"Because you were among this evening's celebrants. I do not trust you with our captives."

"You forget, sir, I am 'friend of the Crown.' You your-self have said it, and it's greatly to your credit. It was I who gave you the warning and I who was responsible for his capture, Captain Hoare," she said.

Hoare preferred to divert her from that issue.

"Nonetheless, I must not habituate myself to having a lady preventing the escape of my adversary, leaving him for me to capture," Hoare said.

"What do you mean?"

"Mrs. Graves crippled the skiff in which my last villain was rowing to safety. . . . Just now, you enabled me to catch Spurrier when you tripped him."

Hearing his name, Spurrier sat up and groaned. The side of his head was bleeding slightly where Selene Pret-tyman had swatted it.

"Ah, yes, Mrs. Graves," Selene Prettyman said. "And how, pray, did she 'cripple' the skiff?"

"She slung a stone. It broke one of its thole pins. He capsized in the surf. I went on from there."

"I must remember to keep out of slinging range of Eleanor Graves, then, must I not?"

Mrs. Prettyman put a slim, strong hand on Hoare's arm.

"But surely, Captain Hoare, you can do better for yourself than a globular widow. Why, she . . ."

Upon seeing Hoare's expression, Selene Prettyman stopped in midsentence.

"That was inexcusable of me, Captain Hoare," she said.

"Yes, madam, it was. I thank you for your intervention with Mr. Spurrier, and I wish you a good evening."

With that, Hoare left Selene Prettyman standing. He summoned the landing party, and departed for Dorchester with the captives. *Mrs. Selene Prettyman could find her own damned way.*

On the way to Dorchester, Hoare instructed Leese to

let all the participants in the ceremony escape, except Spurrier and the hard henchmen who had brought Rabbett and Thoday to the altar in the Nine Stones Circle. In the first place, Hoare reasoned, the folk who had been present at the pagan rite could at the most be no more than Spurrier's deluded devotees—harmless, eccentric perhaps, and now very frightened. In the second place, *Royal Duke,* while a brig herself, had no accommodations for prisoners—no *brig,* so to speak, he told himself half-hysterically. He put the horrid jest in that mental commonplace book of his, against possible future need.

So he merely had Rabbett take down their particulars before releasing them in the town. As Hoare had expected, the clerk already knew most of them. One, for example, was the wife of the town grocer, another a ne'er-do-well ditcher.

"Remind me, Rabbett," Hoare said, "to give their names to the vicar at the Church of All Angels. They committed their sins in *his* parish, I think. He can do as he will with them."

"Yes, sir," Rabbett said. "If you wish, I'll give 'em to Vicar myself as soon as possible."

"I think not, Rabbett. Tomorrow, you must be aboard *Royal Duke.* I need you there."

He heard the clerk's gasp. Was it with pleasure or fear?

"If I may, then, sir, I would like to bid my old mam and da farewell. And pick up my other shoes. For 'tis a long walk to Weymouth."

"Do you ride, Rabbett?"

Rabbett could not, nor, as Hoare found when he inquired, did the otherwise omnicompetent Thoday. So Hoare silenced his conscience and ordered Rabbett to roust out a chaise for himself, Hoare, Thoday, and their prisoner and a wagon to carry Leese, the landing party, and the other prisoners. Spurrier he would keep to himself and interrogate him in the chaise as they rolled south to Weymouth.

While weary, Thoday could still summon up advice for his Commander.

"We might, sir, visit Mr. Spurrier's place of business while en route to Weymouth," he said. "A more leisurely inspection than I had time to conduct during my clandestine intrusion could produce interesting results."

Spurrier must have overheard, for he started. "You will find nothing of interest, Hoare, I assure you," he said.

"Pipe down, you," Leese said.

Hoare followed Thoday's advice. Joined eventually by the weary Rabbett, they searched Spurrier's quarters by candlelight, from stem to gudgeon, not neglecting his bedroom. Thoday set out to test every panel and every floorboard for secret hiding places.

He found one at last and crawled into it, carrying a dark lantern. On emerging, he shook his head.

"Nothing except this old missal," he said disgustedly, holding out the dusty book. "The place is merely an old priest's hole."

It was past dawn when they were through with the turning out of Spurrier's quarters. Thoday sighed.

"I think we have it all here, sir," he said, displaying a small heap of papers. "I fear there is nothing of interest beyond what I found on my last visit, but we can put our discoveries before the—your crew and see what they make of them."

"A very good performance, Thoday," Hoare said.

"Elementary," Thoday replied.

"Did you check the dovecote, Thoday?" Rabbett asked.

"What dovecote? Where?"

"In back of the house, of course. I thought you knew about it."

Thoday vanished downstairs; the other two followed him. Shortly he returned, feathers sticking to his shoulders, holding a pigeon awkwardly away from his face to avoid the bird's bill. The bird looked disconcerted, as well it might. A tiny silvery cartridge was attached to one of its ruby red legs.

"Here, Rabbett. Hold the bird while I take off the message tube," Thoday said.

"I'll take care of it, Thoday," Rabbett said. "When it comes to pigeons, you obviously don't know what you're doing. We Rabbetts have lived among pigeons all our days."

Holding the pigeon gently, Rabbett slipped off the cartridge and handed it to Hoare.

"Here, sir," Rabbett said. "I'll just go and give the creature its reward."

The message was en clair.

" 'Levi,' " Hoare read, " 'Stop. Stop. Stop. Saul.' "

Saul?

"You were very clever, Spurrier," Hoare whispered to the bound man facing him as they jolted toward Weymouth in the chaise. Thoday sat beside Spurrier, Rabbett beside Hoare.

"You juggled two balls at once, very neatly—killing officers of the Royal Navy on the one hand, and disguising the work with Black Masses to beguile—"

"Not Black Masses, man," Spurrier said with a grin of contempt. "What you chanced upon was to be no more than a rite of initiation. If I had been celebrating a genuine mass, as I should have done, it seems, His Royal Highness would not have been so disappointed. And neither you nor your helots would have survived your spying. There I was fatally foolish."

"That is as may be," Thoday said in a flat voice. "What intrigued me is that you built further on the edifice of superstition you first designed. But you made another mistake. I became aware of it just as I saw you about to sacrifice my little friend here. There you and your bullies went, crushing under your feet the fruits and flowers that the neighborhood's innocent nature worshipers had brought to the harvest festival with which you opened that obscene rite of yours."

"That was a dreadful waste, of course," Spurrier replied with a cynical smile. "But what was mistaken about it?"

"It made it obvious that on the first occasion, when you chose the Nine Stones Circle as the place to put the two Captains to death, you had no idea of involving the paganism, or Satanism, or whatever you choose to call the creed that you follow. That notion came to you only when you returned to your quarters after your double murder. It was then that you took garlands of flowers and produce back to the Nine Stones Circle and scattered them about, as if they were left by a cult."

"I don't follow you, Mr. Thoday," Rabbett said. "The whole thing was bad, but what was the mistake?"

"He forgot to tread them down the first time. That was when I all but knew he had revisited the Stones Circle after killing the two late Captains."

Spurrier's lips thinned. Then he shrugged and looked carelessly out the window of the chaise.

"You wrote a two-act play, Spurrier," Hoare said. "One in which you cast the Duke of Cumberland as the protagonist . . . and, I suppose, those poor deluded folk in your congregation as the chorus. In Act I, you tried to show off to the Duke with your silly pagan ritual. Perhaps . . . you knew beforehand that it wouldn't be enough to take him in."

For a fleeting instant, Hoare thought of suggesting that, for some peculiar reason of his own, Spurrier had planned from the beginning to drive him off. That would have made no sense at all.

"In any case," he went on instead, "it was only after he marched off that you commenced Act II, which was to be the climax of the play—the murder of my two . . . Naval investigators.

"What gave you the idea of using that means of covering up your part in the killings?" Hoare went on. "It cannot have been the Duke of Cumberland. Unpleasant . . . he may be, but he was obviously a mere observer of your performance and not an informed participant."

"You'll have to ask someone else that, Hoare," Spurrier drawled. "You are insolent, just as Sir Thomas said you were, as well as stupid."

That he was still naked to the waist and no longer even had the blasphemous cope to keep him warm in the November dawn had evidently not dampened his superb self-confidence.

"Your master, Sir Thomas, has much to answer for," Hoare replied, "and answer for it he will. It's a pity for you that you did not receive his last message before you, er, raised the curtain on your two-act melodrama."

"You are absurd as well as impudent," Spurrier said. "The frog—the man you call my master—he's no more than a useful puppet, an over-the-hill jackanapes with mad pretensions of being the rightful occupant of the throne. It was bad enough that his tadpoles had to be present. D'ye think that if the frog himself had anything to do with it, I could have got . . ."

235

"Got what?"

Spurrier shook his head.

"A different frog, then, Spurrier? A Frog from over the water, perhaps?"

"I have nothing further to tell you," Spurrier declared. "In the first place, you are my enemy. More important, you interrupted a holy sacrifice. So did the Prettyman woman. She will live to regret it, as will you, but not for long. Both of you will regret last night's doings, I promise you on behalf of my masters. My word, yes."

Rabbett's face went white in the dawning, while Thoday's remained impassive.

"So you serve two masters, Spurrier," Hoare whispered. "One on earth, I suppose, and one . . . elsewhere. You will forgive me, I'm sure, if I confess myself a devout skeptic concerning the Deity's existence; that being the case, I must logically doubt the existence of the Enemy as well.

"It is your earthly master that interests me. His purpose I think we know; it is to throw a spoke in the wheel of the Royal Navy whenever he can. The infernal machines your colleague Kingsley caused to be planted in *Vantage* and her sister ships out of Portsmouth were one such spoke; your attempt to decapitate the Navy by decapitating its senior officers was another."

Here Thoday intervened. "I must confess, sir, that the purpose of Mr. Spurrier's essay at gathering in the Duke of Cumberland eludes me. Perhaps he will enlighten me."

When Spurrier had nothing to say, Hoare decided to put up a possible motive to see if he could bounce the prisoner into telling more.

"I rather suppose, Thoday," Hoare said, "that the notion stemmed from Sir Thomas . . . by example, perhaps, or by direction. The bee in Sir Thomas's bonnet, about his being the rightful occupant of the throne now beneath King George—"

"God bless him!" Rabbett declared.

"—yes, Rabbett—is well known. And it is also well known that the Prince's younger brothers, Cumberland in particular, have ambitions of their own in that direction.

"If Spurrier here could stir up the Duke, turn him into a fellow Satanist—if he needed turning, that is—and promise him support from over the Channel, that would be a spoke in the wheel, not only of the Navy . . . but of the entire kingdom, would it not?"

Although Thoday made no observation, his look told Hoare that his point had merit. Spurrier's expression told Hoare he had struck home.

But the chaise was approaching Weymouth, and time was running out.

"Pray tell me about your master," Hoare whispered. "The earthly one, I mean. His name, his whereabouts."

Spurrier uttered an imprecation from between thinned lips. "I have nothing to say to you," he said. "You and your crew are dead men."

That might be the case, Hoare admitted to himself, for it was obvious that Spurrier himself was in deadly fear.

As the chaise drew up to the low scarp overlooking Weymouth, Hoare could see *Royal Duke* hove to outside the harbor, breasting the easy seas that rolled gently in from the Channel. He also heard the sound of bells. It was a confused cacophony, a compound of merry, even jubilant rounds, underlain by a solemn tolling, as if for a great person's death. The ringing must come from every church in Weymouth town.

Once down in the town itself, Hoare thrust his head out of the chaise window.

"What is happening?" he croaked at a passerby, but

must needs repeat himself before the other raised his head. His face was beslobbered with tears.

"It's Nelson," the man said. "Dead, dead. Struck, he was, at the instant of victory."

The party was silent amid the bells until they had hoisted their prisoner into a wherry and were being rowed out to *Royal Duke*.

"I shall never forget this moment," Thoday said in a voice pregnant with feeling. "The morning of November the sixth, 1805. This is the place, and the time, where I was when I learned of Nelson's death."

Spurrier's two hard men were not so hard after all, Hoare found. Questioned separately, both admitted having been present when Spurrier butchered the two Captains Getchell and to having been among the gang that assaulted Admiral Hardcastle and Delancey in Admiralty House. They denied knowledge of the dead Marine, Baker, and knew nothing of his head's whereabouts. When it came to disclosing the names of the person or persons behind Spurrier, their claims of ignorance were persuasive.

"I never seen the Capting talkin' business with no one but Sir Thomas," one said. " 'E'd ride off for parts unknown every few weeks an' come back wi' some new bit o' mischief."

When Leese had convinced Hoare that Spurrier's men had been milked of all the information they had, he had the pair stowed in the brig's bilges. He would not risk setting them ashore here in Weymouth; Sir Thomas Frobisher ruled here. He would take them to Portsmouth as soon as he could; there he would feel safe in sending them ashore under guard for trial and disposition.

Spurrier himself, bound into Admiral Oglethorpe's huge hanging chair in Hoare's cabin, resisted Hoare's most persuasive questioning. As the chair swung with *Royal*

Duke's gentle motion, however, Hoare saw Spurrier's discomfort increasing. Hoare remembered, now, Spurrier's passing remark when he was previously in this very cabin on the occasion of Cumberland's disastrous inspection.

"You go to sea in *this* little thing?" he had asked. "Makes me want to spew just to think of it."

"Your men have laid two murders at your door, Spurrier," Hoare said now. "There can be no question; you killed the two Captains in the Nine Stones Circle. I'm sure we'll find evidence that you killed my Marine, too, and your own followers, the ones my men took captive the other night. You've lost your interest with Cumberland now. You'll hang.

"But if you name your master, the agent of the French, I will try to arrange for you to be shot instead of hanged. It would certainly be less dishonorable, and I understand it is far quicker. Now. We know you go by the code name of 'Levi.' Who, pray, is 'Saul'?"

There was no reply.

He remembered overhearing Morrow/Moreau, the Canadian turncoat, refer to a "Louis" in London. Hoare knew there was a connection between Spurrier and Moreau and that it was almost certainly Sir Thomas Frobisher.

"Who is 'Louis'?" he asked, on the spur of the moment.

"Louis?" the prisoner echoed. "Never heard of him. King of France, I suppose." He clamped his jaw again.

"And where did you go so suddenly after our first encounter in Dorchester?"

Royal Duke gave an extra lurch just then, and Spurrier's color grew even unhealthier. For a moment, Hoare thought the prisoner would tell him, but his lips hardened, and he shook his head.

"I have nothing to say to you, Hoare. I have already

said—and done—too much. Now bugger off."

Hoare watched Spurrier carefully for a few more moments. He might be doing his best to behave like an iron man. Nevertheless, he was sweating and his color worsening.

"Put the prisoner in the forepeak, Leese," Hoare said at last. "Right up in the eyes of the ship."

Going on deck, he beckoned to his lieutenant.

"Get under way, Mr. Clay."

"What course, sir?"

"Brightstone, I think. Yes, set a course for Brightstone. We'll heave to there, and then we'll see what we shall see."

"Aye aye, sir," Clay said.

Off Brightstone, the seas were heavier. *Royal Duke* bucked lightly against them during her approach. When Clay hove her to as Hoare had ordered, the slight roll she added made for a gentle corkscrew motion. There were a few moans from the watch on deck. Two or three of the watch below came topside as well, to join their shipmates at the leeward rail under their petty officers' watchful eyes.

"What now, sir?" Clay asked.

"Remain hove to until further orders, Mr. Clay," Hoare whispered.

"Aye aye, sir. May I exercise the watch on deck?"

"Of course. And you might include those of the watch below who have found business on deck."

With this, Hoare made himself comfortable on the new hatch leading to the pigeons' quarters and settled down to wait. Clay looked his Commander askance for a moment, then began issuing orders.

Three times, the Marine on deck went forward to strike the bell. At eight bells, the watch changed. Still *Royal*

Duke lay hove to. Her Commander went below once, just long enough for a solitary dinner in his truncated cabin.

Before he returned to his seat on the pigeons' hatch, Hoare made his way into the forepeak. He had not yet quite regained his sea legs himself and must clap onto anything he could reach as the brig tossed in the chop off Brighthead.

By now, he thought, Spurrier should be more than ready to cough up the answer to any question he was asked, if he could only be left free to die of nausea in peace. Hoare was averse to torture, but seasickness, unpleasant though it might be for its victims, could hardly be classified as torture. After all, it was well known that Admiral Nelson himself suffered from chronic seasickness. "*Had* suffered," Hoare told himself sadly.

When Hoare opened the little hatch through which his Marines had thrust the prisoner, the stench that poured out nearly left him, too, retching. Spurrier must have puked himself dry by now; he had evidently also lost control of bladder and bowels.

Hoare reached in and gingerly lifted his prisoner's head by its lank yellow hair. The man's face was slack, a ghastly, beslobbered greenish yellow. A dreadful mess washed about his feet, compounded of vomit, excrement, and seawater.

"Come now, Mr. Spurrier," Hoare said, suppressing his own nausea and dodging the other's breath as best he could. "I do not wish you to suffer. Are you prepared to name your master? If so, I shall gladly have Mr. Clay ease my ship's motion and have you brought on deck, into the fresh sea air."

So speaking, he felt himself the worst of hypocrites.

Spurrier's answer was a gurgling cough.

"Well, sir?"

Silence.

Hoare closed the hatch, returned to his perch on deck to wait until Spurrier had finally had his fill of *Royal Duke's* tossing. The breeze picked up, then died down.

Midway through the first dogwatch, Hoare bestirred himself again and summoned Leese.

"The prisoner has been confined in the forepeak long enough to have become really seasick," he said. "Let's see if he is prepared to talk now. Bring him back on deck. If he isn't ready, we'll masthead him."

A few minutes passed; then Leese reappeared. He was alone.

"Where's the prisoner?" Hoare asked.

"Beggin' yer pardon, sir, but 'e's dead."

"*What?*" Hoare croaked. Then, in his normal whisper, "Get him on deck, man."

Summoning one of his men, Leese scrambled below. The two came on deck at last, bearing Spurrier between them. Spurrier's face, yellow-green when Hoare had left him, was now gray-green. His limp body was covered with stinking vomit. He was not breathing.

"Roll him over a barrel, someone," Hoare said. "Maybe he's choking on his own vomit. And call Tracy."

Samuel Tracy, failed apothecary, was *Royal Duke's* nearest approach to a surgeon. He took one look at the prisoner and rose to his feet.

"He's dead, sir," he said.

"No one ever died of seasickness, man," Hoare was about to say, but Tracy forestalled him.

"Someone has now, sir," Tracy said firmly. "Choked on his own vomit, I suppose. Look. He was hitched to a cleat, lying on his back, and couldn't move his head."

"*Damn,*" Hoare whispered. It had been his doing, then. It had been he, Bartholomew Hoare, who had directed that Spurrier be confined up here. He, Bartholomew Hoare, had hoped that the agony of seasickness would compel Spurrier to name his master, despite his fear. That master *might* have been Sir Thomas Frobisher, but Hoare was far from sure. There had been a Byzantine, corrupt quality about the whole affair that did not suit the knight-Baronet's blunt, deluded nature. In any case, here was another death to lay on the altar of his conscience, and this time a useless one. He had blundered again. He had let Spurrier spill his innards to death, indeed, but his voice had spilled nothing.

"Untie him, someone, and clean him up," Hoare whispered sadly. "We must take him back to the authorities."

In Weymouth, Hoare knew, "the authorities" were Sir Thomas Frobisher. He dreaded the thought. He would not do it; he would return to Weymouth, but he would keep his prisoners and his corpse aboard until he could get them to Portsmouth.

"Make for Weymouth, Mr. Clay," he whispered. "I'll be in my cabin, preparing my report to London."

Hoare almost felt sorry for Spurrier. The man had gained standing of a sort in Dorset, as Sir Thomas Frobisher's tame bully. But then hubris had got the better of him. Using that as a platform, he had put himself in the hands of the master agent of the French, the man whose puppets knew him only as "Himself," and set out to spread alarm and despondency among the Royal Navy by beheading its senior officers. And he had striven to enlist Ernest, Duke of Cumberland, in his unsavory cult, only to discover that the jaded royal had, as he had told Spurrier, "by the time I was fourteen, seen more, and done more, than you could dream up in a hundred opium dreams."

Somewhere, an unidentified puppet master was making his marionettes play out a vast malign joke, a joke that would soon be on England if the strings were not cut.

With that thought, Hoare drew himself up at the desk in front of his cabin window, dipped pen in Standish, and began to write his report to Sir George Hardcastle, for him to read and forward to Sir Hugh Abercrombie at the Admiralty.

Chapter XVI

————◆————

SPURRIER'S BODY had been sewn into a shroud of airtight canvas, the forepeak aired out, and the henchmen stowed in less discomfort, until *Royal Duke* could deliver them all in Portsmouth. Hoare had sent Rabbett off in a hired chaise, all by himself, with his report. The clerk promised to place it in Sir George's hands without delay and to see that as soon as that officer had read it, it went on to London. Before he left, the clerk had taken Hoare aside and placed his hand in both of his.

"You saved my life, sir," he declared. "I shall never forget it, or the great adventure in which you allowed me to join. Please, count on me in any situation where you believe I can be of aid."

"I shall, you may be sure, Rabbett," Hoare whispered. "I shall consider you at least an honorary member of the brig's crew."

In truth, as he had noted before, Rabbett had grown during their acquaintance, in confidence of spirit, if not in bulk. He had become all but doughty.

"Oh, thank you, sir." With that, Rabbett relinquished Hoare's hand but continued to speak; he had obviously prepared this speech, and he would speak it to the end, come what may.

"You must be proud, sir," he continued. "Admiral Hardcastle commanded you to track down the villains and rogues who killed the Captains and tried to kill him, too. And that was what you did. It is not given to every man to accomplish . . ." His voice choked. He climbed into the chaise, signaled to the driver, and rolled away. Hoare had forborne to remind Rabbett that it had been he, Bartholomew Hoare, who had sent him into peril in the first place.

"Proud," Rabbett had said Hoare should feel. Hoare laughed sourly. Yes, one criminal group had been dealt with, but it had become clear that it had functioned at the command of another entity. He had scotched puppets only; the puppet master was still at liberty. The Moreau affair had planted the belief in Hoare's mind, and these last events had seen the belief grow stronger. He was sure of it. He would find that entity, wherever it was, and uproot it. But first, he would go ashore and explain affairs to his beloved widow.

As he thrust his head through the hatchway, he looked directly into the eyes of the widow herself, who was about to climb nimbly aboard the yacht from a wherry that must have just pulled alongside. She uttered no word but finished boarding. Then she led him below, as though she had been in command of the yacht for months. Once in the privacy of Hoare's cabin, she reached up with both arms, pulled down his head, and kissed him.

"Well, Bartholomew," she complained softly after some time, into Hoare's uniform coat, "I waited in vain on the tuffet in my parlor for you to come again in glory and ask for my hand. That is what you did after your last

246

triumph. Now that you have triumphed again, will you not do so once again?"

"But I already have, Eleanor," he whispered.

"Not lately," she said.

"I . . . Will you—"

"One knee, Bartholomew. Do not deprive me of this triumphant moment," she said in gentle reproof. "One knee."

JAN 24 2000

22 FEB 2000